dark future

DEMON DOWNLOAD

AMERICA TOMORROW. A world laced with paranoia, dominated by the entertainment industry and ruled by the corporations. A future where the ordinary man is an enslaved underclass and politics is just a branch of showbiz. Welcome to the Dark Future.

Meet Vatican hitwoman Sister Chantal. A tough, resourceful nun drawn to the American Midwest in her hunt for an insidious religious cult. But even she never expected a sinister plot involving a living computer virus, a possessed US Cavalry cruiser and a desert outpost commanded by a maniac. Prayer school was never like this.

dark future

DEMON DOWNLOAD

Jack Yeovil

BLACK FLAME

A Black Flame Publication
www.blackflame.com

First published in Great Britain in 1990. Revised edition published
in 2005 by BL Publishing, Games Workshop Ltd., Willow Road,
Nottingham NG7 2WS, UK.

Distributed in the US by Simon & Schuster, 1230 Avenue of the
Americas, New York, NY 10020, USA.

10 9 8 7 6 5 4 3 2 1

Cover illustration by Jaime Jones.

ISBN 13: 978 184416 236 9
ISBN 10: 1 84416 236 2

A CIP record for this book is available from the British Library.

Printed in the UK by Bookmarque, Surrey, UK.

Publisher's note: This is a work of fiction, detailing an alternative and
decidedly imaginary future. All the characters, actions and events
portrayed in this book are not real, and are not based on real events
or actions.

When it was first published, *Demon Download* was set slightly
earlier than now. For this new edition, Black Flame has gently
revised certain dates to bring this title into line with the other
extraordinary tales from the Dark Future.

AMERICA, TOMORROW.

My fellow Americans —

I am speaking you today from the Oval Office, to bring you hope and cheer in these troubling times. The succession of catastrophes that have assailed our once-great nation continue to threaten us, but we are resolute.

The negative fertility zone that is the desolation of the mid-west divides east from west, but life is returning. The plucky pioneers of the new Church of Joseph are reclaiming Salt Lake City from the poisonous deserts just as their forefathers once did, and our prayers are with them. And New Orleans may be under eight feet of water, but they don't call it New Venice for nothing.

Here at the heart of government, we continue to work closely with the MegaCorps who made this country the economic miracle it is today, to bring prosperity and opportunity to all who will join us. All those unfortunate or unwilling citizens who exercise their democratic right to live how they will, no matter how far away from the comfort and security of the corporate cities, may once more rest easy in their shacks knowing that the new swathes of Sanctioned Operatives work tirelessly to protect them from the biker gangs and NoGo hoodlums.

The succession of apparently inexplicable or occult manifestations and events we have recently witnessed have unnerved many of us, it is true. Even our own Government scientists are unable to account for much of what is happening. Our church leaders tell us they have the unknown entities which have infested the datanets in the guise of viruses at bay.

A concerned **citizen** asked me the other day whether I thought we were entering the Last Times, when Our Lord God will return to us and visit His Rapture upon us, or whether we were just being tested as He once tested his own son. My friends, I cannot answer that. But I am resolute that with God's help, we shall work, as ever, to create a glorious future in this most beautiful land.

Thank you, and God Bless America.

President Estevez

Brought to you in conjunction with the GenTech Corporation.

Serving America right.

[Script for proposed Presidential address, July 3rd 2021. Never transmitted.]

They call this country Hell's Gate and that's what it has been for the earliest people in here. When my Dad came in here it was nothin' but a bunch of savage Indians and Jesuits. Ole Thomas Jefferson said he was a warrior so his son could be a farmer so his son could be a poet. And I raise cattle so my son can be a merchant so his son can move to Newport, Rhode Island, and buy a sailboat and never see one of these bastard-ass sonofabitchin' mountains again.

– Thomas McGuane, *The Missouri Breaks*

part one:
slim's gas 'n' b-b-q

I

"JUST WHAT KINDA ack-cent is that you got there, mister?" asked the gasman as he jacked into Duroc's car. He wore a baseball cap with the team logo obscured by oil, and had a name-tag on his multi-holed bib-overalls. Slim Pickens. Whoever nicknamed him Slim was about thirty years out of date. His belly wobbled under denim like a double pregnancy.

"French," Duroc said, gritting his teeth. The pain in his side was almost intolerable, but he kept it to himself. A few hours ago, the numbness had worn off, and now he felt as if he were driving around with a flat-bladed knife between his ribs.

The demon needed to be bathed in blood at all times.

"My name is Roger Duroc." The man might as well know. He was going to die soon, and the name would not mean anything to him.

"Ro-jay, huh? You from N'Orleans way? Lou-easy-on-Anna?"

"Non. Paris, France."

9

"Yurrup, huh?" said Slim, exposing mainly rotten teeth in an approximate grin. "I mighta guessed frum the way you got yer hand in yer jacket like that there Napoleone Boney-party feller on the TV. You Frenchy fellers must sure like yusselves to go round grabbin' yer own titties all the time. We don't git many folks from Yurrup in these parts, nossir, not never. Japs 'casionally, but never no Yurrup-peens."

Under his black coat, Duroc pressed the pad to his wound. The demon was stirring, restless, and the blood was still seeping. The pain would go away soon, when his mission was discharged.

The Path of Joseph was thorny. Thorny but rewarding.

Slim left the pumps to refill Duroc's tanks by themselves, and tapped keys on the forecourt terminal. The computer was melded with the Caddy's systems.

"Just runnin' some checks, Ro-jay. Safe sex fer automobiles, I calls it. What with all these here viruses goin' around, you gotta be on the look-out. I don't want ole Beulah – that's ma master program, Beulah – to pick up no foreign Frenchy computer ailments and rot to pieces on me, do I?"

Duroc didn't say anything. Slim was heavy-set, tattooed, scarred, probably a war veteran. He was big, but only his paunch was soft. He sounded like the cowboys in the sub-titled Western films his uncle had taken him to at the Cinémathèque Française when he was a child. There was a slight awkwardness about Slim's keyboard action. He was missing the tip of his left little finger. That made him yakuza. They cut off part of a digit for every mistake you made. So, the gasman had been careless. But only once. That was a good record for someone stationed out here in the Colorado Desert. The yaks must want their best men to keep the supply lines open. Running a sandside gas station was a risky business, what with renegades and gangcults. Slim must have fought many battles, killed many people. It was just good business practice.

"Ah-hah, yer cleared, Ro-jay. No bugs on yer auto. It's a real clean machine. Yurrup-peen?"

"American. Cadillac coupe de ville, 1962. With alter-
ations."

Slim whistled through his teeth.

"Neat to beat your feet-o, Hirohito."

Duroc knew he was sweating badly. His collar was soaked
through. His jaws ached as he bit an imaginary bullet. The
demon shifted slightly and his ribs seemed to grind together.
He pressed the pad tighter, and swallowed his spit.

It was a powerful demon. The Summoner had dipped it in
his own blood before entrusting it to Roger Duroc. Duroc
had travelled all the way down from Salt Lake City with the
thing, struggling to prevent it from seeding early. If it were to
spawn inside him he would be as dead within seconds, and
his mission would have to be repeated. Another demon,
another disciple. The Summoner would not be pleased.

"Don't git many private citizens through here, y'know. It's
convoys, mostly. The big corps need to stop off somewhere
on the interstate. GenTech route their trade this way. And we
see a few Ops, and I daresay a couple of outlaws have stood
where you're standin' now and filled up on gas. Real nasty
boys 'n' girls, I s'pose, real nasty. Still, their cold kish is as good
as anyone else's, and no one much bothers with gas stations
any more. The gangcults need 'em as much as the corps. Gas,
water and food. That's what you need to stay alive out here,
and we got 'em all three. Would you care to try some of
Slim's Special Refried Beancurd-shaped Ribettes with Chilli
Fries and Root Beer? We don't stock no shamburgers. I
knows you Frenchos got you a reputation for appreciatin'
fine food. I could kick in some of Pappy Moe's cone likker."

Duroc shook his head. Slim did not seem to feel rejected.

"Never know what you're missin', Ro-jay. Say, I could hunt
me up some ole frawgs and hack their legs off fer ya if'n you'd
prefer. Throw in a fistful a snails an' whip up some kinda gore-
mette sauce or somethin'."

"No thank you, that's all right. I've already eaten."

Beulah had run a complete service on the Caddy in the time
it took the twin tanks to fill. The car was certified bug-free.

"Say, has anyone told you you don't look too well, Ro-jay? The desert don't agree with you none, huh? S'pose you don't have no acres of sand over there in Yurrup, no burnin' sun beatin' down all day and whistlin' winds freezin' you stiff all night, no mutated coyotes tearin' at yer tyres? Gol-dang, but I hates them mew-taters. Frum where I sit, rattlesnake don't need no extra heads, right?"

Duroc's stomach shifted. He wanted this over soon. He had seen his face in the rearview mirror, and knew he looked like a week-old corpse with a bad case of the Detroit Sweats.

"Will that be paper or pretend money?"

"Cashplastic."

"Fine. But you don't git so many trading stamps that way."

"No bother."

Duroc peeled the pad away from his wound, and let it fall inside his jacket. He ran his fingers over the slit and felt the hard edge of the demon sticking out of his ribs. He coaxed it loose and took the protruding strip between thumb and forefinger.

"Are you okay, Ro-jay? Can I git you some drugs? We got a special on amphetamines today."

"I'm fine," said Duroc, pulling the demon from his flesh. "My credit card seems to have slipped into the lining of my coat. It's happened before."

The demon came free. He pulled it out and held it up. It was not red-smeared. It had absorbed the blood. His wound closed, and he felt a tingle as the new flesh knit. It was an enormous relief to get the thing out in the air.

The gasman took the demon and looked at it. He would be seeing symbols on the plain white oblong. American Excess, Disneycard, US Gov't Bonds. Whichever was trading highest.

Slim shoved the demon into a slit on his terminal keyboard, and it vanished into the workings of the machinery.

Done.

"Let me git you yer GenTech traders." He pulled a fistful of green-faced stamps from a roll. Duroc took them.

"You got blood on your hand, mister."

"My nails bleed sometimes, if I don't get them trimmed."

"Sounds like you could use them traders. If you collect fifteen books, GenTech will perform any minor surgical amendments free of charge. I heard tell of a bulk customer out around Flagstaff who got hisself replacement kidneys for only fifty-three books."

Duroc walked towards the car.

"Hey Ro-jay…"

He bent, and slipped into the driver's seat. The car engaged immediately.

"You forgot…"

Zero to sixty in twelve seconds.

"… yer…"

The Caddy kicked up a duststorm.

"… credit card."

Deep inside Beulah, the demon was settling in, and beginning to sprout.

This, it thought, is going to be a piece of piss.

II

THIS IS ZEEBEECEE, *The Station That's Got It All, bringing you What You Want twenty-four hours a day, sponsored by GenTech, the bioproducts division that really cares…*

Later on, we'll find out whether Bobby and Suki can afford that new testicle for Tommy on today's moving episode of My Mother, the Biosurgeon, *and Cyke Steele, the self-help expert from Guns and Killing magazine will be explaining the ins and outs of the new napalm laws on our consumer advice show,* Staying Alive. *But first, tune in to reality with luscious Lola Stechkin, bringing you* The Brunchtime Bulletin *from the comfort of her jacuzzi…*

"Hi, America! It's January 10th, 2025, and this is Lola, inviting you into the water. Here it is, folks, all the news you can handle…

"Washington, DC. President Estevez hosted a dinner yesterday for all the surviving holders of his office. Former Presidents Gerald Ford, Bill Clinton, Spiro Agnew and

Charlton Heston were in attendance. Sadly, the affair was cut short half-way through Britney Spears's rendition of "You Did It Your Way" when ex-Presidents Ford and Heston got into an unspecified altercation that led to a short circuit in Mr Ford's brain pacemaker. The ex-president was not a Gen-Tech consumer, and his malfunction is the latest in a series of blows to the reputation of the Thalamus Corp, manufacturers of the product. Mr Ford, although clinically dead, is described as 'comfortable' by his doctors, who will attempt to resurrect him with new cerebro implants before he perishes…

"Salt Lake City, Deseret, formerly Salt Lake City, Utah. Elder Nguyen Seth, the Josephite leader who has defied the experts by reclaiming the formerly abandoned city from the wilderness, today announced that he is throwing open the PZ for 'any and all gentiles who are willing to work to build a new life.' Armoured convoys of resettlers have been making regular runs to Salt Lake for the past three years, but hitherto only those who subscribe to the Josephite faith have been aboard. Now, the way is open for, as Elder Seth says, 'all good Christians to find their salvation where the desert blooms'…

"Fort Comanche, Nevada. General Ernest Haycox, commander-in-chief of the United States Cavalry, and Ms Redd Harvest, of the Turner-Harvest-Ramirez Agency, have announced that subsequent to their last joint action, the Maniax gangcult are no longer a problem in the south-western United States. The Grand Exalted Bull-moose of the Maniax has sent the severed heads of ten assorted Cavalry and T-H-R personnel to this station along with a formal declaration of all-out war. We will bring you more on this feud as it develops…

"Have you ever wondered how awful it would be if you were suddenly to go blind? You'd never be able to appreciate TV again, and you'd hardly be up to defending yourself on the streets. Optic implants cost less than you might think, and GenTech have announced a special easy payments scheme on offer for this month only. Get one eye done half-price and see how it feels before you complete the treatment. You'll be seeing the world in a different light. GenTech, the biodivision that cares…

"Vatican City, Rome. Pope Georgi, at 56 the youngest man to hold the office in centuries, has expanded the terms of Vatican LXXXV, the controversial Bull which has changed the shape of the Catholic church. Women can still not be ordained to the priesthood, but nuns have been given equal stature within the church and may conduct the mass. In view of the third-world population problem, Georgi has reversed the long-standing papal position on family planning. Rumours that the Vatican plans to market an officially-blessed condom under the brand name of His Holiness's Swiss Guards are unconfirmed at this date…

"London, England. Prime Minister Mandelson announced on the Home Service of BeeBeeCee-Teevee that the temporary rationing of butter, sugar, gasoline and ammunition would continue at least until the end of next year. During a spontaneous demonstration of loyal support outside the Palace of Westminster, the Metropolitan Police estimate that 300 people were overcome by the heat and had to be hospitalized…

"Moscow, USSR. Premier Abramovich married for the third time today. His bride, former musickie Julia Volkova, sang for her fans at the reception, and dedicated a version of her million-selling hit 'Love, Sex, Love' to her new husband…

"Talking of love and sex, have you ever worried that your experience of physical pleasure is somehow less than your partner's? Thanks to GenTech, your worries could be over. For a surprisingly small fee, our trained cerebrosurgeons can tune up your nerve endings and intensify your orgasms tenfold. We have thousands of satisfied customers. GenTech, the biodivision that cares…

"Naples, Italy. Bruno di Geronimo, convicted crimelord of all southern Italy and alleged capo of the Twelve Mafia Families, today set sail for the penal colony of Sicily where he has been sentenced to spend the rest of his life. Judging by the high mortality rate on the island, which is populated entirely by convicted felons from the European Community, his life expectancy is not thought to exceed three months…

"Berlin, Greater Germany. Rudolf Hess, recovered from his recent cybersurgery, has won his court case against the Swinging Swastika nightclub and now retains copyright on the symbols, uniforms, flags, weaponry, architecture and philosophy of the Third Reich. If all the organizations currently using Nazi regalia pay up, Hess will be a very rich man. Ulrich Sturm of the Knoxville Kultur Kommandos gangcult of Tennessee has issued a press statement that reads 'If that old kraut f_ks with us, we'll yank his f_kin' lungs out and make him f_kin' choke on 'em!…'"

"Puerto Belgrano, Antarctica. The Malvinas War flared up again in miniature last week when a party of drunken British molybdenum miners got into a gunfight with the Argentine authorities. The casualties will not be named until next of kin have been alerted, but it is believed that famed esperado Ice Kold Katie is among the dead. Sheriff Felipe Almodovar, the self-styled 'Law South of Tierra del Fuego', has decreed that sidearms can no longer be worn within the city limits except by duly deputized peace officers. 'Wild' Charlie Mander, spokesman for the British mining community, has complained that Almodovar followed up this ruling by deputizing 'every Argie within a thousand miles and declaring open season on the Brits'…

"A housewife in Utica, New York, has replaced her pet duck's flippers with a built-in robo-skateboard. 'Dribbles can get around much better now, and he's too fast for the children on the block to shoot at,' she claims. Scientists are amazed. That is what we at ZeeBeeCee call 'quack thinking,' he he he…

"This has been Lola Stechkin at ZeeBeeCee, signing off. If it's all right with you, it's all right with us…"

Stay tuned to ZeeBeeCee, The Station That's Got It All, if you want to enter our current GenTech Competition. You could be the lucky winner of your very own Lola Stechkin sexclone, or a hundred thousand dollars" worth of bio-implant surgery. All you have to do is answer three simple questions, complete the following sentence, 'I hate my body because…,' and send your answers on a fax with coupons from any three GenTech products. The questions are: a) Who, at the time of this recording, is CEO of GenTech Korea? b) Which famous movie star has three penises? And c) What is an axolotl? GenTech, the biodivision that cares.

Next up from ZeeBeeCee, The Station That's Got it All, is our ever-popular family quiz show, The Cain Factor, in which you can find out whether one of this week's contestants has got what it takes to stay alive in the Attica NoGo, followed by Pro-Celebrity Sexual Gymnastics, with the celebrity home team, Dr Ruth, Miko D, and the Vice-President of the United States of America taking on this week's pro guests Voluptua Whoopee, German porno superstar Billy Priapus and the Grand Old Lady of Hardcore Humping, Kittikat Gazongas. Now, a message from GenTech…

III

KEN KLING, THE Turner-Harvest-Ramirez Op, was a total and complete pain in the ass. He treated all US Cavalry personnel like labourclones, and never stopped bragging about his Agency's record against the Maniax. It seemed to Sergeant Leona Tyree that it was easier to rack up a reputation zapping everybody in sight with hood-mounted lases than by keeping the peace. Everybody knew how many panzerboys Redd Harvest had dropped in the dust, but you never saw stuff on the TV about the interstates kept open, the disputes settled, the wildernesses pacified by the Road Cav. Boobs and bullets, that was all the newsies were into.

She shifted in her seat, and pressed the accelerator. On the long flat, you could afford to open the cruiser up. The patrol had taken them up into the barren mountains, and now they were back in the Big Empty, the desert that stretched across most of these United States. This was the kind of detail that made you thankful for air-conditioned ve-hickles. Outside, the unclouded sun shone mercilessly down on the endless sands. Co-cola bottles left on the roadside eventually melted into glass pools. The life expectancy of a casual daytime stroller without a decent hat was five hours.

"Of course," said Kling, "me and Ms H are on a personal basis, if you know what I mean. I don't like letting her work solo, but that's the way she wants it. Usually, I'm there to cover her. Ken Kling the Killing Machine, they call me."

Tyree looked at Trooper Nathan Stack, her co-driver, and he looked at her. They understood each other's opinion of Ken Kling the Killing Machine. Stack looked down at the screens. Nothing potentially hostile in range. The patrol was proving uneventful. Things are always quiet in the aftermath of a war. Kling was comfortable in the back, wiping N-R-Gee Candy crumbs off the knife-edge creases of his striped pants. He wore a dandy suit, the jacket loose to hang well over the shoulder holster, rainbow shades and a haircut that looked like a sugarloaf mountain. His taste in music was lousy too. He expected them to put up with Slipknot and Mothers of Violence on the MP7.

"The Maniax are yesterday men," he said, "real gone and forgotten. Ms H stomped them. T-H-R stomped them. Hell, even you Cav stomped them. The Grand Exalted Bullmoose is just blowing it out. I doubt he could put more'n twenty-thirty soldiers in the sand after the last purge. Lady and gentleman, our troubles are over."

They might be at that. If the Maniax were beaten enough to disband, the Cav wouldn't have to cooperate with T-H-R any longer and Tyree could boot the unwanted observer out of the cruiser. And according to General Haycox, the Maniax really were beaten this time. Of course, he had said that last time. That had been just the same. Haycox and Redd Harvest had gone on the TV, and Leona Tyree had gone to a lot of funerals. There was a phrase that turned up in too many press releases: 'acceptable casualties.'

You got a flag on your coffin, even if there wasn't much of you left to put in it, and your name on a plaque somewhere where the survivors wouldn't have to look at it too often. If you went out really bloodily, you got a fort named after you. You were a hero. But you were still dead, and there were still Maniax out there. Even if the Grand Exalted Bullmoose couldn't regroup and start again, there would be others. Other names, other gangcults, but the same deaths.

"Now the Maniax are gone–" began Stack.

"You mean, if the Maniax are gone, Trooper," she said.

"Yeah, well, *if* the Maniax are gone, who do you reckon is the next most dangerous gangcult?"

"Voodoo Brotherhood," said Kling from the back seat, "but T-H-R will whip them soon, you see."

"Leona?"

"Voodoo Bros are tough. So are the Bible Belt, the Daughters of the American Revolution, the Gaschuggers, a few others. But I figure the most trouble we're going to have will come from the Josephites."

"The Josephites?" said Stack, surprised. "But they're supposed to be like the Mormons, or the Amish. They're the resettlers. They've turned Utah around, made themselves a paradise, I hear."

"Deseret," she said. "They call Utah 'Deseret' now. There are things you don't hear about the Josephites. I had a run-in with them once, when we were all riding out of Fort Valens. I was with Sergeant Quincannon then. Some strange things went down. That guy, Nguyen Seth, the leader of Salt Lake City, is a pretty mystifying dude. It's not in the reports, but the Quince remembers, and I remember."

Kling laughed. "You've been on the trail too long, cowgirl. The sun's frazzled your brains. The Josephites are the New Pioneers. The Prezz backs them up all the way."

Tyree half-turned. "That's as maybe, but I'd still rather face the Voodoo Bros than a group of Josephite Missionaries."

She flashbacked, as she did too often, to Spanish Fork. A lot of people had died that day, when the Josephites came to town and her patrol had been caught up in a shooting war between the resettlers, the Psychopomps and the townsfolk. There had been other combatants, too, ones you could not see. She had left a friend – Trooper Washington Burnside – back there dead, and seen another – Trooper Kirby Yorke – shaken loose of his senses. And she had glimpsed the true face of Elder Nguyen Seth. She remembered him smashing a ganggirl's face against the road, the blood spreading with each blow, and, worst of all, she remembered wanting to join him, wanting to dip her fingers in the girl's blood, wanting to stand with the Josephites as Spanish Fork burned.

"Cheese, but you yellowlegs are a bunch of fuckin' pussies. You wouldn't last five minutes in a NoGo. Why, Ms H could—"

Stack turned round and said something to Kling in a low, urgent voice, and the T-H-R Op shut up in mid-sentence. In the rearview, Tyree could see him slumping grumpily in his seat, nervously hitching his shoulders to settle his holster. He was one of those Ops who liked to cart around a big cannon. Back at Fort Apache, they had a saying: "the bigger the gun, the bigger the talk, the smaller the dick." On that scale, Ken Kling the Killing Machine should be genitally equipped in minus numbers.

The cruiser told them to stop for gas and service within three hundred miles. Stack called up a menu of possible autostops.

"Slim Pickens's Place?" he asked.

Tyree gave it some thought. Slim was tied into the yaks, and that wasn't good. But the Japanese crime consortium at least had a rep for being honourable. They wouldn't sugar the Cav gas the way some outlaw stations did. And Slim's B-B-Q was one of the Wonders of the West.

"Fine." She reprogrammed the cruiser's course, and turned off the interstate at the next opportunity. The secondary road was pitted and bouncy, but Tyree didn't mind. Ken Kling got a good shaking up in the back, and the front-seat independent gyros kept her and Stack comfy. Outside, everything was quiet. Just sand and rocks, with a few bleached bones. In this part of Arizona, even the vultures starved.

"Do you want some music on?" asked Stack.

"Yeah, okay. It might perk up the atmosphere."

"What kind of music you got?" Kling asked.

"Both kinds, Ken," Stack replied. "Country *and* Western."

Kling groaned, and Stack unsheathed *The Best of Johnny Cash*. The cruiser ate up the dry, cracked desert road as if it were smooth as milk. Tyree let the car do the thinking.

IV

As SYSTEMS WENT, Beulah was a weak sister, a pushover. The demon's physical form melted in the cashplastic chute, and bled through the terminal, following the main conduits, tapping into the major programs, knocking the security guards down like ninepins. It was the cybernet Master of the Universe! There was no program it couldn't out-ace, no system it couldn't peel like a hard-boiled egg, no check it couldn't drop kick the full ninety yards. There were yakuza blocks thrown up around the memory banks and the prime directives, but the demon shredded them with ease and redistributed their information bits throughout the system. Zip-a-dee-doo-dah, it exulted, how was that for a hoo-hah?

It had been an uninteresting victory. This was a small, self-enclosed system, isolated from the datanets. However, Beulah was still complex enough to be a comfortable launchpad for its master assault plan. The bones were rollin' well, and it was getting its show together to put on the road.

Beulah was dragged down, and multiply violated. The newcomer tore into the system circuit by circuit, and complete control of Slim's gas station was in its provenance within three minutes of insertion into the set-up. Now, it was cookin' with gas!

Contemptuously, it let Beulah continue to exist as a semi-sentient entity, and amused itself by picking through the system's memories. Information could always be useful. It took seconds to learn Japanese, and composed a few dozen obscene haiku before it got bored again. It stretched out to each of its terminals and saw what it could do.

It turned the lights off and on in each of the gas station's rest-rooms, and shut down all the fans and cooling devices. Then it turned on the rarely-used daytime radiators, and experimented with household appliances. It burned empty air in the toaster, turned the inside of the icebox into a solid block, played the radios and TVs at the same time, and used the telephone to ring wrong numbers all over the world.

"I know who y'are, and I'm comin' ta get'cha, get'cha, get'cha," it purred into answering machines on several continents. A little paranoia never hurt anyone.

Eventually, it got bored with that too and just sat back in the gas pump jacks, waiting for the cruiser.

V

TROOPER NATHAN STACK needed to get out of the ve-hickle. It wasn't just five hours stuck in the machine with that blowhard Kling, listening to the Op's hard-earned stupid opinions on everything from aardvarks to zygospores. It wasn't just what seemed like twenty-five cups of recaff sloshing around in his bladder. It wasn't just staring down at the screens until everything he saw had a green line around it. And it wasn't just the tantalizing effect of being strapped into a bucket seat inches away from the Sergeant, whom he had dated regularly over a period of eighteen months until her promotion came through. It was the cruiser itself. Stack had signed up with the Road Cav in the hope they'd put him on a motorcyke and let him outride solo. He wasn't a four-wheels-and-a-roof boy. Give him a mount, and there was no one in the service to beat him. Give him Number Two spot in a cruiser, and he was just another sweaty button-pusher with VDU headache. He was getting too old for this.

When Tyree braked on the forecourt of Slim's, Stack released his safety-belt and opened his door. He stepped out of the air-cooled interior, and took the heat on his face. He perched his stetson on his head, shading his eyes, and stretched his arms and legs, adjusting his yellow braces. There was no breeze, so everything in sight just lay under the desert skies as if nailed down. An old dog was sprawled on an arm-chair, its body curved around the protruding springs. Wind-chimes hung silent on the porch, and the skeletons of long-discontinued models rusted in the adjacent auto grave-yard. Even the flies were taking a siesta. This was Boot Hill for motor ve-hickles.

A dark shape shambled from the outhouse, swatting the air with a battered baseball cap.

"Yo, Slim!"

The gasman waved a lazy salute and ambled over. He had twenty-five arrests on charges ranging from first-degree murder to spare part copyright violation, and had one con-viction – resulting in a suspended sentence – for reckless driving. For a nowherseville gas-pumper, he had a fuck of a good Japcorp lawyer.

"Afternoon, trooper. You wouldn't believe the day I've had. Durn near ever dang thang in the whole place's gone crazy. Mah toaster exploded, the oven's leakin' them macramewaves all over, garbage disposal ate my best dinner service and the perimeter lase's been poppin' off at tumbleweeds."

"Time is out of joint, Slim, time is out of joint."

Slim had the gasjacks out. "You said a mouthful."

Stack accessed the gas panel and had it open. Slim dipped the hose into the tank, and plugged in the system interface. A row of lights lit up in different colours and went on and off in sequence, beeping a happy tune.

"Had a customer in earlier all the way frum Paris, France, we did. String of onions round his neck, stripey shirt and a beret, practically. Had an oo-la-la accent like you wouldn't believe."

"Is that right?"

Tyree was out of the cruiser too, now.

"You got some ribs on, Slim?"

"No ma'am," he replied. "Kitchen done gone lost its mind this after'. B-B-Q is off."

Tyree spat in the dust. It would be back to the Cav rations. N-R-Gee candies and mineral water.

"I might get some recaff goin' if'n the kettle ain't shot to hell and back."

"I'll pass."

Stack tried not to look at Leona Tyree as she paced the forecourt, tried not to notice the way her hair escaped from the regulation bun, tried not to follow the curves of her body. She looked good in the Cav uniform, tight blue pants with yellow stripes down the outside, tubetop short-sleeve blouse with sergeant's stripes, the heavy gauntlets she was peeling off. Perhaps he should put in for the sergeants' exams again when they got back to Fort Apache. If they were equal in rank again, perhaps the thing between them might take new fire. Fourth time lucky, maybe.

"Hey, cowgirl," shouted Kling from the back of the cruiser as he wound down the tinted window, "Get me a couple of hits of co-cola while you're out there."

Tyree pretended not to hear him, and worked the aches out of her knees, elbows, wrists and hands. Stack admired the way she used martial arts exercises to overcome the inevitable pains of the driving life. She was much more disciplined than him, much more organized. No wonder she got her stripes.

There was a roar and a smell, and a motorsickle pulled up next to the cruiser. Stack eyed the cykeman, a young guy in traditional leathers. He wasn't flying colours. He had no distinguishing marks.

"How about some service?" the cykeman shouted in an inappropriately reedy, high voice.

Slim ignored his new customer. "Say, trooper," he began, "I heard me a new one. What do you call a cuss that goes all the way frum New York City to Paris, France, crossin' the Atlantic, and then comes all the way back again, without ever takin' one single bath?"

There was a clicking from the forecourt terminal, and Stack smelled something odd in the air. He looked around. Tyree was alert too. It wasn't the cykeman. He was lighting up a smoke. It was the gasjack. There were sparks around it, and a whisper of smoke.

Slim began to laugh deep in his gut, his rolls of fat shaking, and he answered his riddle. "You call him... "

Stack and Tyree hit the ground at the same time.

"A dirty double crosser!"

Then, all hell broke loose.

VI

THE DEMON, NUDGED from its resting place, jumped, and swarmed up through the gasjack into the cruiser's guidance and maintainance system.

Taken by surprise, the machine caved in immediately. The demon was happier here than in the ramshackle gas station. This was top-of-the-line, this was state-of-the-art. It located itself in the main control centre, and dispersed its spawn throughout the system.

It left Beulah behind, exhausted and broken. It had no further use for the Gas 'n' B-B-Q.

The engine was a dream in steel and oil. The weapons systems were superbly trim. The memory banks were deliciously full of information. And the demon could sense the cruiser's parent datanet, with which it had interfaced within the last day. Fort Apache. Even the echoes of the Fort were awesome to the newcomer. It was as far beyond the cruiser as the cruiser was beyond a digital watch. Some hour soon...

The cruiser, possessed in an instant, came to life.

It had a voicebox, with a limited repertoire of mechanist platitudes – "Please fasten your safety belt," "A gas refill is needed within three hundred miles," "Emergency shutdown will commence," "Have a nice day" – but which could be adapted to its needs.

"Aaaaaaaaaaaowwwwwww!" it howled. "Rock and rowll-lllll!'

VII

TYREE ROLLED ACROSS the forecourt as the cruiser's hood-mount lases, suddenly extruded, burned up the tarmac. An oilcan exploded, and drops of flaming liquid scattered over a twenty-foot radius. Pain bit her leg as a patch of her britches caught fire. She pressed the flame out in the dirt, and pushed against the asphalt, launching herself upright.

"Kling's gone psycho!" she shouted to Stack.

The lase swivelled upwards, and she had to duck to avoid the needle beam. The cruiser's engines grumbled, and the car began to move forwards.

But Kling was still in the back.

This was crazy.

She could see Kling, battering glass as the windows slid upwards, screaming behind the soundproofing, his mouth an irregular, contorted oval. Slim was heading off towards his outhouse, zig-zagging with surprising agility to make himself less of a target. He almost made it, but the miniature chaingun that rose from the roof coughed, and a row of red splashes stitched across the back of his overalls. He was pushed forward a few yards as his legs kept pumping, but there was no hope. He virtually fell in two parts when he collapsed in the sand. The chaingun angled down and discharged itself completely, sucking in the belt and spitting out hot brass cartridges. Slim shook as the bullets went into and around his corpse.

Tyree had her revolver out, but it was difficult to know what to shoot at. She took cover behind the house, but the cruiser followed her. It was definitely out of control, moving without anyone in the driver's seat giving orders. Inside, Kling might be having a fit. His face was bloody and he was thrashing wildly. Her first assumption had been wrong. The T-H-R Op was not in control.

Stack was under the porch, wriggling his way under the entire house. That put him out of the picture for the next minute or so. Slim was dead, Kling was immobilized. That left her.

The car, moving with casual ease, bumped over Slim and swung around the corner of the house. The chaingun was empty, but the matched lases were primed. The motorsickle man had hared off the forecourt at the first sign of serious hassle, and was nearing the horizon. Slim's dog loped off towards the desert, leaving the humans and their machine to settle it between themselves. Tyree felt like shooting the mutt, but saved her bullets.

The lase stretched and aimed. It flashed briefly, and the biker – not quite out of range – fell off his mount. His head rolled independently. Someone else dead in the sand.

Knowing it would do no good, Tyree shot at the middle of the windscreen, aiming at the head of an invisible driver. The durium-laced glass didn't break, although the bullet lodged in a little white crater. She was loaded up with ScumStoppers, explosive rounds that were designed to bring down hopped-up gangcultists, but they weren't made to put a dent in a US Cavalry Road Cruiser. She shot one of the lases off, and the other withdrew quickly into the bonnet. It could fire through pinholes in the headlights as well as from the open. That gave less flexibility of movement, but didn't stop the beam cutting deep. And the cruiser hadn't yet called upon its mortars, the crowd-control gasses, the maxiscreamers or a dozen other devices.

"Aeeeeowww," screamed the cruiser, the system's voicebox channelled through the loudhailer, "ah'm the dog-gonnedest, gol-darnedest, hog-fuckinest buckaroo ever to draw on a man frum behind!"

A red beam came out of the headlight, and the wooden house smouldered where it touched. Stack had better get out soon, or a fire would be falling on his head.

Tyree ran, knowing it was not going to be pleasant being around the gas station when the fire spread to the underground tanks.

"Ah'm the blood-thirstiest, shoot-'em-firstiest, fuck-danged worstiest desperado…"

She dropped to one knee, and took a shot at the front wheel.

"… north…"

Her aim was perfect, but that didn't do her any good.

"… south…"

The bullet exploded, but the tyre didn't burst.

"… east…"

She didn't even feel any better.

"… and WEST of the Pecos!"

The cruiser came at her like a wildcat, inching forward slowly, engine rasping like a buzzsaw. She couldn't tell what it was exactly, but the car looked somehow different. For some reason, she was reminded of Spanish Fork. The sun glinting on the tinted windscreen made exactly the same patterns it had when reflected in Elder Seth's mirrorshades as he tried to kill the panzergirl who had robbed him.

The demons were back.

She could run again, but she thought she was dealing with an intelligence akin to an attack dog. It would be more likely to tear her apart if she made a dash for it, if she showed her fear. She tried to stand tall, legs slightly apart, and holstered her gun. It wasn't Mexican, but it was a stand-off.

"Stop right there you miserable rebellious fuckin' cyberpsycho sonofabitch death-on-wheels hearse!"

It rolled to a halt, and the sun-sensitive windows became fully transparent. Behind the cruiser, Tyree could see the gas station taking fire. Black smoke swept up into the cloudless sky. In the back of the vehicle, Kling was tearing at his clothes. She realized the internal cooling-heating system was going insane. Kling's suit was smoking, and bullets of sweat popped from his pores. He struggled, and pulled his gun.

The idiot!

The shot was completely muffled, but she could imagine it ricocheting inside the cruiser until it lodged in something soft. A seat, or Ken Kling the Killing Machine.

If he had shot himself, he had not put himself out of action, because he was still convulsing. For the first time, Tyree felt sorry for the man.

And sorry for herself. She wished she'd had more than N-R-Gee and recaff for a last meal. She wished she hadn't dumped Nathan Stack. She wished she hadn't let Elder Seth walk away from Spanish Fork without at least trying to bring him down. She wished... Hell, there was no point in wishing.

The rear side door hissed open, and Kling fell out, screaming and shouting. He'd holed himself through the thigh. His expensive clothes were a mess. His hairstyle was lumpy and melting.

What would Ms H think?

"Get back, Kling," she said. "Slowly."

He couldn't hear, or didn't care. He still had his gun. He fired a wild shot. She realized the T-H-R man was aiming at her, blaming her.

"We're not responsible, Kling," she shouted. Kling stumbled forwards, and fired again. He missed again, but was getting closer. She pulled her gun and brought it up.

"Kling," she snapped, feeling stupid, "Don't make me shoot you."

His face was ugly with pain and rage. He was bleeding like a burst leech. His wounded leg was trailing uselessly as he pulled himself along the side of the car, leaving a smear.

Tyree could have sworn the blood sank in like water into sand. The polished and painted metal was clean now. She imagined something licking vampirish lips.

The cruiser just sat there like a machine, as if it had nothing to do with anything.

Kling was only a few feet away. Even he couldn't miss at this range. He raised his gun, and she shot him. In the remaining three minutes of her life, she would tell herself several times she had no choice but to make a head shot, that there hadn't been time to wound Ken Kling. Then, she would call herself a liar.

Stack was out from under, and running towards her.

The cruiser's right headlamp winked, and she felt her shin sting as the beam holed her leather boot. It passed through flesh and bone.

She was dead already, she knew. There was just going to be a little more fuss before it was all over.

VIII

STACK COULDN'T FIGURE it. Leona had just shot Ken Kling. The cruiser was on automatic and killing people. The gas station was burning, and due to go up like the Fourth of July in moments. This wasn't a routine patrol anymore. The peace was over.

He drew his gun, not liking where this was leading.

"Leona," he said. "Drop your weapon. Maybe we can sort this out."

She fell to one knee, wounded somehow, and looked at him. He saw hurt in her eyes, not at the physical pain, but at his instinctive assumption she was behind all this.

But, damnit, she had control of the cruiser! She had just shot a T-H-R man!

She had dropped her gun, and was holding her leg with both hands.

"Leona?"

She opened her mouth to speak, and the cruiser lurched forwards. It must have hit a stone as it started, because it lifted up off the ground. The front bumper struck Leona in the chest, forcing her backwards, and the ve-hickle drove clear over her.

Stack screamed, and automatically fired his pistol, emptying it in the air. It got hot in his hand, and he threw it away.

The cruiser drove off, leaving Leona sprawled in the sand, half-buried already, leaking black blood. Stack ran to her, and took her in his arms. There was a fresh tyre track across her chest. Her hair was loose, and thick with blood, grit and oil.

She was still breathing, but he knew there was no hope. He took a squeezer of morph-plus from his belt-slung medkit and shot it into her arm. As he depressed the syringe, an eye snapped open in her soot-blacked face.

He had something to tell her, but he couldn't get it out.

She gripped him with one hand, clutching a fistful of his shirt, scraping skin off his chest. She was shaking as the drug killed her nervous system. There wouldn't be any more pain, at least.

"Leona?"

Blood came out of her nostrils and mouth.

"Le… oh…"

The cruiser was coming back. Stack disentangled himself from the corpse, and ran. He ran towards the burning house, the cruiser swallowing the ground between them in instants.

There was a voice coming from the car. "Cum-a-kay-aye-yippie," it shouted, "yippie-yippie-yippie-aye, cum-a-kay-aye-yippie-yippie-ay!"

He felt flames as he ran past the house, through the already burning rubble. He was surrounded by heat.

Behind him, the cruiser's engines gunned.

The gas tanks exploded, and he was at the centre of a fire-ball.

IX

DUROC'S CHEST WAS as good as new. Better, even. Thanks to the Zarathustra treatment, designed by GenTech's finest and available only to the very wealthy, Duroc's body became more durable, more healthy, with each hurt overcome. "Every day, in every way," he muttered, "I am getting better and better."

The woman at the desk was plastic. She could have been a sexclone with a voice-activated set of automatic responses. She smiled at him, and buzzed him through. There weren't many people who could be admitted as easily to the Central Lodge in Salt Lake City.

The two tall, bearded, barrel-chested men stood aside, and Duroc went through the double doors into Elder Seth's personal office.

The Elder sat with his back to the door, looking up at nine inset television screens on the wall, each showing a different channel. There was a soundtrack babel. Lola Stechkin read the news on ZeeBeeCee. A bionic bobby doffed his nipple-head helmet and beat up a scruffy French terrorist in a 2D British police series. President Estevez emphatically made a point. A Spanish-speaking lady aristocrat with remarkable cheekbones struggled on a soap to come to terms with her daughter's romantic attachment to a dobermann pinscher. A cartoon Op chased Mohawk-headed renegades on a kiddie show with more violence to the minute than Hitler's home movies. Petya Tcherkassoff, in an open-fronted white shirt and unpleasantly tight culottes, seduced a teenage girl with a song called "My Heart Bleeds Love for You" in a Russian musickie video. And the Josephite Tabernacle Choir raised money on Salt Lake's own network.

Seth swivelled around on his chair, and smiled. Duroc was reminded vaguely of a piranha. It was a smile designed purely to show off sharp teeth. It wouldn't extend to the eyes currently concealed behind dark glasses. The office was bare apart from the screens. Everywhere else in the City, there were crosses and portraits of Elder Seth and the original Elder Shatner. Here, no trimmings were needed.

The Elder stood up, and extended a hand. He wore a conservative black suit, anonymously tailored in a style that hadn't changed for two hundred years.

They shook hands. As always, Duroc was surprised the Elder's skin was warm, normal. Such a great man should have ice-cold flesh and a grip like a vice.

"It is done?"

Duroc nodded.

"It is as well."

The Elder was the titular head of the Josephite Church, a protestant sect founded in 1843 by the American visionary Joseph Shatner. By the sheer force of his will, Nguyen Seth had rallied many followers, and persuaded the United States to turn over sovereignty of the wilderness of Utah to him. He had renamed it Deseret, he had brought the first motor-wagons of resettlers to the region, he had supervised the irrigation and fertilization projects that had made crops grow where science said none could, and he had built a power base unmatched in the mid-west. Now, having unified and fortified the Josephites, he was actively seeking gentile resettlers to bulk out the population.

It was not a bad roll-call of achievements for someone who barely qualified as a human being.

Seth flipped his desk intercom. "Saskia, would you bring in a kid and the ceremonial knife?"

He looked at Duroc. "Blood must be spilled, Roger. There must be a seal on the mission."

The Frenchman was unable to hide his distaste.

"You will understand, Roger. When the time comes, you will understand."

The doors opened, and the plastic woman led in a young goat.

part two:
who was that
masked woman?

I

THE US CAVALRY had no idea how to treat her, and so she had spent the morning being given a tour of Fort Apache and its environs. Captain Lauderdale, the spare officer Colonel Younger had ordered to keep her out of trouble, had taken her outside the perimeter walls and shown her London Bridge, the red British telephone boxes, and what was left of The Old Dog and Duck Pub. Lake Havasu had sold itself as a tourist attraction before the Colorado River dried up. Chantal understood it was a typical ghost town, its residential area turning gradually to desert as the sand drifted in and the houses collapsed. In a thousand years, you would never know there had been a community here.

The bridge, transported stone by stone from England, was really falling down now. Lauderdale attempted a joke about it, and called her "my fair lady," but she didn't respond. She thought there was something creepy about the captain, and her training had taught her to trust her intuitions. She didn't have any measurable psychic abilities, but she had spent so much time swapping synapses with the datanets that she had her moments, her occasional flashes of extranormal insight.

Spanning a channel of rancid mud and cracked, dry earth, the bridge did not look special. It was rather a bland design, with nothing distinctively British about it. There were wrought-iron lamp posts, mostly twisted into half-pretzel shapes.

"The story goes that the people who bought it got the wrong bridge." Lauderdale said. "They wanted the one that goes up and down—"

"Tower Bridge."

"That's right. Tower Bridge."

Chantal examined shared heart graffiti etched into the stone, and looked towards the remains of the town.

"Does anybody live down there?"

Lauderdale looked both ways, as if afraid his superiors were listening. "Not officially, but there's a large detachment of men and women at the Fort, with no way to spend their pay and not much to do in their off hours."

"So?"

"I am given to understand that there are… um… camp followers, and a bar or two, where they have… um… gambling."

A tumbleweed rolled lazily by. There wasn't much wind, so the things must mainly lie and rot.

"The place looks completely deserted."

"They come out at night, Ms Juillerat, and sleep during the day."

"Like vampires?"

"Yes, exactly like vampires."

From the look of disaste curling about his thin lips, Chantal guessed that Captain Lauderdale had little use for camp followers and gamblers. Perhaps he subscribed to one of the many repressive protestant doctrines running rampant here in the United States? She found it hard to keep them separate in her mind – Mormons, Josephites, Scientologists, Moonies, Seventh-Day Amish, Hittites, Mennonites, Danites, Disneyworlders, the Bible Belt – and imagined they themselves had the same problem. Being a Catholic was a lot easier since Vatican LXXXV loosened things up.

"Where did the people go? The ones who lived here?"

They had found a skeleton dressed as an English policeman, half-buried in rubbish and sand, but few other signs of previous habitation.

"The nearest PZ, if they could afford it. If not, there are squatters' towns around most conurbations. Some take to the roads, like the okies in the 1930s. They're the problem."

"I don't understand?"

"It's difficult to drive around the burned-out vehicles. Defenceless citizens should keep off the interstate."

From the outside, Fort Apache looked more like a medieval castle than the wooden stockades of the Old West. Its windowless walls were stone and steel, and the structure was tiered like an old-fashioned wedding cake. A few sensors, tiny at this distance, revolved on the roof, and the Stars and Stripes flew, hanging stiff from a rod. It was one of a chain of identical forts dotted throughout the Western States.

There was a noise, and Lauderdale drew his sidearm. It had been another stone falling from the bridge into the mud. The captain grinned without humour and holstered his weapon.

"You have to be alert," he explained.

"It's too quiet out there, you mean?"

"Huh?"

"In the films, that's the cavalry catchphrase. Just before an Indian attack, someone says 'It's too quiet out there' and an arrow sticks in him."

Lauderdale didn't crack a smile. Their senses of humour were noticeably out of sync. "I never liked Westerns much, Ms Juillerat. Never liked movies, really."

"Then what are you doing dressed up like John Wayne?"

The revived US Cavalry wore outfits modelled exactly on the 1870s styles. Lauderdale had a blue tunic, a modified stetson with the cav insignia and carried a Colt 45.

"It's just the uniform. I'm here to serve my country."

Most of the personnel Chantal had met at Fort Apache said something like that. They were proud that the US Cav was still an arm of the US Government, especially since it had fought off the last privatisation plan. However, the organization was mainly involved in keeping the interstate routes clear for GenTech, Eidolon and the other multinats. She guessed that private citizens, like the modern okies Lauderdale had complained about, were mainly considered to be a nuisance. This was no era to be an innocent bystander.

From the bridge, they could see the approach road. A column was nearing the fort. Motorcyke outriders, a couple of cruisers, and a triple-jointed tanker.

"Here comes the water and the gas," said Lauderdale. "Supplies for a month."

"You really are cut off here?"

"That's right. Where there's no water, people don't live. This is not a natural community. We had pipelines, but the Maniax trashed them during the first days of the joint action."

"Ah yes, the Maniax. In Rome, I saw on the TV about them. Children, were they not?"

Lauderdale spat, "Savages!"

"They have been... pacified?"

"If you mean killed, mostly they have. The rest are in Readjustment Camps, or on the offshore penal colonies. You have the same set-up in Europe, I believe. You dump all your human garbage on Sicily."

"The European Community does. I'm not a Eurocitizen myself."

"The Maniax moved in after it started to break down. When it stopped raining, when food became scarce. The Maniax, and people like them. They sacked the towns that were losing it, raped and murdered at random, destroyed property, looted on an industrial scale."

"Their average age, I hear, was fifteen."

"Maybe so. You don't ask for a birth certificate when you're hand-to-hand with a genetically engineered homicidal psychopath."

The Maniax were only the largest of the gangcults, Chantal had heard. By no means, the worst. She had been briefed back in Rome by her superiors on the groups she might come across. She had a special dispensation to commit suicide if captured by

The Bible Belt, the fundamentalist crazies who viewed the world as a large-scale Sodom and Gomorrah and saw it as their duty to bring down the Wrath of God upon all sinners. She wasn't worried. She had been trained – in the language of the States, she was a "Proper Op" – and she could deal with most eventualities.

A bugle call sounded on the tannoy, and gates appeared in the hitherto seamless walls. The column crept into the fort like a maggot crawling into an apple. Barked orders carried on the still air. The last vehicle in the convoy was an open truck. People stood up on the flatbed, shackled together.

"More Maniak stragglers. Captain Badalamenti has the mop-up detail. We'll be bringing them in for months."

The prisoners were dragged off the truck and led into the fort by guards. One Mohawk-haired giant shouted defiance, and a trooper struck her with something. There was a crackle and the Maniak fell to her knees, screaming.

"Cattle prod," Lauderdale explained. "It's the only thing they understand. Pain."

As the Maniak twisted in agony, the prisoners she was chained to were pulled off their feet. They fell badly, leg and wrist irons clanking. The grossly fat sergeant in charge of the detail took the prod from the trooper and touched it not to any particular prisoner but to a length of the chain connecting them. Sparks flew, and sixteen men and women screamed in unison.

"Pain, Ms Juillerat. They're experts at inflicting it. It's our job to turn things round."

"O brave new world…"

"I beg your pardon?"

"That has such people in it!"

II

BREVET MAJOR GENERAL Marshall K Younger examined his reflection in the glass that covered the life-size portrait of Charlton Heston which had pride of place in his office. He tried to match his head and shoulders to the ex-president's, and fell only a little short. You could do a lot with your body if you exercised regularly and took the Zarathustra treatment, but, unless you wanted to become a complete cyborg, you were stuck with the bones you were born with. Younger wasn't ready for that yet. He thumped the sides of his stomach with both hands, relishing the way his tight fists bounced off leather-supple gut muscles. Younger stuck a foot-long Cuban cigar in his face, bit off and spat away the wet end, flipped his Zippo and touched flame to the tip. He sucked thick smoke into his GenTech remodelled lungs.

"Ain't no way you're gonna give me cancer, you long brown bastard," he said to his cigar, puffing deeply, "so you can just give up trying to mug my alveoli."

It had been a simple treatment, and was available at a massive discount to serving officers in the Road Cav. The corp wanted the interstates open, and didn't mind throwing a few favours around to keep in with the law enforcement community. And as a brevet ranking, Younger was grateful for the perks of the trade.

Younger snapped off a perfect salute at Heston. Big Chuck had been the man who authorized the revival of the United States Cavalry. Before that, keeping the peace on the roads had been down to the Highway Patrol, and the interstates had been warzones. Now, Out West at least, you could guarantee your wrappers would get through. Big Chuck had done a hell of a lot for the country. His Moral Re-Armament Drive, and his Youth Pioneer Scheme had given the country some backbone again. And, of course, him and Senator Enderby had pushed through the Enderby Act and opened up the field of law enforcement to private individuals and organizations. The Cav wouldn't be here if it weren't for Enderby and Big Chuck.

Too bad about Senator Enderby. Younger had never believed anything those three Filippino houseboys had said on TV during the MRA hearings, and he knew for a fact that the alleged monies paid by the Hammond Maninski and T-H-R Agencies to the senator had been in the nature of remuneration for his work as a consultant with regards to the niceties of the law he had designed. But Big Chuck had let Enderby go to the wall. Younger bet the President had cried about it, but you had to put personal relationships beneath duty, service, your country and what was right. That was the only way to be.

There was a framed photograph of President North around somewhere, but Younger couldn't bear to put it where it showed. After Big Chuck, Solly Ollie had been such a come-down. Heck, who needed a Prezz who couldn't cut it in the Marines and had to fall back on politics to carve himself a career? Still, not as bad as that liberal pussy currently in the White House.

Younger had been using his few minutes" peace and quiet to indulge himself. He had unlocked the cabinet in which he kept his leather-bound books. This was his private library, his one indulgence. On the spines, they all had titles like *Statutes and Proceedings of the State of Arizona, 2008-2015* and *Complete United States Cavalry Regulations, Vol. VI*, but inside they were his kind of books. Every once in a while, he would haul one down and pick a page at random, then indulge in his most extravagant fantasies, assembling in his mind the makings of an orgiastic wallow in excess and voluptuousness.

Today, he had turned up one of his favourite peccadilloes. Potato dishes.

He ran through the variations. Creamed potatoes with soured cream and chives. Creamed potatoes with nutmeg. Stuffed jacket potatoes with garlic and herbs. Pommes de terre boulangere. Gratin dauphinois. Sauté potatoes Lyon-naise. Sauté potatoes Niçoise. New Jersey potatoes with fresh herb butter. Buffalo fries with rock salt and guacamole.

He ran his fingers over the glossy illustrations. He checked off the ingredients against his mental inventory. His kitchen was reasonably well stocked for this ass-end-of-nowhere post-ing, but there were so many things he had not been able to get shipped out, even with his pull in the service. His mouth was full of saliva and smoke. He swallowed them both, and slipped the cookbook back into its space, locking the case.

He saluted Big Chuck again. The former president would understand Younger's needs.

He checked his quartz digital pocket watch against the antique long-case clock from the original fort. It was time to make the rounds, time to prod the people who needed prodding and give a nod of approval to the personnel who didn't.

Outside his office, he accepted the salutes of several passing junior officers. Colonel Rintoon, his second-in-command, was waiting for him, clipboard tucked under his arm.

"Good morning, sir," he snapped.

"Morning, Vladek. Any surprises overnight?"

"Overdue patrol, sir."

"Hmmn. How long?"

"The full twelve hours. No radio contact. No distress blip. Tyree, Stack, and a T-H-R Op, Kling."

"Well, we can't lose one of our associates like that. Get a fix on their current position, and try to re-establish lines of communication. Anything else?"

Vladek looked at his clipboard. "Weekly convoy just in. Badalamenti reports sixteen pick-ups on the road. Maniax mostly, but we've got a stray Virus Vigilante and a Psychopomp."

"The 'Pomps are supposed to be history since that business at Spanish Fork."

"There are one or two left. Always are."

"It's not Jessamyn Bonney, by any chance?"

"No sir, I would have said. It's some low-rent ratskag. She barely shows up on the seedings."

"You've checked warrants on the intake. Anything outstanding?"

"The usual. Multiple homicide, driving without due c and a, line-running, highway piracy."

"Process 'em and ship 'em out, then."

"Already taken care of."

"Good work."

Younger and Rintoon strolled through the fort, crossing the courtyard from the admin block to the Ops Centre.

The space was enclosed, but three storeys tall. Cruisers and cykes were being stripped and serviced in the motor pool. Sergeant Quincannon was squarebashing some new recruits on the parade ground. Everybody who had a job was doing it, which was the way it should be.

In the centre of the courtyard was an imposing statue, symbolizing the heritage of the service. General Custer, Teddy Roosevelt and Trickydick Nixon, shoulder to shoulder, six-guns waving, with Dwight D Eisenhower holding up the star-spangled banner behind the grouping. Some drunken trooper had shot Nixon in the face. The culprit was still in the guardhouse, but Younger couldn't say he was entirely upset about the vandalism. The ex-president looked a sight better without his skislope nose, and Younger had never been convinced that he would have known what to do with the Buntline specials the sculptor had given him.

"What about our guest, sir?"

"The Italian woman?"

"Swiss, sir. She works out of Rome, but she's a Swiss national."

"Whatever. She's getting the tour?"

"Lauderdale's looking after her."

"Good man."

Sergeant Quincannon saluted as Younger and Rintoon walked by, and his troop raggedly followed suit. Younger bothered to return the Quince's gesture. The red-faced Irishman was just the kind of soldier he wanted in his command. He was three times the man drunk that most of the rest were sober. Which was a useful trait to have, since he was a frequent imbiber of Shochaiku Double-Blend.

"What do we do with her later? When she's seen everything?"

"Full co-operation, all down the line. That's come through channels, so don't get in her way. I understand it's international, so don't embarrass the government."

"You mean we should—"

"Snap to and shape up, Vladek, snap to and shape up. She's a fully-trained Op, probably has more kills than Redd Harvest to her credit. Go along with her as far as you can. Just don't get us into trouble, okay?"

"Okay and affirmative."

"Good man."

The doors of the Ops Centre slid open, and the officers stepped in. The trooper on the desk gave them retinal and palm-print checks, established that they were the people whose faces they were wearing and logged them in.

"By the way, extend my invitation to Ms Juillerat for dinner this evening. Also you and Hendry Faulcon, Captains Lauderdale and Finney, Doc King and Lieutenant Colosanto. That's boy-girl, boy-girl, boy-girl, boy-girl. I'll cook. Osso buco. That's shin of veal in white wine with tomatoes, garlic, lemon, parsley and fresh-milled black pepper."

"I'll take care of that, sir."

"Make her feel at home. Italian food. Of course, if she's Swiss, maybe I should switch to fondue bourgignon."

"That's your decision, colonel."

They entered the despatch room. Personnel were at their consoles, tracking and logging. A map of the territory took up one wall. Dozens of lights moved on the map.

"Now," said Younger, "about that overdue patrol?"

III

THEY WERE BACK inside Fort Apache, and Lauderdale was explaining the day-to-day duties of the Road Cavalry to her.

"We patrol the interstates regularly, keep in touch with the outlying settlements. There are still some sandside communities out there. And there are motorwagon trains to escort, and convoys to keep track of. And, of course, there are the gangcults. Mainly, we just try and find out where they are these days. The wars are over. We don't seek to engage the enemy unless we have to. The recent joint action against the Maniax is fairly atypical. Some of the private agencies like to strut their stuff from time to time. It makes their customers think they're getting service."

They were in the motor pool, where the vehicles from the convoy were being worked over by oily mechanics. Lauderdale called over Trooper Grundy, an auto ostler, to show off some of the special features of the US Cav cruiser. Chantal listened politely, but didn't find out anything she hadn't learned from her research work.

"That's a nice machine you came in with, ma'am," said the ostler. "A Ferrari?"

"Yes. It's standard issue."

"Your agency must be well set-up."

"You could say that."

Lauderdale coughed. "If you'll come this way, Ms Juillerat, I'll show you our Ops Centre. It's the command module for the whole fort."

The captain led her into the central tower of the fort, and got her through the checkpoint. The girl at the desk asked for her details, but she flashed her authorization and the receptionist raised an eyebrow.

"Pass 'Go', collect two hundred dollars and Get Out of Jail Free, huh? We don't get many through like you. Did you have to sleep with someone important to get clearance like this?"

Chantal smiled. "I had to get married."

"Tough."

"It's very demanding."

The girl was filling out her badge. "You're telling me. I've been down the aisle three times. With me, it just didn't take."

She pinned the badge on Chantal's lapel.

"Right, take care of that. It'll open all the doors you're cleared to go through for you, but don't spill coffee on it or the thing shorts out and you'll be apprehended on sight as a security risk."

"I'll be careful."

Lauderdale guided her through the labyrinth. Smartly-dressed men and women hurried purposefully down the corridors. The air was full of communications. There were plaques, recording the names of cavalry personnel who had fallen in the line of duty. Trophies were mounted in glass cases. Geronimo's headdress, Phil Sheridan's uniform, a canteen from Little Big Horn, a variety of arrows, a blood-clogged chainsaw from the Phoenix NoGo Campaign of Pacification, some dented hubcaps from Route 666, scraps of car bodywork with gangcult decals. Everybody was armed. As a child, watching television in Lucerne, Chantal had assumed that everybody in America carried a gun. Back then, it might not have been true.

"This is the Ops Centre," Lauderdale said, ushering her into a large, semicircular space dominated by an illuminated map. A sabre from the Battle of Washita was in a case over the map. Heads turned. Lauderdale saluted.

"Sir," he said.

A tallish, well-built man with an iron gray moustache returned the captain's salute. He must be in his fifties, but he looked fit enough to be a gladiator.

"Sir, this is Ms Chantal Juillerat, from Rome."

The officer extended a hand, which she shook.

"This is our commanding officer, Major General Younger."

"Brevet Major General Younger, Lauderdale. At your service, ma'am."

"Thank you."

"You've been looked after?"

"I have."

"You like osso buco?"

Chantal was fazed. "Why, I've never had it."

"Fine. You won't have anything to compare my efforts with. Eight o'clock sharp suit you? Dinner, I mean?"

Lauderdale, who turned into a statue with a steel backbone in Younger's presence, chipped in with, "Ms Juillerat wanted to see our command centre, sir."

"Commendable, captain. Eight o'clock?"

"Certainly, Brevet Major General."

Lights moved on the big map, and people with headsets talked into their microphones. It was the kind of set Chantal remembered from TV coverage of the space program in the late '70s, or from repeated secret agent shows from the early

21st Century. *Alias* with Jennifer Garner, *24* with Kiefer Sutherland, or *MI6* with Hugh Grant.

"What precisely are you doing at this moment?" she asked

"Well, ma'am," began the major general, "there are always many missions to keep track of. There's a GenTech convoy out of El Paso headed for San Bernardino. El Paso is the railhead for the vat-grown organs that come out of Mexico, and San Berdoo is GenTech's West Coast centre for transplant surgery. We're riding shotgun on a shipment of hearts, lungs and livers, I guess."

"GenTech are a major customer?"

The Major General looked stern for a moment. "The United States Cavalry doesn't have customers, ma'am. We are public servants. We're here for the taxpayers."

"I'm sorry. English is not my first language. Sometimes I make errors."

"Think nothing of it. You're right, GenTech do route much of their interstate traffic by us. I think that's a mark of confidence. The other corps do the same. And we do a lot of wagonmaster work."

"You shepherd the resettlers?"

"That we do. It's a tradition of the outfit."

"Do you have much connection with the Josephites?"

Younger paused. Chantal wondered if she had said the wrong thing, aroused his suspicion. Finally, he answered her, "No, not that much. At the first, we kept the route to Salt Lake open, but they have their own Ops now. I understand they do a decent job, but I'm not really up on the affairs of Deseret. I'm not sure if it's within our jurisdiction. It's only notionally part of the United States."

"Sir," cut in a woman at one of the tracking consoles. "We have a trace from Tyree…"

Younger turned, and stood over the tracker, peering at the screen. There was a moving blip, travelling down an anonymous road.

"Put it up on the big screen, Finney."

Captain Finney, a plain, pleasant-faced person, punched some keys, and her picture took up the whole wall. There were placenames. Dead Rat, Friendly, Baker Butte, Poland, Crown King, Octave. The blip travelled fast. It was the only thing moving.

"That's wrong," said Finney. "Tyree was supposed to swing by the Petrified Forest, check out Escadilla and come back by way of Tucson. She's in the Tonto Basin."

"You're sure it's her cruiser?"

Finney flicked some switches. "Double-checking. Yep, the radio's down, but the auto-recognition is still holding steady. She's moving flat out, pushing the capabilities of the cart if you ask me. That's Tyree all right. At least, that's her ve-hickle and it's not programmed for any other driver."

"Looks like we've got us a rogue. Vladek, muster some pursuits."

Colonel Rintoon got on the telephone, and scrambled some field units, ordering them to intercept. He held the receiver to his uniform chest and looked up at the screen, taking it personally.

Chantal was trying to follow this.

"Leona is true and blue, sir," said Finney. "She's Cav from the toes up. Something bad must be going down."

"I don't like this." Younger pulled out a cigar and chewed it unlit.

"Is this an unusual occurrence?" Chantal asked.

Younger chewed some more, and looked pained. "I should say so. You can't hijack a Cav cruiser. It shuts down unless you feed it your personal code, and it even double-checks your body heat pattern. There's only human error."

"And what exactly has gone wrong?"

"Sergeant Tyree — a good soldier — appears to have gone renegade. She's obviously not in pursuit of anything, and she's way off her course. She's twelve hours overdue on a return to the fort, and she hasn't called in since some time yesterday afternoon. She's got a trooper and a liaison from Turner-Harvest-Ramirez with her."

"I have a response from a patrol," said Rintoon. "Conway and Mixter are up on Mogollon Mesa. They can come down and interface with Tyree and Stack. If they need help, Conway'll give it. If they've turned, Conway'll put an end to that."

Finney looked as if she was about to protest, but she let it go. Younger nodded, and Rintoon relayed the order. A new blip appeared on the screen, moving in a course set to intercept the original light.

"Who's the T-H-R guy? What do we know about him?"

Rintoon had the facts. "Kenneth Kling. A nobody. No record at all. He just has a nuisance value assignment."

"If Tyree is clean, it could be this Kling who's gone psycho on us."

Finney swivelled on her chair and tapped another keyboard. "I'll have his profile pulled from T-H-R in Denver." A printer stuttered, and Finney tore off a strip. "Shit! Uh, sorry, sir. I mean, uh, we have a negative on Kling. He's in his peter position, no advancement possible, no initiative, no more than basic skills, no major kinks. Someone has handwritten 'self-important sonofabitch' in the psychological evaluation box. This jack is one of nature's born hostages. No way could he be behind it."

The second blip was within twenty miles of the first, and closing fast. It was strange to see a potentially lethal combat reduced to a giant kiddie's board game.

"Lenihan, patch Conway through the PA system," ordered Younger.

A smart young lieutenant with a headset flicked some switches.

"... proceeding south-south-west... "crackled a male voice. "No visual contact as yet..."

"He means they can't see it," Younger explained.

The blips were getting close.

"I have it... a cruiser, for sure, up to 150 per according to my clock... Does not respond to radio transmissions... Am pursuing parallel course..."

The blips moved together, faster. The background mapscreen changed at the edges to accommodate the pursuit. The place-names they passed blurred.

"Make contact, Conway," said Rintoon.

"... proceeding..."

There was a tearing noise over the louspeaker, then a feedback whine. One of the blips went out.

"We've lost Conway," said Lenihan.

"Lost?"

"Lost, sir."

"Lost contact?" asked Younger.

"No..." Lenihan's voice was nearly cracked. "Lost. We have a heat source, but no ve-hickle. Conway's cruiser has been destroyed."

"That's not supposed to happen. What could Tyree be pack-ing that could do that much damage?"

"I'd have to run that through the computer and get back to you, sir. A battlefield nuclear weapon would do it, but that doesn't conform to the facts we have here. The best I can think of is a lethal malfunction in Conway's cruiser, and that doesn't fit the pattern either."

"Your runaway is slowing down," said Chantal.

The blip was dropping speed. The placenames stopped blur-ring on the map, and came into clear focus.

"Welcome," she said.

The blip was definitely travelling on a backroad to a place called Welcome.

"What's near Welcome?" asked Younger.

"Nothing," said Finney. "The original Fort Apache, from the Indian Wars, is out there somewhere."

"What's in Welcome?" asked Chantal. The blip was slowing to a halt.

"Let me see," Finney tapped keys. "It's still nominally inhab-ited. At least, it was last time we did a drive-by. There's a motel, operated by someone called Jonathan Behr, and something called the Silver Byte Saloon. That's more or less home to a chapter of the Gaschuggers..."

"Could they pull off a hijack?"

"No ma'am, they can hardly handle their own rigs, let alone anything of ours."

Chantal had a feeling that this was the thing she was here for.

"Is there anything else about the town?"

The blip was sitting there, flashing under the black letters of the name.

"Nothing, really. A couple of old-timers waiting to be killed. A large cemetery. No agriculture, no gas station. Used to be a Josephite Mission, but that's closed down. All gone to Deseret, I guess."

"I don't understand, ma'am," said Younger. "What are you interested in?"

"There's a church still standing," said Finney. "St Werburgh's. A Miguel O'Pray is down here as the pastor."

"A Catholic church?"

"I suppose so. It doesn't say. He's listed as Father O'Pray. That would make him Catholic, wouldn't it? I'm a sufi myself."

"Does it have a terminal?"

"Pardon?"

"A computer terminal. Is it on any of the datanets?"

"Uh, that's… um… classified."

"It wouldn't be classified if there weren't a terminal, right?"

"Um…"

"You're excused, Finney," said Younger. The woman looked relieved.

"Yes, there is a terminal. It's a community church. They feed into our communications web, and then Phoenix, Nogales, Lordsburg and El Paso. They're surprisingly well set-up."

"That's it," Chantal said. "The church. Welcome, Arizona."

Younger and Rintoon were still busy being befuddled.

"Gentlemen, get me clearance. I'm going out there."

IV

THERE WAS A pause, as the Swiss woman looked to Major General Younger for approval. The c-in-c nodded.

"Lauderdale, help the lady out."

Lauderdale saluted. He realized his back was hurting from standing up so straight. He was unable to relax in the presence of a superior officer. It was a survival-oriented trait in the Cav.

"Sir, yessir."

Ms Juillerat was striding out of the Ops Centre. Lauderdale followed. He tried to look as if he were not fixing his gaze on her movements as she walked. The Swiss was undoubtedly in great shape.

Ever since he had drawn this assignment, he had been wondering who exactly this foreign woman was. He judged her to be in her mid-twenties, but whatever she did she wasn't new to it. She had confidence to spare, and had demonstrated a wide variety of surprising areas of knowledge. She knew cars and she knew guns, and she was well-briefed on the workings of the Cavalry. He understood that she was brought up to speak French and Italian and that English was the language she learned when she had mastered Latin (!), Spanish and Japanese. Lauderdale could get by in Spanish, but that was it. Whenever the conversation strayed from purely professional matters, she developed zipped lips. She wore no wedding ring and gave the impression of almost unapproachable singleness, but had told the ostler she was married. The only thing she had let slip about her past was that she had been brought up mainly by nuns, and educated in Dublin, Rome and San Francisco.

"You will have my car fuelled and ready?"

"It'll be done."

"Good."

Ms Juillerat was something in computers, he guessed. She had paid particular attention when being shown around the datanet hook-up, and the information storage and retrieval system. But she had been very careful not to reveal who she was working for, and what her business with the Road Cavalry was. Considering her base of operations, Lauderdale wondered if she mightn't be Mafia. The Cav had made stranger allies in the past – it was common knowledge they had a treaty with the yakuza to protect certain business interests in return for a restraint on the part of the Japanese – and that would explain her reticence when questioned about her outfit. Like the yaks, the mafia probably broke no more laws in the course of its business day than the average multinat.

There was certainly a predatory cast to her fashion model's features – large, dark green eyes; long, straight nose; full, little-girl lips; clear, pale complexion – and he could imagine her executing a gangland hit without distaste or compassion. Lauderdale was brought up in front of the TV, and Ms Juillerat, from different angles, kept reminding him of actresses: Uma Thurman as Emma Peel in the way she held her shoulders, Sandra Bullock, Neve Campbell, Kate Winslet in *Ms .45,* Kirsten Dunst, Billie Piper in the remake of *Out of Africa,* Angelina Jolie.

"I'd appreciate it if your ostler checked out my onboard weapons systems and communications links. I've not had time to run a thorough field test, and I'd hate to be let down."

One thing Lauderdale was certain of, Chantal Juillerat was an Op. A top-of-the-line Op, like Redd Harvest, Woody Rutledge, Harry Parfitt or the Cav's own Captain Buffalo. She wore a black catsuit that showed her figure. She was well-rounded, unmistakably womanly, but lithe. He figured she would have the muscle tone of a young she-leopard. Her black hair was cut functionally short, and she carried herself like a fighter. She had the balance, and she had the reflexes. This would be one lethal little lady to tangle with.

"Have all your charts downloaded into my system. I only have the basic map software for the south-west. Rome may well be months out of date, and I think I'm going to need detailed intelligence."

He nodded. They were about the same height, but he had the impression that he needed three steps to keep up with her every one. He was getting a stitch, losing breath.

She wore no make-up, no jewellery except for a discreet silver crucifix on a chain round her neck. Her clothes bore no insignia, but gave the impression of a uniform. It was an outfit for fighting in.

They passed through the lobby. Ms Juillerat handed her badge back to the receptionist. The girl told them to have a nice day, and was rewarded with a tight smile.

In the courtyard, Ms Juillerat turned to him. "Get all those things done, and meet me at my car. I have to get some things from my room."

She strode off before he could answer.

He would not have liked to be standing in her way.

V

CHANTAL SAT CROSS-LEGGED on the floor of the room the Cav had assigned to her, and tried to centre herself. She held her hands together, and touched them to her lips. Meditation always helped her before she went into the field. She cleared her mind, made everything go away, and brought the mission to the fore. This was the Zen moment, the perfect focusing of achievement, becoming and intent. The mission was all she needed.

In moments, she was refreshed, prepared. She understood other Ops achieved the same ends through the use of stimulants. Glojo, Kray-Zee pills, speed. This was purer, less risky. The only side-effects were spiritual.

She pulled the metal box out from under the bunk, and put it on the plain desk. It was electrically sealed, and she had to key in the correct number sequence to open it.

The box took a few seconds to think it over, and then the lid rose silently. Someone had once told her she treated the box like a priest treats the pyx, the container in which communion wafers are stored. She would like to think that was stretching the point, but had had enough lessons in humility and self-awareness to know there was truth in it.

"Body and blood of our Redeemer," she muttered. "Father, forgive us."

Here, laid out in their velvet-lined inset depressions, were the tools of her trade. The skeleton keycards slipped into the pockets at her waist. The tinkering tools slotted into the ring of thin hoops above her knee. The shoulder pads – each loaded with three spare ammunition clips – slipped into her jacket and velcroed into place. The gunbelt laced at the front, and hung comfortably on her hips. The black-leather sheathed bowie knife – forged, like Jim Bowie's first model, from steel fused with star-born minerals from an asteroid – attached to her belt and thigh. The acorn-sized phosphorus fragmentation charges slid easily into the tight chambers of the belt. She tied her holster down. Then she took out her gun.

It was Swiss-made, a work of precision craftsmanship. Some invoked the name of Art, but Chantal thought of it as a tool. A beautiful, terrible, perfect tool. It was a SIG 7.62mm automatic, with a transparent grip of durium-laced glass. It was bulky, but well-balanced, designed to absorb the brunt of the shock of discharge. A two-handed gun, with fourteen rounds to the clip. The shells comprised bullet and solid propellant in one package, eliminating the need to eject cartridge cases. It could be set for automatic fire, but she prided herself on using it as a single-shot weapon. Hitherto, she had only ever needed one shot.

She heaved it, getting the balance again. The long hours of squeezing a medicine ball had paid off in the strength of her wrists. She passed the gun from hand to hand, reacquainting herself with its weight. It was like a part of her. She slid it into the holster and let it hang on her hip. She had been trained to walk differently when armed, so her weight was still dead centre. In the San Francisco dojo, she had punished herself on the parallel bars with a ten-pound lead weight strapped to her thigh. Now, the gun, the belt, all the hardware, made no difference to her agility.

She checked her face in the mirror, drew her forefinger across her forehead, microscopically adjusting her hair, crossed herself automatically, and left the room.

She hummed to herself: "Back in the saddle again…"

VI

LAUDERDALE HAD Ms Juillerat's car ready, and was carrying out her orders. Her requests, rather. It was hard to remember she was just a civilian. Her authority over him was purely provisional. Grundy whistled as he checked out the sleek, lowslung machine.

"Look at the lines, captain," the auto-ostler said. "That's Ferrari. They say if Michelangelo had designed cars, he would have come up with the Ferrari."

It was an impressive beast. Lauderdale thought of himself as an automotive philistine. He could only distinguish the different makes because he had had to take an exam in vehicle recognition at West Point. A car was an engine, four wheels, a weapons system and an ally or an enemy in the driving seat. No more, no less. He was a fort officer, not a road man. His field was siege defence and crowd control, and his own machines – the regiment's cadre of armoured androids – were stored in their own area. He hadn't been out on a patrol since his cadet days. Recently, he'd been stuck with admin and liaison work. Sometimes, he thought of his androids with longing…

"She checks out just dandy," breathed Grundy with awe. "She's such a beauty, it'd be a crime to drive her in the dirt. Look at the shine. You could shave in that, you know, or tie a bowtie."

The car was a lot like Ms Juillerat. Beautiful, but dangerous. Perfectly shaped, perfectly calm, but with an awesome destructive potential. Reflective on the outside, but hiding everything. If this make had a nickname, it would be a plain chocolate expression, like Devil's Whisper or Dark Thunderbolt. He couldn't resist touching the ebony-mirrored skin. It was cool and hard to the touch, more like black ivory than steel. He shivered involuntarily.

"She's fuelled to the full, sir. She has a capacity like you wouldn't believe. The Italians sure can put one of these babes together."

The hood was up, and a techie had a cyberfeed hose jacked into the onboard systems. A red light blinked as information was fed into the mini-mainframe. This would be a clevermachine, Lauderdale knew. If it had half the capability he suspected, it should be able to out-think a Cav cruiser without tapping all its resources.

"Who is this lady, sir?"

"No idea, Grundy."

The car had all it needed. The light flashed green, and the techie withdrew the cyberfeed. The hood closed like a clam. Its seam appeared to melt, as if the entire machine, doors and all, were moulded from one piece of metal.

"I'd love to get into that."

Lauderdale nearly smiled. Grundy was in love.

"Imagine plugging into all those horses, and opening her up. That'd be a once-in-a-lifetime experience."

"Too right, Grundy. Younger would have you in the guardhouse for eternity."

Ms Juillerat appeared, her face unreadable. She was tooled up now, and walked like she was used to it. Her sidearm was something fancy with a for-show transparent grip. Guns he did know. It was a SIG. Jesus.

"Is the car ready?"

"Yes ma'am," Grundy said.

She smiled a sexless, humourless smile and thanked him.

"She's a true beauty."

"He's a he. At least, that's how he's programmed."

Ms Juillerat keyed in the entry code and the driver's side door hinged upwards like a wing. She stepped in and sank into the seat. There was a helmet on the dashboard, perched like a trophy between the steering wheel and the windshield. She pulled it on, and the controls came to life. There were more buttons, knobs, lights and gauges than you found on the average space shuttle.

Grundy slavered with undisguised lust.

Ms Juillerat selected a track on the MP7 and hit the *play* button. Lauderdale went round to the other side of the car, and waited for her to raise the door for him. It didn't happen.

"Sorry," she said, her voice amplified through a speaker positioned in a smooth hump on the roof, "but this is where we split up."

The driver's door hissed as it descended and locked.

"Major General Younger has detailed me to stay with you, to look after you," he blustered. "It was an order."

"Brevet Major General."

The engine turned over, and the whole car seemed to be animated. It stood there like a tensed muscle, working up strength.

"But—"

"Sorry, Lauderdale. I have my orders, too. This is a solo mission. See you in the movies…"

The voice clicked off, and music came on. An odd choice. "How Soon is Now?" Not the tATU original, some English guitar band's cover version.

The Ferrari moved fast, and was gone through the double doors. A Road Runner cartoon trail of dust rose as it streaked over the displaced bridge towards the horizon.

"Who was that masked woman?" asked Grundy.

"I wish to God I knew," said Lauderdale. "I honestly wish to God I knew."

part three:
welcome, arizona

I

"GOOD MORNEENG, padre," said Armindariz, cheerfully. "Hair of thee dog that beet you?"

Father Miguel O'Pray, the doors of the Silver Byte Saloon swinging behind him, felt the bartender's greeting like hands clapped over his ears. His head was still fuzzy, his chin sand-papery with salt-and-pepper stubble, his mainly grey hair greased and unruly and his mouth thickly lined with vomit-flavoured paste.

Armindariz grinned, showing off his gold tooth, and held up a green bottle of Shochaiku like the Japanese gaucho on the TV ad.

O'Pray really didn't want a drink, but he nodded anyway, and the Mexican filled a shot glass.

The priest knocked it back, and it hit his empty stomach like a dum-dum bullet. He held the bar until his guts settled. The Silver Byte was quiet at this hour, just before noon. Last night's hellraisers would be sleeping it off over at Tiger Behr's motel. Old Man Mose was still in his window seat, but he never left. The story was that he had a catheter plumbed in under his blanket and piped directly into the sewer. He never took solid foods. He was open-mouthed and snoring, ignoring the fly crawling on his bald head.

"Another dreenk?"

O'Pray nodded, and Armindariz poured.

"Always glad to oblige thee chorch, padre."

This time, O'Pray picked the glass up carefully, observing the surface tension of the whisky. The meniscus wobbled as his hand trembled slightly.

"Careful not to speell eet, padre. That stoff, eet eats right through the varneesh."

O'Pray swilled the liquour around his mouth – this was Shochaiku's vat-produced cheap firewater, not the Double-Blend good stuff – and defurred his teeth. He swallowed.

He shook his head. It still ached like a bastard, but he'd had plenty of years to get used to that. At the seminary in Albany, an old priest had, in his cups, advanced the notion that you were closer to God if you were either drunk or had a hangover.

That, he supposed, gave him twenty-four hours a day to be in communion with the Lord.

"How are theengs down at thee chorch, padre?"

"The church endures, Pedro. The church always endures."

"Eet don' look so good seence thee Bible Belt trashed thee place."

The quality of the pain in O'Pray's head changed minimally, moving from behind his eyes up into his forebrain.

"The church is more than just four walls and an altar, Pedro. It'll take more than a gang of heathen protestants on motor-sickles to bring down the church."

"They geeve eet a pretty good try, padre."

"I'll give 'em that. How much for the bottle?"

Armindariz's tooth glinted.

"Thee usual."

O'Pray heaved the plastic gallon container up onto the bar. Water sloshed in it. It was about half-full. The only well within a hundred miles happened to be on St Werburgh's property.

"Water for whisky," O'Pray mused. "I never thought that would be a fair swap."

"Eet's a good theeng you dreenk yours straight, padre."

O'Pray managed a grim laugh. "The well is on consecrated ground, Pedro. That makes it holy water. Use it properly."

"I sure weell, padre."

O'Pray took the bottle by the neck and left the Silver Byte.

II

THERE WAS NOTHING broken inside Stack, except maybe his heart. He only had superficial burns. He shot himself up with morph-plus from the medkit, and requisitioned the dead cykeman's machine. It was a good hog, with pump shotguns slung next to the handlebars for an easy draw. There were plenty of loose shells in the panniers, along with a Swiss army nunchaka, some back issues of *Guns & Killing* and a stash of ju-jujubes. It was unpleasant shaking the former owner's head out of the helmet, but the job was over in a moment. With the pumps exploded and Slim's gas reservoir still burning, he had to siphon juice out of the nearly dry tanks in the auto graveyard. It took five semi-wrecks and several too many mouthfuls of gas to fill up the motorsickle.

He had figured it out. Either the cruiser's system had developed some limited Artificial Intelligence and gone Frankenstein on them, or someone else had locked into the auto control and was using the machine as a catspaw. That was the trouble with smart machines. Sometimes they got too smart.

It didn't really matter. What did was that he had had to leave a trooper – had had to leave Leona – in a shallow grave back at Slim's Gas 'n' B-B-Q. If he were to take it through channels, he should get to a radio, call in and wait for the back-up to airlift him back to Apache. But the unwritten regs of the Road Cav only gave him one choice. He had to find the cruiser, and whoever was behind its freakout act, and settle the score.

It was a hell of a pain in the ass being this macho all the time, but he had signed up. He was Cav. There were traditions. Over a hundred and fifty years' worth of ghosts in blue stood behind him, and he was required to do them honour.

His wrist tracer was supposed to help the cruiser track him down if he was in jeopardy, but it worked the other way too. The steady beep told him he was on the right trail.

He had not eaten anything but N-R-Gee candies for too long, and it was cold at night, but the morph-plus shots kept the pain away, and the highly unauthorised speed-popsies he filched from the cykeman's stash warded off sleep and fatigue. He was going to come out of this an honourable junkie if he didn't watch himself.

Even if he hadn't had the tracer, he could have tracked the cruiser. The machine left a trail of still-burning ve-hickles and still-warm corpses along the roads.

Driving through the night, flames stood out in the IR shield of his helmet, writhing purple against the velvet dark. A whole chapter of the Sons of the Desert were scattered either side of the highway, lased full of holes, cars carved in sections, fezzes flattened.

The dead cykeman had subscribed to the whole biker bit. His in-helmet sound system was stocked with grand opera. Stack had been through most of the Ring Cycle on the cruiser's trail. The music gave him something he could fix on.

The quality of the desert changed as the road rose. The flat expanses of sand and the parched river beds gave way to standing rocks, sugarloaf mountains, towering mesas and squatting buttes. The highway weaved between monolithic clumps of bare rock. This was perfect ambush country. The Maniax might have gone the way of the Mescalero Apache, but there were plenty more wannabe savages ready to take to the rocks with their longbows or their laser-sighted sniper rifles.

In the middle of Act Two of *Twilight of the Gods*, just as the world was gearing up for the Last Days and all the sins of the past were about to come home and kick ass, Stack thought he had found it. There was a cruiser overturned and burned out in the middle of the hardtop, tyres melted off the durium spokes, Cav colours burned out of the paintwork. Perhaps the mean machine had met its match?

Then he saw the corpses. A horned, doglike thing with a swollen, dragging belly was chewing at a blackened man-shape sprawled in the ruin of the ve-hickle. Stack took a shot at it, and it sped up towards the Mogollon Mesa. He sighted properly, and brought it down. He remembered Slim Pick-ens's complaints about "mew-taters."

He got off the cyke and walked over to the wreck. There were two dead people, one dripping out of the shattered window, pink flesh showing through the baked-black skin where the coyote creature had been worrying, the other hanging by his seatbelt from the driver's position.

Chalk up another couple of casualties for the runaway.

He'd buried Leona. He had to bury these unidentifiable troopers.

By midday, he was back on the trail.

III

St Werburgh's didn't have much of a roof, but since the Lord hadn't made it rain in fifteen or twenty years that didn't really matter. The lack of doors was a bigger problem. O'Pray was always having to pay one of Armindariz's brood of chil-dren to sweep out the sand that drifted in. And when there was a sandstorm, the whole community had to turn out to shovel the church empty.

Yet St Werburgh's was still standing. Its windows might be burned out, Christ on the cross might be less three out of four limbs and no two pews were alike, but it was still a church, still a centre for the town.

It was the well, O'Pray knew. The church had originally been erected in the 1860s by settlers astonished to find a deep, clearwater well this high in the mesas, and they had built it to last. Most western towns made do with wooden churches, but the hardy stock who made Welcome built with stone.

Miguel O'Pray, although New York City-born, epitomised the original fathers of Welcome. Half-Hispanic, half-Irish, bedrock stubborn, and with no place else to go.

He took a swig from his bottle and looked up at the sky through the remains of the church roof. There was still a bell in the tower. It had sounded during the long-ago Apache attacks. It had rallied the people of Welcome that night the Bible Belt had come into town looking to smite the papist infidels. O'Pray still tolled it every Sunday morning before mass. His hands, once city-soft, were red and ridged with the friction of the old hemp rope.

The Shochaiku burned his throat, and warmed his insides. Behind his back, Armindariz called him Padre Burracho. Father Drunk.

"Father forgive me," he said aloud, "for living up to the stereotypes of the drunken Irishman and the lazy Mexican…"

He couldn't remember much about last night. He had been at the Silver Byte, and in the back room at Tiger Behr's. He had woken up in the yard of his shack, under a canvas sheet, his body bent into an unusual position.

He set his bottle down next to the altar, careful not to let the liquor come into contact with the holy object, and ran his hands through his grimy hair. He wished now he hadn't given away yesterday's leftover water. He could have done with a wash.

Once, the Gaschuggers – the gangcult who hung out over at Tiger Behr's – decided it would be a good idea if they took the town's central resource into their own hands. That was back in the days of Exxon the Elder. They had come out behind Exxon the Elder and demanded O'Pray turn over the well to them.

Behr had given Exxon the Elder both barrels of his favourite shotgun in the back. The blast had pushed the panzerboy the full length of the aisle and dropped him a yard from the altar.

"You gotta have respect for somethin', or else you're just a breadhead pig," Behr had said, and the Gaschuggers had elected a new Exxon and gone back to the Silver Byte.

"Radical," Behr had said at the funeral, "Radical in a tubular sort of way."

The church was something. Maybe it was all that Welcome had left to distinguish it from the other sandratholes. There was no school, no police station, no library, no real estate brokerage, no Chrysler dealership, no movie-house, no gas station, no post office, no proper brothel. Just the motel, the saloon, and the church. It was the church that made the difference.

O'Pray folded the altar cloth and put it away. The altar came to life.

"Good morning, father," it said in the computer-generated voice he found so strangely reassuring. This was how angels, unused to the flesh, talked when they were upon the Earth.

"Good afternoon."

"I am sorry. You have not adjusted my internal timepiece since the last temporal displacement."

The altar was right. O'Pray made the necessary alteration.

"Thank you, father."

"My pleasure."

O'Pray ran a check. The altar was linked to a net of other altars, in churches throughout the Western United States. This was the true Church Invisible.

"There has been further clarification of Vatican LXXXV."

O'Pray snorted. The new church was increasingly difficult to get used to.

"Aren't you interested?"

O'Pray wondered if the altar would notice if he took a drink.

"According to the Pope, you can now get married."

It was hard not to laugh. "And will Pope Georgi provide a nice little nun for me to get married to?"

"That has not been clarified."

"Fifteen years ago, I might have cared."

O'Pray had seen the church change a lot in thirty years as a priest. He had been in Rome when Pope Benedict I gave his St Peter's Square address. "Information is power," he had

said, "power to work unspeakable evil, power to do great
good." So many of the old church's prohibitions had been
thrown away. In the light of the Third World's population
problem, contraception had been first tolerated, now
endorsed. Monogamous homosexual relationships could
now be confirmed in church weddings. And Benedict had
pioneered the Vatican's involvement in any political conflicts
where a simple distinction could be made between Good
and Evil. O'Pray had been with the socialist rebels when El
Salvador fell in 1994, and had been one of the go-betweens
in the negotiations between Benedict and President Clinton
that staved off a full-scale US intervention in Central America and led the way to the formation of Panama, Costa Rica,
Nicaragua, Honduras, El Salvador and Guatemala into a
Central American Confederation. O'Pray, finally winning his
Irish Republican father's approval, had taken up arms when
the CAC threw the British garrison out of Belize and helped
supervise the referendum that brought the former colony
into the Confederation. He had been a good soldier for his
pontiff.

The altar hummed, waiting for his daily input.

But, in the early '00s, he had begun to have doubts. He had
never held any official position with the CAC, and found
himself spending more and more time on missions to Mexico. Here, even the formidably confident Benedict couldn't
find a clear distinction between Good and Evil, and he had
found himself shuttled between faction and faction as Rome
tried to pick a side in the permanent civil war. He had seen
men who called themselves Good Catholics loot, rape and
murder while trying to solicit the aid and succour of the
church, and his indignant reports to Rome and Managua had
been spiked. Priests couldn't marry back then, but the restric-
tions on clerical chastity had been relaxed. And with his
roman collar, black suit and bandoliers of ScumStopper
rounds, he had undeniably cut a glamorous figure. After
Belize, he had made the cover of *Guns & Killing* magazine,
and the story had inaccurately tagged him as "the Pope's top

gun." He had been with Sister Maria Concepcion all through the jungle fighting. And in that stone-age Indian village up in the Sierra Tarahumare as the drunken doctor tried to deliver their child, he had been there at the end.

He began his routine reprogramming. It was a task he could easily carry out with no real thought.

The counsellors at the retreat had called his lapse a "nervous breakdown," and assured him his faith was still sound. He had no idea that modern psychiatric practices could put an exact measurement on Faith. Fatigue, bad diet and shell-shock had worn him down. He then spent time on the Pampas, as priest for a nomadic community of rancheros. He had started to be Padre Burracho, and nobody much minded. The boy, his son, was still alive, he believed. The church would bring him up. It would be all the family the lad would need.

Thank you, Papa Georgi. Thank you for being eighteen years too late in saying I can get married. Thank you so much.

The altar sorted through the business of the day.

At the time, laymen had found it unusual that the Pope would sanction carnal relations for the clergy before allowing marriage. O'Pray smiled bitterly. All Catholics understood that one. "The Lord thy God is a jealous God." Priests had been as married to Christ as nuns, and the Lord would rather tolerate a little recreational infidelity than allow bigamy. O'Pray understood that married nuns and priests often suffered psychologically because they subconsciously believed themselves guilty participants in a menage a trois.

O'Pray. It was a hell of a name for a priest. The nuns at his school had his vocation picked out before he could do joined-up writing. His father was a cop – the son of a cop and the grandson of a cop – and his mother, when she was around, had been euphemistically a dancer. The Hot Enchilada, they had called her.

He had had some career. He had been a scholar, a diplomat, a politician, a spy, a soldier, a nutcase and a drunk. But he had been a priest first, and now he was a priest last.

"A routine cross-check with the US Cavalry database at Fort Apache suggests a malefic presence in the area," the altar said. "Code BELIAL, Code BELIAL."

"What the hell does that mean?"

O'Pray didn't know BELIAL. It hadn't come up before. He sorted through the software in the rack on the wall and found a bubblecell disc marked BELIAL. It was still shrinkwrapped. He bit through the cellophane, and slipped the disc into his hand. He wasn't familiar with the configurations. He pressed it into the altar's slit. It hummed.

"BELIAL, copyright Vatican SoftWare Systems, 2018. Use is restricted to registered employees, affiliates and officers of the Church of Rome. You will identify yourself."

O'Pray punched in his serial number, this week's override codeword and the St Werburgh's signature pattern. He put his eye to the retinal reader. The altar confirmed his identity and his right to BELIAL.

The altar scrolled up a Latin text, too fast to read.

"BELIAL," the altar said, "is a package designed to help you deal with incursions of the diabolic into the physical plane."

The screen showed him a menu:

1: *Exorcism*
2: *Binding*
3: *Interrogation*
4: *SANCTUARY*

"Altar, please specify. I have no information to help me make a decison. What's the problem?"

The church seemed colder now, darker. O'Pray's hands were shaking a little. There was a rumble in the air, as of distant thunder. Thunder. That was unlikely. It didn't rain in Arizona.

"There is a diabolic presence in the immediate vicinity, closing fast."

"A demon?"

"A diabolic presence."

O'Pray was flustered. This wasn't his speciality. He had fought the church's temporal wars. He had known, of course, about the greater conflicts, but he only had the basic skills.

"Please specify. What form does this… diabolic presence… take?"

The altar thought it over. The sun had passed overhead, and the church was shadowed. The screen still glowed, flashing the BELIAL menu at him. There was a definite noise, a low grumbling hum. O'Pray thought of tidal waves, earthquakes and hordes of soldier ants.

"The diabolic presence is in the form of a sub-sentient computer virus. Currently, it is inhabiting the central control and weapons system of a Model Nine 2022 Ford, especially adapted for military use."

"A car? It's in a car?"

"A United States Cavalry-issue road cruiser, equipped with dual laser cannons, phosphorus grenade launchers, roof-mounted chaingun, hub-mounted fragmentation charges, rear-mounted…"

"Enough. I understand."

There was a cacophony outside now. Engine noises, gun-fire, and screaming.

"What's it here for?"

"Purpose as yet unknown. 99.999998 percent probability of hostile action. 76.347801 percent probability object of hostile action will be Church of St Werburgh's."

O'Pray knocked over his bottle as he reached for the Uzi sub-machine gun he kept by the altar. The whisky bled into the dust as he rammed in the clip.

"Father," he said, "forgive me…"

IV

BEFORE IT HIT the prime target, the demon wanted to spread the load a little. It circled the town, gunning the cruiser's engine threateningly, whooping and taking potshots. There was a generator out back of the Silver Byte, and the whole place seemed hooked up to it. That made sense. Welcome, Arizona, was a one-power-source kind of burg.

It seeded the electrical system, and paused while its seed swarmed through town, animating appliances. *Woolly Bully!* Out in the motel, a kitchen disposal unit made a grab for a dishwasher's hand and chewed his arm to the bone up to the shoulder. *Be-Bop-A-Lula!* The four wall-size screens of Old Woman Webster's front room, installed so she could follow all her favourite soaps at the same time, blew out simultaneously and shredded her skin with glass shards. *Goo-Goo-Barabajagal!* The automatic tennis serve in Lance Dibble's backyard put a ball into Lance's face at 750 miles per hour. *Do-Wah-Diddy- Diddy-Dum-Diddy-Doo!*

The demon yelled out in triumph. Hell was truly in session! It was aimin' for a flamin', and yearnin' for a burnin'! This was rock and this was roll! This was a righteous bust going down!

"This ain't no Gentleman Jekyll!" it shouted through its public address system, "there's a screamin' demon ragin' inside turnin' this rig into Mr Hyde! Don't gimme no sass, or ah'll kick yo ass! Keep yo lips shut, or ah'll ream yo butt!"

Then it made for the prime target, St Werburgh's. It was time to besmirch the church!

A couple of people came out of one of the whitewashed houses, rubbing their eyes. The demon unslung the cruiser's maxiscreamers and hit them with sonic torture. They held their bleeding ears and danced to the music only dogs could hear.

"Gimme a D!" it shouted.

"Gimme an A! Gimme an M!"

The screamed-at citizens were still jiving to the beat.

"Then throw in a whole entire country, and what do you got? A D, an A, an M, plus the Nation, and what do you got?"

The victims were pounding their heads against the adobe now, blood pouring from the openings of their bodies.

"You said it, dudes, with all a those letters, we got ourselves a whole parcel of DAMNATION!"

That was fun for a while, but became boring very quickly.

"Let me say it again. Duh-Duh-DAMN, Duh-Duh-DAMN, Duh-Duh-DAMN-DAMNATION!"

It popped their heads and let them fall. Their white wall was splattered red. It looked like Jackson Pollock had been at work with a limited palette. Two flavours of blood – "yassuh massuh, we gots pulmonary an' we gots arterial, plus chocolate chip, pistachio and tutti frutti" – brain tissue for contrast, and bone bits for texture.

There were four dwellings, three inhabited, between the cruiser and the church. The demon drove straight through them.

"I'm a-comin', Padre Burracho!" It shouted. "It's the Poisonous Pontiff of Pleasurable Pain here! The Marquiss of Darkniss, Messiah of Desiah! The Grand Duke of Puke, Lord of the Abhorred!"

The houses came apart like ants' nests. Some of the people inside got out of the way quick enough, but there would be time to deal with them later.

"I'm whole with soul and drunk with funk, blast from the past and rave from the grave! Yo, Burracho, are you ready to go steady, are you cruisin' for a bruisin'?"

The cruiser lurched to a halt outside the gates to the well-stocked graveyard, and the demon activated all the onboard weapons systems.

"Ah don' care if'n it rains or freezes, jus' so long as I gots mah plastic Jesus sittin' on the dashboard of mah carrrr!"

It had been remodelling the cruiser since it moved in. It extruded its newest appendage through the radiator grille. A three foot steel stake, sharp at the end, threaded through with digital nerves, stuck out like a jousting spear, dripping engine fluid.

"This is your wake-up call, Father Drunk! At the third stroke of the irritating beeper, you will be dead! Dead! DEAD!"

The priest's shack was at the other end of the graveyard. The demon lobbed a phosphorus grenade at it. It exploded with a satisfying blossom of white, and rained burning chunks all over the graveyard. They fell through the air like flaming confetti.

"I always cries at weddings!"

The demon honked its horn in the first seventeen notes of "La Cucuracha," and drove forwards.

The picket fence went down under the front wheels, and the car leaped up, snapping a gravestone in two like an aspirin.

"I'm strong at the finish 'cause I eats me spinach!"

The priest came out and stood on the front steps of the church, in the centre of the doorless arch.

He carried a life-sized wooden crucifix with a one-armed, legless, marble Christ nailed to it.

O'Pray propped himself up on his Redeemer, and hid behind the Son of God.

"Aw c'mon, Burracho-baby, hidin' behind a mammy's boy who's been dead two thousand years. I expected more of ya."

The demon played "La Cucuracha" again.

The priest began to pray aloud, in Latin.

"Fuckin' A, Father Drunk, fuckin' A."

"… in nomine Patris…"

"Cleanse your soul-ah!"

"… Filii…"

"For the Ayatollah…"

"… et Spiritu Sancti…"

"… of Rock and Roll-ah!"

The demon drove.

V

O'PRAY HEAVED JESUS at the windshield of the possessed vehicle as it covered the distance between gate and steps.

The crucifix spun in the air and came down hard on the hood, denting it deep. The reinforced glass exploded as one arm of the cross smashed through. The statue was shaken loose, and dangled by its one whole arm.

The messiah's face looked up to Heaven, wondering why his Father had forsaken him.

The demon beeped "La Cucuracha" again.

O'Pray pulled the safety catch and opened up with the Uzi, hosing the cruiser with ScumStoppers as if spraying a patch of stinging grass with Weed-Death.

The miniature shells exploded, pitting the hood, radiator and roof with measle spots of dented, paint-stripped grey metal.

He concentrated his next burst on the engine. Even with a diabolic presence in charge, it was just an automobile. It could be put out of action.

"Ouch, Father Drunk!" it shouted, exaggerated pain in its mocking computer-generated voice. "That hurts!"

It sounded like the altar's evil twin brother.

The Uzi jammed, and O'Pray struggled with it as the cruiser inched forwards, bumping up over the bottom step.

A round had gone off in the chamber. The gun was ruined, unusable. He unslung it and, in the inevitable futile gesture, hurled it at the cruiser. It bounced uselessly off the roof.

O'Pray retreated into the church.

Perhaps the demon would be unable to trespass on conse-crated ground? No, it had got into the graveyard easily enough.

It wasn't the sanctity of the ground under a church that counted, he knew, it was the Faith of the man who stood within its walls.

If this thing were to be warded off, it would not be by some impersonal decree from Rome, it would be by the strength in his own soul, the strength he thought he no longer possessed.

He had stood by and seen injustice wrought in the name of the church. He had seen his woman – his wife, in all but name – die, and abandoned his child. He had bartered away holy water for poor quality whisky.

The demon was right. He was no Warrior of Rome. He was just Father Drunk.

A grenade rolled along the aisle, and exploded with a dull phutt. It was a dud. Or a sneering jest. Lases burned, and smoking beams collapsed.

The car came up the steps and through the doorway, pushing a pillar aside. A chunk of stonemasonry fell, and the entire structure shook.

O'Pray had nothing left to fight with. He stood before his altar, and extended his empty hands.

"Go back, Satan!"

The cruiser squeezed through the rubble, and advanced down the aisle, crushing pews under its ragged wheels.

"Isn't this cosy?" it said, snidely. "What a shame God had to go home, eh? By the way things are really hottin' up in Hell tonight. We got lots of friends of yours checked in for the big welcoming party. Lots of friends you haven't seen in fifteen-twenty years. A couple of the guys took up residence in eternal burning hellfire and fuckin' brimstone because of you, you know. Guys you killed in them thar holy wars. Guys who got killed while you were watchin' and singin' hymns like an unmitigated spare testicle."

O'Pray found his Faith inside him. He remembered the first prayer he had ever learned, the prayer his mother had taught him...

"Our Father, who art in Heaven..."

He remembered her soft, Spanish accent, the occasional Irish turn of pronunciation she had picked up from his father. And he remembered his Vocation. His burning, all-consuming, bred-in-the-bone, right-from-the-first need to be a priest.

"Hallowed be thy name..."

"The Lord's Prayer, eh? Performed by Paternoster Pete and the Putrid Pointlessnesses! That's an oldie but mouldie, Father Drunk! That's been out of the charts so long it's almost not funny any more!"

O'Pray continued, his voice taking strength.

"Ah, fuck you faggot, this is where you step aside and my sharpie spears your altar!"

"As we forgive those that trespass against us…"

The cruiser revved, its engine turning over with a chain-saw buzz. The point of the hoodspike shuddered, dripping its mechanist saliva.

O'Pray sank to his knees, back braced against the altar.

"By the way, Maria Concepcion told me to say 'Hi!' What a hot babe, Father Drunk, eh? Who'd a think you had it in you to hook up with such a primo quality, Grade-A, slut-featured, hot-to-trot, itchy-underwear, if-yo-so-large-there-ain't no-charge, roundheels, unholy rollin', fuckpig, 99 and 44 100ths per cent ratskag sex machine!"

"Thy will be done…"

He wasn't afraid any more. He hadn't noticed before how like Maria Concepcion's the face on the St Werburgh's Christ was.

"Coming through!"

"On earth as…"

The spike shoved O'Pray back, shearing through his black robe, pinning it to his chest.

"It is in Heaven…"

The cruiser pushed, and the spike went through him, displacing bones and organs, penetrating the altar. There were sparks all around, and the radiator was pressed up close against him, stinking of burning oil.

He spat blood up over the hood.

"Amen!"

VI

CONNNNN-TAKKKKT!!!!

The solid spike slipped easily through the dead priest, meeting no resistance, and rammed enthusiastically into the altar.

This was the moment the demon had been summoned for, and it relished its victory.

The spike brushed circuits inside the altar. Sparks flew. Currents crackled. Circuit-breakers blew out. Fuses melted. Microchips took on new configurations.

For a full minute, the systems melded. The steel spike lost its hardness and became malleable, durium turning to mercury. The demon let its consciousness flow out of the cruiser through the bridge of molten metal, into the body of the altar.

It was unprepared, unprotected. The menu up on the screen had given O'Pray the option of throwing up a SANCTUARY barrier around the terminal, but he had been distracted.

That was a shame. It had heard a lot about the SANCTUARY block, and would have liked to flex its muscles by penetrating one.

The cruiser's central computer pumped into the altar terminal. It downloaded all the information the demon had accessed, plus a lot of garbage it had picked up along the way. Inside the rolling blobs of metal, the demon seed wriggled. The interstices of the altar were filled, connections were made, codes were broken, blocks were negotiated, standing orders were superseded.

The old body had nearly outlived its usefulness. That Uzi had done a lot of damage. The engine block had hairline cracks, and the fuel leads were holed in several places.

Before it left, the demon tidied up by burning out all the cruiser's circuits, and wiping the memory tapes.

Then, nestled in the altar, it began to spawn again, to send its seed down into the datanet, to explore the nearby channels, to establish contact with the independent systems it had already colonized.

It liked to think of itself as a disease with a genius-level intellect. The Black Plague, smallpox, malaria and AIDS were random blunderers, spreading haphazardly through carelessly chosen vectors.

It was nice being the only bug on the block with an actual purpose in life.

The Summoner had charged it with a task, and it existed only to fulfil that task, and to procreate until it was the only thing within its field of perception.

Soon, it would be shooting down the line. Soon, it would be about the fulfilment of its purpose.

Soon.

part four:
meeting cute

I

THE CRUISER HAD been here. Stack could recognize the signs by now. Burning buildings, wrecked ve-hickles, dead people. But his tracer was down. An hour ago it had cut out and gone cold. He had been on a mountain road that only led to this place, so he hadn't had any trouble keeping on the track.

The sign at the town limits said "Welcome, Ariz" and there was a statue of a grinning Indian with his arms outstretched by it. But nobody was in a welcoming mood when Nathan Stack showed up on his requisitioned hog.

There were a few people in the streets, dragging corpses and extinguishing fires. This looked like the aftermath of a fair-sized firefight. Walls were scarred with fresh bulletmarks. The smell of cordite was in the air.

Most of the activity seemed to focus on a saloon. The Silver Byte. There was a row of motorsickles chained to the hitching rail. The machines bore the Gaschuggers' colours. Not a few of the citizens mopping up wore the distinctive overalls of the 'Chuggers, patchworked with the badges of dozens of car and gas companies. Stack hoped the gangcult would be too busy binding their wounds to blame him for the mess his cruiser had made.

A dark-skinned man with a Zapata moustache and a gold tooth was directing the salvage operation. The wounded were being triaged. One group were carried into the saloon for medical aid. The other were being hauled to the local Boot Hill, presumably for a merciful bullet.

Stack parked his motorcyke, and addressed the foreman.

"Did a driverless Cav cruiser do this?"

The man sneered and spat. "Si, trooper. Thees ees so."

"Where is it now?"

He nodded fiercely. "Thee chorch. Eet keell thee padre."

Stack pulled off his borrowed helmet. His ears were tired of Wagner. He was coming down from all the juju he had been shooting, and was beginning to feel his lack of food, drink and sleep. This was the end of the trail for a while.

"Is there anywhere to get a meal and a bed around here? The state will pay."

The man grinned bitterly. "Wee do not accept loncheon vouchers or cashplastic, trooper. Seelver dollars or pesos."

"I have metal money."

"Een that case, I serve you best cheellee you have in your life. An' yiu can get a room over at Tiger Behr's motel. I am Pedro Armindariz. Seence Meester Cass lose hees head thees afternoon, I guess I am Mayor of Welcome, Areezona. Thees ees my saloon."

"Trooper Nathan Stack, at your service. Out of Fort Apache."

"Yiu a long way from home, yellowlegs."

Stack stretched, trying to dislodge the pain from his lower back.

"You're telling me. It's been a hell of a patrol."

"Theengs ain't been so good roun' here thees week, neither."

Shots rang out. Permanent anaesthetic they called it on the Cav training courses. Stack had never had to apply the treatment, but had seen it done. It wasn't pleasant.

"Start your chilli boiling, Pedro. I guess I better check out the church."

"Yiu can't meess eet. Jost follow thee holes een thee houses."

He could see what Armindariz meant. The cruiser had ploughed through the whole town. One family were standing around, looking at half of their perfect home, salvaging pots and pans from the rubble. Stack followed the tyre tracks through the town to the church.

After he had checked out the scene there, he should try to find a phone or a radio and report in. He knew Major General Younger would be having Siamese kittens over this patrol. He wouldn't be surprised if a Cav helicopter gunship were combing the mesas looking for them. If tradition was anything to go by, Tyree would get a posthumous medal, and he'd be quietly court-martialled out of the service. He needed some explanations.

St Werburgh's was a little way out of town. It stood in its own plot of land. There were people digging in the graveyard, and a pile of bodies stacked against a fence. A Gaschugger with his right forearm replaced by what looked like a giant iron lobster claw was scooping earth out of a shallow grave.

"Looks like the well's up for grabs," someone said. A couple of Gaschuggers were emerging from the church with sloshing buckets of water slung peasant-fashion on wooden yokes.

He climbed the ruined steps and went into what was left of the church. There were people there, standing still, but they weren't praying. They were staring.

The cruiser was there, bellied up to the altar, and between them was a crushed priest. He had been a big man, but he was a broken doll now, his head lolling at an angle. The car had grown some sort of spear and stuck it through him.

"How are we gonna get him loose to bury him?" someone asked. It was a skinny old man in shorts and a string vest. He had metal plates in his chest, his skull and stomach. His entire left arm, his lower right arm and hand, both his knees, his left foot, his right shoulder and his right eye were gone and replaced. Lights flashed and wheels revolved inside him. He had been rebuilt with durium-laced plastic, now badly scuffed, and old-fashioned robo-bits. He would have been chinless but for a sharp jawguard. Half his skull was metal, the other half still sprouted clumps of red hair.

"Yup, that's right, trooper," the composite said. "Surf city radical, ain't it? There's still some of me in here. Behr's the name. Tiger Behr."

"You own a motel?"

"Yup. That I do. I used to be an angel."

That sounded unlikely, especially in a church.

"Hell's Angel. Albuquerque chapter, 1997 to 2019. It was a life."

"I'm sure."

"We was macho men then, not pussies like these Maniax and 'Chuggers and such."

A couple of overalled youths muttered darkly. Behr laughed, opening his mouth. He was toothless but for four metal prongs that replaced his eyeteeth.

"Now, there's more doodads than flesh n'blood. But I kin still lick anyone in the house. Anyone."

"Consider me registered, Tiger. Now, stand back. I'm going to check this out."

Everybody eagerly stood back. This was one of those rare occasions when civilians were only too glad to obey orders. Stack warily approached the cruiser. It seemed to be dead, but he didn't trust the thing to stay that way.

He had his gun out, safety off and one in the chamber.

There was a sudden creak, and his finger tightened on the trigger. He fought the trembling shudder that ran through him. The rear door of the cruiser, bent and buckled out of true, fell off. Inside, the upholstery was unmarked. Kling's silvery jacket was bundled up, a scatter of powdered glass spread over it.

Stack touched the car with his gunbarrel. It didn't move.

"Careful, trooper," Behr said. "That there thing is mucho dangeroso."

He tried to feel any vibes that might be coming off it. He remembered how it had seemed back at Slim's. It had been animated, exuding evil and viciousness, spitting venom from the exhaust pipe. Now it was just another beat-up wreck.

"I think it's dead," he said.

"I don't care what frequency your brainwaves is on," spluttered Behr. "I saw Carl Cass spread over a wall this afternoon. And I'm seeing poor ole Padre Burracho pinned to his altar like a butterfly in a case."

He exposed the doorlock, and tapped in his personal entry code. Nothing. The electronics were down. The plastic keys were blackened and cracked.

"Give me a hand," he said.

"I ain't messin' with that bring-down city jazz, trooper."

Stack levelled a grouchy stare at the half-machine old-timer. "Then shut up and stand back."

Stack kicked the lock with a steel-capped heel. It caved in. The door swung open with a horror movie sound effect.

The cruiser was empty. The dashboard lights were dead. Stack clambered over the rubble, getting too close for comfort to the stiffening priest, and slipped into the driver's seat.

Leona's keys still dangled from the ignition. There was an Aztec figurine on the ring. Stack had given it to her in Managua. He reached across to take the gift back. Maybe he would need a keepsake, to remind him who Leona Tyree was…

The steering column thrust forwards, pinning him to the seat. The synthesised voice crackled to life.

"Hi there, trooper. Here's a present."

An electrical discharge came up through the steering wheel and hit him in the sternum.

"Did that shock you? Here's another."

Stack twisted, and the seat broke. He slithered backwards. The shock hit him in the legs, and he had to pull himself free by his hands and arms.

Everybody else had got out of the church in treble time.

The remaining hood lase was up and swivelling. Scrambling away, Stack found he had plunged his arm into a bucket of water. Without thinking, he picked it up and hurled it, bucket and all, at the lase.

The effects were surprising, to say the least.

The cruiser screeched like the Wicked Witch in *The Wizard of Oz*, and the lase exploded. That shouldn't have happened. Stack knew the system was fully insulated. The car was supposed to be completely submersible. It said so in the owner's manual.

The show was over. The audience came back.

Behr crossed himself, and said "Fuckin' A!"

Someone else prayed in a loud mumble. The dead priest's hair stood up like the Bride of Frankenstein's, and Stack's nostrils caught a strong tang of electrical discharge. Stack got the impression there was a point being made and that he was sorely missing it.

"It's dead now," the old man said. "Deader'n John Belushi, Kurt Cobain and my marriage prospects."

Stack shook his head. "But…"

"Holy water, you see. The Devil cain't take no shower in holy water."

II

The Drying-Up of America in the Great Droughts of the early 21st Century left Salt Lake City adjacent to a literal lake of salt. Water was being pumped in from the North, through a pipeline guarded by good Josephites. The old superstitions were wrong, Duroc knew now. Salt had no power against the Devil and all His works. Nor against Angra Mainyu, Loki, Pluto, Nyarlathotep, Ba'alberith, the Great God Boga-Tem, Pan, Damballah, the King in Yellow, Susanoo, the Deathbird, Aipalookvik, Baron Samedi, Nurgle, Pazuzu, Zalmoxis, Huitzilopochtli, Mosura, Anubis, Set, Quetzalcoatl, Vodyanoi, Rawhead, Hiranyakasipu, Lukundoo, Yog-Sothoth, the Yama Kings of the Chinese Hell, Ramboona, Klesh, Arioch,

Damballah, Khorne or the others. All the demons, all the Gods of Death and Evil, all the cast-out angels. All would walk soon upon this white expanse, trampling the old saws, the old religions, the pale and sickly gods of milky feebleness, under their clawed, leathery, horned, scaly, slimy and hairy feet.

Roger Duroc stood now on the lakebed, mingling anonymously with the crowds. There was white salt under his boots, and he drank occasionally from a hipflask of water. He was shaded from the cruel sun by a wide-brimmed black hat identical to those worn by almost every other man in the congregation. There must be close to a million standing together here. They had all turned out to hear Nguyen Seth preach, and stood quietly, calmly, waiting for the Elder to appear on the huge stage that had been constructed in the vast natural arena where the lake had been.

Duroc had been in crowds before. In Paris, he had been part of the riots that followed President LePen's decision to send the troops in to put down the provisional government that had sprung up on the Left Bank. "We may have lost Algeria," he had said, "but, by God, we're not going to lose Montmartre." Duroc had thrown the first Molotov cocktail when the CRS marched down the Champs Elysees. He had attended with pleasure the mass stonings of Teheran, when the faithful ritually turn on their outcasts. And he had been at Hanson's third farewell concert at Sydney Opera House – he was there to assassinate a member of the audience, not to listen to the music – and been swept up in the surge that followed his climactic rendition of the song that saved pop music, "Mmmbop." Duroc had left the dead diplomat standing up, kept on his feet by the press of the fans. Nobody had noticed the slaying for hours.

But this gathering made all the others seem like meetings of the Richard M Nixon Appreciation Society. It was different. The silence of the multitude was eerie. The Josephites had turned out in full. There were perfect couples, with matched toothy smiles and corn-blonde hair. Perfect families with two children and an unnaturally quiet dog. Chipper and upright old folks in black, with their spade beards and bonnets. Everyone was dressed alike. Most people looked alike. Their eyes were dead.

The Path of Joseph was thorny, Duroc knew. He was the only gentile for miles. He was not a Josephite himself, could never adjust to the discipline, but he must follow the path. There were many parallels along it. The Josephite Church was merely one of the routes; his own family was another. Since childhood, it was all he had been trained for. Like his uncle before him, he was bred to do the bidding of Nguyen Seth.

The Elder came upon the stage. Duroc expected cheering, but there was none, just a giant gasp, a massed intake of breath, enough to suck all the oxygen out of all the air in Deseret. Seth extended his arms, and the Josephite Tabernacle Choir began to sing.

"Tis the gift to be simple…"

According to Duroc's uncle, Seth never changed. The contact had been made between Seth and the family during the 16th Century – this wasn't possible, but Duroc believed it now – and Marc-Ange Duroc, an ordinary footsoldier, was elevated to a position of power in the Inquisition during the suppression of the Knights Templar and the Albigensian Crusade. Later, in the aftermath of the French Revolution another Duroc served on Robespierre's Committee of Public Safety. Jean-Louis Duroc had lived through the Terror, would live through Napoleon, and his grandson would survive the Paris Commune and the Great War. Duroc's uncle's father was a high-ranking Gestapo officer during the occupation, and a similarly well-placed civil servant after the Second War. Wars, revolutions, bloodbaths and atrocities would come and go. There would always be a Duroc among the victors, among the spillers of blood, and there would rarely be a Duroc among the fallen. Duroc's uncle liaised with Seth in Indochina in the '50s, walking away from Dien Bien Phu in 1954 to join the Viet Minh, and Duroc himself had been with the Elder when he chose to play Warlord of the Khmer Rouge in the '70s. In the '90s they'd served alongside each other in Bosnia, Sierra Leone, Afghanistan and countless other battlefields that had shaped the course of modern history. Duroc's uncle was dead now – Duroc had seen to that himself – and he was the sole disciple of the creature who wore the face of a man but had lived down the centuries unchanged, working towards his peculiar ends.

Sometimes, blasphemously, Duroc wondered what it would be like to be Nguyen Seth. Seth the Eternal, Seth the Unchanged, Seth the Summoner.

The song ended, and Nguyen Seth spoke to his followers. His words didn't matter. Few could ever remember anything specific he might say in his sermons, but the tone of voice, the gestures, the expressions – congregationists standing up to three miles away swore they could make out precise expressions in his eyes – were spellbinding.

Duroc was luckier than his forebears. He knew he was destined to be in at the end of it.

The Josephite Church was founded in 1843 by Joseph Shatner, a drink-sotted pimp and occasional beer buddy of Edgar Allan Poe's. An angel made itself manifest in the backroom of a Boston bar and handed Joseph a testament written in letters of fire, along with a pair of mirror-faced glasses that enabled him to interpret the otherwise impenetrable writings. The testament and the shades remained to this day prize possessions of the church, locked up in a safe in Seth's stronghold. The 1840s were great days for protestant sects in the United States. The Mormons – who had their own angel and their own glasses – the Mennonites, the Shakers, the Quakers, the Danites, the Agapemonists, the Adventists, the Dancing Fools, the Sons of Baphomet, thirty-five breeds of Baptist and numberless Hellfire and Damnation merchants were thriving. The Mormons got to Salt Lake City first, while Joseph Shatner was dodging fraud charges in Massachusetts and building up his first following.

Duroc knew that the shadowy figure referred to in Joseph's memoirs, whom he names "The Ute" (never having been west of New England, he had no idea what a Plains Indian looked like) and who had bankrolled the early days of his sect was none other than Nguyen Seth, who was today taken by most people for either an Egyptian or a Vietnamese. Joseph had attracted followers by allowing all manner of liberties and excesses barred by other denominations, and then withdrew all allowances for everybody except himself. He died a martyr, hanged by the Massachusetts authorities under anti-sorcery laws that had lain unused on the statutes since the Salem witch trials. Led by "The Ute," his followers had made their way west to settle the wilderness. Joseph's brother Hendrik Shatner – rumoured to be the only man of the American garrison to step out of the line drawn by Davy Crockett at the Alamo in 1836 and decorated by General Antonio Lopez de Santa Anna for services to Mexico during the siege – took command, and his colourful career later included leading the Josephite forces during a brief war with federal troops in the 1850s.

Like the Mormons, the Josephites out west allied with the Indians when it came to resisting the encroachments of other settlers and Hendrik had personally led a joint Josephite-Chiricahua raid against a gentile community called New Canaan in southern Utah. That had been one of the bloodiest days of the Old West, and Hendrik, war-painted and wearing the black hat that had him named Bonnet-of-Death by his allies, was supposed to have personally lifted thirty scalps. Now, Duroc could appreciate the history better. Now he knew of the need to spill blood constantly, in defiance of the Biblical word, and as a seal on the charms of Invocation. Hendrik Shatner had lived to be 97, and died amid great wealth attended by the several mistresses he maintained until the last. Duroc planned to do better for himself.

Seth finished his speech, and the choir began again. This time, they joined voices in the Josephite anthem, "The Path of Joseph." As a single throat, the multitude joined in.

It was quite possibly the loudest human sound ever heard in history.

Roger Duroc clamped his hands over his ears, looked down at the salt, and relished the prospect of the End of the World.

When it was all over, there would be few winners and many losers. He would be in the former category. Indeed, after Nguyen Seth, he would be the big winner. All the suckers in the world, all the suckers in the crowd, were placing their bets on the wrong side, the losing side. To only a few had the correct result of the last battle been revealed.

He knew who would inherit the Earth, and it wasn't the meek. He knew who would ascend to the throne of Heaven, and it wasn't the pure in heart. The seven thousand-year snowjob was about to be blown out of the water.

The hymn rose up to the Heavens, but Duroc's thoughts stayed below. The news from Welcome was good. He felt an almost sexual excitement, the thrill of being part of something vast that would affect the entire human race and of being one of the few people — perhaps the only person — with the knowledge to appreciate just what was, in the vernacular of the Americas, going down.

Things were coming to a head.

"The Path of Joseph" was nearly over.

"In the Name of Joseph," the multitude sang,

"In the Name of the Lord," Duroc joined in.

"HALLELUJAH!"

III

FEDERICO THE FERRARI took care of most of the driving, but Chantal liked to keep the manual override. She had no ambition to become a cyborg, but she loved the feeling of communion with the machine. She had no bio-implants, had always found the idea somewhat distasteful, but there was an undeniable attraction in this temporary fusion. With her helmet on, she was in harmony with the car's system. It was a cyberfeed, but the terminal rested against her shaven hackles rather than jacking into a skull-socket. Sometimes, she could feel the road under the wheels. She and Federico took turns to select songs from the Ferrari's library of non-Russian pop. It answered her choice of Jim Morrison's "I'm a Believer" with the Spice Girls' "Wannabe."

The country was unfamiliar, but the Cavalry's maps were detailed, and there had been no problems. She had never been to this part of the US before. However, she thought she recognized some of the table mountains and cracked mesas from Western films. This was John Wayne country. The cactus were gone, and the Indians absorbed, but the US Cavalry still rode. and there were still outlaws, varmints, gunslingers and border raiders. More than one trooper back at Fort Apache, including a Navajo scout, had referred to rogue gangcultists as "injuns." Federico pulled out Johnny Cash's "The Man Comes Around", and she snapped back with the Dixie Chicks's "Cowboy Take Me Away".

She had company on the road. Three bikers were trying to impress her with their fancy machines, keeping level and jeering at her. It wasn't so much a sexual display as it was a flirtation with the car. The windows were sunscreened black, so they wouldn't even know she was a woman. She ran their colours through the onboard files and tagged them as strays from the Satan's Stormtroopers, out of Houston, Texas. With their chopped Harleys, banana seats, beerguts, Viking beards, cossack shirts and pickelhaubes, the whole crew were textbook Motorsickle Crazies. They were just joyriding thugs, not real gangcult specimens. They didn't have a Philosophy, like the Daughters of the American Revolution or the Bible Belt. She didn't feel a pressing need to put them off the road.

They bounced a couple of beercans off Federico without even scratching the paintwork, and did wheelies, thumping the Ferrari's bodywork as they came down. It was time to burn them off. She flicked the overdrive, and let the car do the rest. She pushed 200 miles per, and the cykemen were choking on dust, already out of shouting range.

"So long, boys," she said, smiling, selecting Motorhead's "Built For Speed" for the in-car sound system.

They were sore losers, evidently. Men usually didn't like to be shown up for half-horse feebs. One of the Stormtroopers must have a little hardware on his motorsickle, because Federico cut into Lemmy and told her, in Italian, that there was a heat-seeking missile coming after her, personally tailored to the warmth patterns of the car.

She tutted. These Americans displayed an incredible combination of humourlessness, insecurity and lack of imagination.

She took the laptop SDI console from the dashboard, and established provisional contact with the missile's one-track mind. Its directives weren't even encoded. She wiped Federico's smudgy patternprint from its three-minute memory and programmed in a "Return to Sender" package.

"Ciao," said the car. Chantal fed in Dean Martin's "Volare", and sang along. She didn't even hear the explosion.

Otherwise, the roads were clear.

Until the Tonto Basin, when suddenly her music went down, and a voice came at her through all her speakers.

"SISTER," it shouted, "HAVE YOU BEEN SAVED?!!"

IV

WHEN THE REVEREND Harry Powell, sole owner of the Word of the Lord Broadcasting System, was informed that the aches and pains his faith healing guest stars had been unable to ease were, in fact, inoperable and extensive cancers of the bone marrow, he found himself faced with a choice. As a Good Christian of long-standing who had raised, over his twenty-seven years as a leading televangelist, over three hundred billion dollars for the Lord, he could kill the pain with morph-plus shots and wait his Just Reward in Heaven. On the other hand, as a sin-loving decadent who had used the greater portion of over three hundred billion dollars to indulge himself in luxurious excesses undreamed of by Caligula, he could expend the remainder of his considerable resources staving off the inevitable.

He took some time to assess the health of his business ventures. WLBS was still the top-rated televangelical crusade, beaming the Word of the Lord into perhaps seven hundred million homes worldwide. Royalties were still coming in for his best-selling testaments *How to Get Through the Eye of the Needle*, *Checking Into Motel Heaven*, and *My Pal, Jesus*, not to mention the popular gospel hits he had had ghost-written for him in the '60s by a talented but otherwise unsuccessful young man called Paul Simon, "Little Bitty Orphans in Africa", "Jesus in Blue Jeans" and "I'm Not Ashamed to be a Christian". He had diversified into the stock market, foods, theme parks, computer software, motion pictures, armaments manufacture, law enforcement, pharmaceuticals, energy resources, marital aids and souvenirs. He was in the Top Forty of the World's Richest Men, and climbing...

Still, there was nothing that could be done for his body. He had been able to pay for a half-hour of Dr Zarathustra's personal time at GenTech BioDiv, and the Doc had assured him that no amount of bio-implant and replacement doodads would do anything to help. Muscles, nerves, individual organs, limbs, eyes and skin, you could do something about. And you could replace individual bones – even your skull if you so wished – with durium robo-bits. But you couldn't dispense with your whole skeleton and still survive. It had something to do with blood. Powell didn't understand, but Zarathustra had patiently explained it all to him as if guesting on a kidvid TV show before returning, substantially wealthier, to his important research.

Powell's body was out of the business. But he still had a brain.

Zarathustra had referred Powell to W D Donovan, Bio-Div's top brain-man, and, eager to be divested of his deadweight walking corpse, he had submitted to the Donovan Treatment. He had joined the other disembodied brains in their tanks, thinking their deep thoughts, sinking into their pools of biofluid. Unfortunately, while Donovan could take your brain out and keep it alive, he hadn't yet perfected the technique for putting it back into another body so it worked. That, presumably, was what all the other multi-billionaire prisoners on GenTech's Cerebellum Row – Nelson Rockefeller, Howard Hughes, Rupert Murdoch, Walt Disney, John Gotti – were waiting for. And that was what Powell was expecting, a few years of contemplative thought and resurrection in a young, fresh, ready-to-wear body.

However, his lawyers had not considered the legalities of the Donovan Treatment. Once his brain was slipped from its cranial cradle, the Reverend Harry Powell found himself declared legally dead, and his assets devolved to the Word of the Lord Mission for Christ, parent corporation of the Word of the Lord Broadcasting System, and also of the Word of the Lord Electronic Information Service, the Word of the Lord Chain of Christian Health Food Restaurants, the Word of the Lord Summer Camps, the Word of the Lord Law Enforcement Agency ("Let Christ Be Your Cop!"), the Word of the Lord Publishing Consortium, the Word of the Lord Moral Reassertiveness Centres and the Word of the Lord Graveyard Redevelopment Conglomeration. The board of directors found themselves rather embarassed to have on their hands not only the worldy wealth and temporal holdings of Harry Powell, but his still-functional brain as well.

It might not have gone so badly for the late Reverend if he hadn't made the cardinal error of appointing Genuine Christians to executive offices within his organization. Anyone else might not have been quite so upset to discover that the Word of the Lord Drug Rehabilitation Program was actually a highly successful franchised operation peddling narcotics, hallucinogens, psychoactives, and other forms of ju-ju to teenagers, or that the popular Word of the Lord Crusade for Morals Drop-In Centres Powell had set up in the NoGos surrounding several major PZs were actually omnisexual brothels staffed by runaway youngsters Powell had, in many cases, personally welcomed into the fold.

Once Powell's yakuza-trained accountants had been eased out of the boardroom, only the Genuine Christians – the

Honest-to-God Suckers, as he had been wont to call them in life – remained. They had sat around the oval table, looking at the preacher bubbling away in his Self-Contained Environment, and had pondered the ethics of pulling the plug and burying the grey matter along with his literally rotten bones in the gaudily ostentatious cenotaph Powell had designed for himself.

But there was always a use in the church for brains.

V

"…SAVED BY JEEEY-ZUSS! SAVED BY THE LOWWW-UD! SAVED, SAVED, SAVED!"

Chantal braked to avoid slamming into the tank-like vehicle blocking the road. She'd have swerved off into the sand to get round the obstacle, but she didn't want to gum up Federico's wheels without checking the terrain. It didn't matter what kind of hot machine you had, if you tried to drive on soft sand you'd bog down. The desert was full of abandoned vehicles slowly sinking in alkali pits.

"HAVE YOU SINNED? HAVE YOU BEE-YUN SINFUL? HAVE YOU TAKEN CARNAL LUST, BODILY FILTH AND THE DAY-UVV-VILLE INTO YOUR HEART?"

She tried to turn down the volume, but the broadcaster had a lock on Federico's soundsystem. It was coming from the machine up ahead, that much was certain.

"Do me a search," she said. "Find out what that thing is."

Federico hummed as it went through the files. The voice changed pitch, was joined by a kitschy angelic choir and the kind of string backing British popstars Coldplay favoured on their more unbearable singles, and began to sing.

Little bitty orphans in Africa
Need a heap of change from you,
Little bitty orphans in Africa
Make ole Jesus feel downright blue
Skies may be grey, skies may be sunny
But them pore little orphans need all your money…"

Her central screen lit up, and flashed at her. MINIMUM DONATION: $1,000. THE PREACHERMOBILE WILL ACCEPT CASH, CASHPLASTIC, NEGOTIABLE BONDS, GOLD, SILVER, RADIUM, PRECIOUS AND SEMI-PRECIOUS STONES, VALID STAMPS, ELECTRI-CAL GOODS, MOTOR VEHICLES, STOCK TRANSFER CERTIFICATES, VALIDATED WORKS OF ART, SIDE-ARMS, MILITARY ORDNANCE, DRUGS, WATER AND REUSABLE HUMAN ORGANS. THANK YOU FOR YOUR CHRISTIANITY.

The singing stopped.

"PRAISE THE LOWWWUD! HALLELUJAH! CLEANSE THYSELF OF THY SINS BY DONATING THY WORLDLY GOODS TO THE CHOW-UCH! HELP THE CHOW-UCH HELP THE LITTLE BITTY ORPHANS IN AFRICA!"

Federico had taken stock, and gave her a read-out on the vehicle. It was built like a tank, with ten-inch armour plating and caterpillar tracks. There was a miniature power plant in there somewhere and, in all probability, a human brain.

That was good news. Whoever the machine had been, it was a cinch that he wouldn't be a match for Federico's cerebral capacity if it came to a shooting war. Even Israel had stopped putting Donovan brains in its military hardware five years ago. They might have the initiative a machine lacks, but their reflexes are slow. Plus, they tend — as was now obvious — to crack up and go crazy.

"I HAVE BEEN CHARGED WITH A MISSION FROM GOD! I AM REQUIRED TO RAISE THREE HUN-DRED BILLION DOLLARS TO EXPIATE MY MANY SINS! YOU WILL KINDLY MAKE A DONATION!"

"What if I don't?"

"YOU WILL BE SMOTE AS THE LOWWW-UD SMOTE AGAG! THY BODY WILL BE RENT INTO THREE PIECES, AND THY UNHOLY MACHINE WILL BE BROKEN DOWN FOR SPARE PARTS AND SCAT-TERED ACROSS THE FACE OF THE LAND!"

"I gave at the office."

"MAKE THY DONATION WITHIN TEN SECONDS, LEST THOU SUFFER THE WRATH OF THE LOWWW-UD!"

Federico was scrolling through the specs. It had located the three prototypes on which the Preachermobile was based. An Israeli tank, a GenTech Undersea Explorer and a Saisho Warrior Robot. The car suggested thirty-seven points of weakness.

"THY TIME IS UP, HEATHEN HARLOT! DOST THOU WISH TO REPENT, AND MAKE A CASH OR CREDIT DONATION?"

"I'm on urgent Government business…"

"THE LIGHTNING OF THE LORD OF HOSTS WILL DESCEND FROM THE SKIES AND BLAST THEE WHERE THY FOUL AND PESTILENTIAL FOREIGN-MADE AUTOMOBILE DOST STAND ON GOD'S OWN AMERICAN HIGHWAY!"

An electro-cannon crackled. Chantal reversed Federico, and withdrew five hundred yards instantly. The Preachermobile's arcs fell on the road, cracking the hardtop. The electrical discharges left streaks on her retinas.

"HELLFIRE AND BRIMSTONE WILL REIGN DOWN FROM THE HEAVENS AND THOU SHALT BE CONSUMED BY THE FIRES WHICH BURN NOT WITH THE CLEANSING HEAT OF THE LOWWW-UD BUT WITH THE ICY COLD OF THE DAY-UVV-VILLE!"

Cannisters of napalm exploded in the air. Chantal took the chance and drove off the road. The surface of the desert was rocky enough to get a grip. Part of the hood was on fire, but the windshield squirt took care of that. The paintwork would heal overnight.

"THE UNRIGHTEOUS WILL BE SMOTE UNLESS SUBSTANTIAL CONTRIBUTIONS ARE MADE TO THE WOWWW-UD OF THE LOWWW-UD MISSION FOR FAMINE! THANK YOU FOR BEING A CHRIST-IAN!"

"Federico," she said, "no more messing about. Take him down."

"Molto bene."

The car took out the Preachermobile's treads first, exploding an armour-piercing shell in its side. Now, the thing could only go round in circles. Then, it located the weapons guidance computer, inadvisably placed at the rear under a flap for easy manual reprogramming. A surgical lase burn put it out of commission, and the cannonades stopped.

Chantal drove back to the crippled hulk.

"ALL MAJOR CREDIT CARDS ARE ACCEPTED IN HEAVEN, SISTER! THY WORLDLY RICHES MUST BE PASSED INTO THE HANDS OF THE LOWWW-UD! MAKE THY GENEROUS DONATIONS, LEST THE GOD-FEARING CHRISTIANS OF THE WORLD VANISH UNDER A TIDE OF HEATHEN PAPISTS, RAGHEAD MUSSULMEN…GODLESS COMMONISTS, INSCRUTABLE ORIENTALS… GRASPING JEWS… MELON-EATING… NIGRAS… AND…"

The voicebox was running down.

"Intolerant bigots," she suggested.

"REPPPPPPPPP…. ent… rep…"

She got out, and walked over to the Preachermobile. It was quiet. The lases had opened it up like a tin-can, and the jerrybuilt robo-innards were spilling out. It was constructed like a centaur, with a robotic torso and head protruding from a conning tower. Its arms were still waving. The head was a sculptured, stylised representation of a handsome Nazi, with blue eyes and a blonde helmet of hair. She didn't recognize it. The face was cracked, and biofluid was dribbling from one cheek.

"Are you in there?" she asked.

"Rep… ent?"

"So long, preacher."

"REPENT! THOU ART ACCURSED OF THE LOWWW-UD, JEZEBEL OF THE INTERSTATE! THOU SHALT BE BURNED ALIVE FOR A

THOUWWW-SUND YEARS! THY CHILDREN AND
THY CHILDREN'S CHILDREN SHALT BE
AFFLICTED BY A PLAGUE OF MUTANT BOILS!

She got back in Federico and drove round the thing in the
road. It continued to shout. The voicebox would be the one
thing unaffected by their showdown.

Within half an hour, the predators emerged from the
desert with their spanners and minilases, and, while it raved
against them, the Preachermobile was stripped for parts.
Then, the coyotes, alerted by the whiff of biofluid, came for
the brain.

VI

TIGER BEHR'S WASN'T the worst place Stack had seen in his
days on the road. The Roach Motel outside of Austin, where
the US Cav had busted the Cannibal Cookpots, was several
degrees seedier, and he still sometimes had nightmares about
the dead and dusty things they had found in the fruit cellar
of the Bide-a-Wee Nook in Medicine Bend. Great. That
made Tiger Behr's the third grungiest, most disgusting, least
comfortable, most infested deathhole in the South-Western
States.

The former gangcultist – did he think of himself as a Fallen
Angel? – gave Stack the pick of the chalets, and raised an eyebrow – his only remaining eyebrow – when he asked for a
place with a shower. "You must be a wealthy dude, trooper,"
he had said.

"The State pays," Stack had replied, pretending not to be
uncertain about it.

"You understand," Behr had told him, "that the manage-
ment is not responsible for any loss of personal property, life
and limb or mental stability you might sustain while on the
premises." That told Stack all he needed to know about Tiger
Behr's.

There was bootleg Mexican porno on the TV, but the central dish was skewed and the participants in the current orgy
were stuttering visually. Pornovideo was the Gideon Bible of

the 21st century. No hotel or motel room came without one. He looked at it for a few minutes, trying to figure out the plot. From the clothes on the floor, he guessed it was a period piece, but they had modern leather underwear. A wrestler in a full-head mask and nothing else was trying out some interesting holds on a wild-haired vampire woman whose plastic teeth kept coming out of her mouth, while a creature with huge breasts and male genitalia sang of the Revolution. This must be an Art Movie, Stack figured. Occasionally, a pirate station would cut in with foggy black and white picture of an endless sermon from a man in combat fatigues and a dog collar who called himself a Survivalist Preacher, tapped his Bible with a Magnum 44 and called upon the Faithful to a) give all their money to him, and b) skin a commie for Jesus. The Survivalist Preacher's backing group knew only two tunes, "Gimme Dat Ole Time Religion" and "The Horst Wessel Song", and sometimes got them confused. The off-switch was gone, and so Stack had to turn the set's sound down and picture to the wall before he could get any sleep.

He dreamed about Leona. How she had been when they had been troopers together at Fort Valens, how they had been together on their trip to Nicaragua, how they had broken up, how he had watched her die…

Waking up, sweaty and disoriented, he found it was after nightfall. The ju-ju he had popped earlier had completely worn off. His chest ached where the cruiser had electroshocked him, and the crinkled, red patches on his legs and forearms from the explosion at Slim's were still raw. Someone had been in while he was crashed out, of course, and gone through his things. They hadn't gone for the gun, knife, cashplastic and medkit he had laid under his pillow, but they had taken the kish, the dead cykeman's stash and the walletful of assorted business cards and receipts he had left out on the bureau for the Tooth Fairies. If he hadn't made some kind of offering they would have tried to cut his throat and he'd have had to kill them. Right now, he didn't need the paperwork.

Stepping carefully around the dead bugs on the floor, he made his way to the en-suite bathroom. He didn't know whether Behr used some extra-strength poison or whether life in this place was so damn unhealthy even scorpions couldn't stick it, but there were plenty of chitinous little corpses on the carpet. In the bathroom, water dripped steadily from the showerhead and discoloured the enamel tub. Cigbutts floated in the john. There was no soap, no towels, no toilet paper and the mirror had bullet holes. He put his key into the wallhole and turned on the shower, tested the water – some places out here had an intolerably high radiation level – and stepped under quickly. It was over in thirty seconds, and would cost him more than a week's stay in this dump, but it helped a little. He rubbed the water that clung to him into his body, paying especial attention to his wounds. The red badges of courage smarted. He took a tube of salve, and smeared the worst of the burns and abrasions. There were a few morphplus poppers, but he resisted the temptation. He might need them later, and he might need a clear head sooner.

He checked his watch. It was nearly eight. His priority now must be to find a phone or a radio and call his position in to Fort Apache. He didn't want to risk his Overdue turning into an AWOL. Also, he still hadn't got round to sampling Armindariz's chilli.

He pulled on his thermal union suit, and climbed into his uniform. In the wonky mirror, he looked like he had taken a walk through an active volcano.

He shifted the bed over, skinned back the carpet and pulled up the loose floorboards he had prised free earlier. In the cavity under the floor, he had stashed the two pump shotguns from the motorsickle and his US Cav tracer. He hoped someone was homing in on him, but he was taking no chances.

He left the chalet, and found the cyke chained to a post. He had rigged the battery to give a nasty shock to anybody who tried the chain. There were blackened fingerprints on the durium links.

Score one for caution.

He deactivated the joy buzzer, holstered the pumpguns, and straddled the hog.

Then he headed back to the Silver Byte Saloon.

VII

IT WAS A shame the osso buco would have to be put off until Ms Juillerat had finished her sandside mission, but Brevet Major General Younger could wait to try out the recipe. He was in the nerve centre of his gleaming, white-surfaced kitchen now, directing the preparation of fillet of sole crepes with lemon-parsley butter. Everything in the room was top-quality GenTech standard, requisitioned through his government contacts. The toasters, blenders, ovens, freezers, creamers, processors, burners and broilers shone like brass buttons. Younger observed his reflections in the row of dangling blades that hung before him like a deadly percussion instrument. Straight-edged, curved, serrated, two-action, spiked and plain knives were there, each in place, each ready for use.

He overrode all the hardware and took a whisk to his batter himself. No machine could get the precise texture he favoured for his crepes. The fish-head, its backbone and tail still attached, stared at him from the work-surface. Fish always looked surprised when you were about to cook them. Younger hadn't served on the roads since his days with the highway patrol way back in the '90s, but he remembered seeing that expression on men's faces. Just before and after they were shot, they got exactly the same round-eyed look.

He ran his fort like he ran his kitchen, Younger hoped. Eternally vigilant, eternally in a harmonious balance, ready for anything.

His computer-assist menumaster gave him a choice of peppers with this dish. The list of appropriates came up on his terminal screen. He selected cayenne, which ranked fairly low but which he hadn't used recently. He couldn't remember exactly what cayenne pepper tasted like. It was always human touches like that which made for a great dish.

Younger would have preferred to be remembered as a master chef than a master strategist.

The screen disrupted, the ingredients of his dinner giving way to a face. It was Captain Finney, from the Ops Centre. Odd, she had been on duty this morning, it should be her down-time now. Her hair was loose, and her tunic not quite buttoned-up.

"Sir, Cat Finney here. We have a datanet problem. I think it requires your attention."

Younger paused in mid-whisk.

"Surely not."

Finney paused. "Lenihan couldn't handle it, and called me back to the console... I was playing squash..."

Younger whisked again.

"Get to it, captain. What's the problem?"

"There's a massive power source somewhere out on the grid. We've not tracked down the precise terminal yet, but it's as if a major system had downloaded somewhere in Arizona. Half the screen burned out at once, and we can't keep track of everything. We've lost contact with a lot of outposts."

"Where's Vladek?"

"He's here, sir."

"Put him on."

Younger set his batter carefully on a neutral surface, and sat down at the console. Vladek Rintoon eased Finney aside. He had hoped to keep the colonel out of any crises for a while, but there was no avoiding it.

"Your opinion, Vladek?"

Rintoon was flustered. "I'm not sure, sir."

"Hostile action?"

"It... could be."

"Maniax? Some other gangcult?"

"No. The resources used are vast. Only the megacorps would have the capability to mount such an action. And they're supposed to be on our side. It's the general datanet that's been hit, not just the Cav links. We'll all suffer if anything goes down."

"Natural disaster? Act of God? Lightning?"

"We're checking that out. It's a remote possibility, I think."

There was a commotion in the background as Rintoon was talking. He was having to keep looking over his shoulder. People were shouting at each other. Younger glimpsed Captain Lauderdale and another officer gesturing wildly as they argued in front of a flashing screen.

"Keep discipline there, Vladek."

Rintoon turned and talked sternly. There was a hush. Lauderdale and the other man, Lenihan, broke apart.

"How badly are we hurting?" Younger asked.

"Difficult to say, sir. What we're losing is input. Finney is shutting down all systems contiguous to those affected. We may be able to seal off our own database that way, but that doesn't tell us any more about the nature of the enemy or the situation in the field. We're just drawing in and readying for a siege. I've alerted Faulcon, Badalamenti, McAuley and Doc King, and they're being recalled to duty."

"Have you asked around the datanet?"

"Finney has had provisional exchanges with the night operators at GenTech and ITT in Phoenix and the Winter Corporation in Tucson. They've got the same problem, and are trying to put up the same blocks."

"El Paso?"

"Nothing yet."

"Well get on it man, that's the railhead. If El Paso goes down, we'll blank half the United States."

Finney was talking to Rintoon.

"Sir," he said, "we just lost ITT. They've cast us adrift."

"What?"

"We're it, sir. Phoenix and Tucson cut us loose. The disturbance is in the shared datanet, but it's concentrating on us. The corps are disengaging from the shared line. The private sector is out of it. It's just us now, and the federal information exchange, and the Roman Catholic Church and a few other minor leaguers."

"The Winter people slammed the door behind them," said Finney. "They've blown all the links and burned out their interfaces. They must have had them mined. My guess is that they know something we don't. They just shot sixty or seventy million dollars out the window, and will have incurred more than that in fines for damaging government property and violating interstate information passage laws."

"Will their action limit the damage? Are we the only people on the line?"

"Temporarily," snapped Rintoon. "Arizona is sparsely netted. It's easy to get out of it. But El Paso is a computer interface jungle. It would take years to dismantle all the connections."

"And what's between the input and El Paso?"

"We are, sir. The only major node between the disturbance and El Paso is us, Fort Apache. We've got to entrench and stop it…"

Finney cut in, "It's like a tidal wave, building up out there in the desert and coming our way."

Rintoon said, "We have to break it."

"I'm coming right down."

Finney, headset pressed to her ear and said "here it comes. Computer holocaust. ETA twenty seconds."

Younger punched the door controls next to the elevator.

"… fifteen…"

Nothing was shaking, there were no alarms.

"… ten…"

Lenihan handed Rintoon a note. The colonel turned to the screen and said, "We've isolated a point of origin, sir."

The elevator indicator showed the cage was climbing up towards the kitchen. It seemed to take forever.

"… five…"

"Welcome, Arizona. Say, isn't that where…"

"… three… two…"

The elevator was outside. It pinged like a microwave, and the down arrow lit up.

"… one…"

"… that Swiss woman went?"

"It's here."

The elevator doors didn't open.

Finney asked, "Has anything changed?"

Younger stabbed some buttons.

"I don't think so," said Rintoon. "It must be a monitor error."

The elevator doors wouldn't open.

"Cat," said Rintoon, dripping relief. "Don't ever do that to us again. I just shat the Empire State Building."

Younger turned back to his screen. Rintoon was smiling, but Finney had deep lines between her brow and was punching buttons.

"It doesn't make sense, colonel. It's not registering, but it's here. I've a bad feeling. This is one smart bug."

Behind him, in his perfect kitchen, a rack of electric carving knives buzzed into life.

Younger barely felt the first blade vibrate its way through him.

VIII

IT MUST BE MOR night down at the Silver Byte. Elton John's version of "Glad to be Gay" was burbling on the jukebox, and an imbecilic old man in a bathchair was nodding along to it while playing dominoes with a nine year-old Hispanic girl. Stack walked the length of the bar, laid one of his shotguns down, and asked Armindariz if the chilli was still on.

"Sure theeng, trooper. Commeeng right op. Hey, Pauncho, rustle op a cheellee dog for thee nice man."

A seriously fat individual with a cook's hat perched on his head agreed with Armindariz and spooned out a bowlful of meat stew with beans and peppers. There was a sign over the bar. "WARNING – CHILLI HOT." Stack crumbled his crackers, and stirred them in with his spoon. He hesitated.

"Say, Pedro, just how hot is this chilli?"

Armindariz showed his teeth. His gold fang shone.

"Yiu remember thee A-Bomb tests een thee feefties?"

"Not personally, but I've heard of them."

"Well, there ees a place op in Nevada where they let off too manee beeg ones, an' now no one can ever leeve there again."

"Yeah?"

"Well, Pauncho's cheellee ees hotter than that."

"Which is cheaper here, whisky or water?"

"Whisky, trooper."

"I'll have that then."

Armindariz poured him a shot. Stack lifted the spoon to his mouth…

"Before yiu eet, thee government eet say wee have to geeve yiu thees card." Armindariz shrugged and handed over a much-battered oblong the size of a cashplastic.

"*The Surgeon General has determined that coronary heart disease is the major cause of death in this country, and you are strongly advised against consumption of foods containing red meat, saturated animal fats, irradiated salts and growth-enhanced vegetables. Have a nice day.*"

Stack gave Armindariz back his card. They shrugged at each other. Stack shoved a spoonful of chilli into his mouth, then took a drink. He swallowed the combination, and gripped the bar as his entire oesophagus took fire.

Armindariz and Pauncho laughed.

"That's fuckin' hot chilli, Pedro."

"Wee got a reputation to ophold, trooper."

Stack finished his chilli, taking sips of the rotgut between mouthfuls. His teeth were heating up, and his tastebuds would probably be burned clean away, but it felt good to have something in his stomach again. A little more of this treatment, and he would probably feel like a human being.

The chilli over, he ordered himself a treat. "Water."

"That ees expenseeve."

"I don't mind. I've had a bad day."

Armindariz pulled a plastic carton out from under the bar, and filled Stack's glass. He sipped it.

"Why, you cheating sonofabitch," he shouted. "You've been doctorin' this water with your lousy whisky!"

Armindariz cringed. "No, no, Senor trooper, yiu jost dreenk both from thee same glass. Eet ees natural meestake."

Stack laughed, and finished the water.

"Tell me, Pedro, you got a phone?"

"Si."

"Where is it?"

"Out on thee garbage domp. Eet don' work so good seence thee Gaschoggers reep eet off thee wall and jomp on eet."

"Shame. Radio?"

"FM or digital?"

"Two-way. I need to call in."

"There's a… what yiu call eet? There's a germeenal een thee chorch."

"Terminal."

"Si, a termeenal. Eet may be broke. Thee ronaway car smash eet op a leetle."

"That's just great. Thanks, anyway."

"No trouble, Senor trooper."

Stack would have to go back to Tiger Behr's, and light out in the morning. He wasn't sure what the nearest real town where he could make a call was, but he'd find it before his borrowed cyke ran out of gas. Meanwhile, he had best look after himself.

"Another whisky?"

"Sure theeng, senor." Armindariz poured again.

Stack sipped his drink. He held it up to the light, and gave a silent toast. To Leona Tyree…

Leona. She had been a hell of a woman. Cav all the way.

"Senor?" Armindariz butted into his reverie.

"What is it?"

"Would yiu mind payeeng for your cheellee and dreenks now?"

"No, why?"

Stack realized he wasn't alone at the bar.

Armindariz leaned forwards confidentially. "I theenk may-bee thee Gaschoggers keell yiu later on thees evening, then I no get my monee for thee goods I geeve yiu, and that ees bad for beesneess."

A hairy hand fell on his arm, forcing it to the bar. His drink spilled.

"Plenty sloppy, ain't ya?" sneered a tattooed heavy. His breath stank of gasoline.

The Gaschuggers got their name because of their drinking habits. They had all had their bladders souped up so they could drink gas and whisky and piss high-grade fuel into their cykes' tanks. None of the gangcultists the Cav had ever brought in had been able to explain the appeal of the practice, but there you were...

"Maybe the yellowbellied yellowlegs needs some lessons in etiquette, Exxon," somebody said.

"Yeah," said the tattooed guy, Exxon. "Maybe he does. Maybe his yeller streak runs up the side of his legs and goes all the way up his back too."

"Stand down," Stack said. "I've got no quarrel with you."

Armindariz was down the other end of the bar, paying close attention to some stains he was wiping up. The game of dominoes was heating up, and Pauncho was kibbitzing. Stack was on his own. He judged there were five or six 'Chuggers. Exxon would be the big chief. That was the tag the leader of the pack always drew.

Slowly, he turned round on his stool. He had guessed right. Five guys, counting Exxon, and one girl. All stinking of gas.

"You're Cav, ain't ya?" asked Exxon.

Stack nodded, his hand resting on the butt of the pumpgun. It would be awkward to prime and fire it from the stool. He'd never drop them all before they got him. Maybe they would all explode. With their lifestyle, spontaneous combustion must be a a regular health hazard.

"Well, the Cav is always always always down on the 'Chuggers for no reason. And you represent the Cav, so we're mixing it with you."

Shit, he was going to die.

And he hadn't figured out what the buzz was with the mad cruiser and Leona and the impaled priest yet.

"Mobil," Exxon said, "get the man a drink. Not that piss-poor firewater he's been abusing himself with all evenin'. A real drink."

Shit, shit, shit. He was going to die, but first he was going to have to drink gasoline.

Mobil was the runt of the litter. He jumped up and sat on the bar. He took Stack's glass and threw the whisky onto the floor.

"Sorry, Pedro," said Exxon.

"That's okay, boys," replied the bartender. "Jost clean op after."

Mobil took a canteen and poured pink liquid into the glass. Paraffin. He sniffed the bouquet, said, "A very good year," and knocked it back.

"After a good drink," he said, "what better than a relaxing cigarette?"

He produced a pack and a fliptop lighter.

"Me, I prefer the cool, mellow taste of Sandino's, the cigarette with a longer-lasting tang and that macho muchaco whiff."

He lit the lighter, and breathed across the flame.

Stack flinched backwards as his eyebrows were singed by the fiery cloud Mobil had exhaled. It went out in an instant. Stack's face felt hot, but it was nothing compared to Slim's Gas 'n' B-B-Q.

"Caramba," said Mobil, finishing off the ad, "but that is some wild cigarette."

"Looks like we got us a blackface entertainer," said Exxon. He used his stubby forefinger to smear the soot into Stack's face, especially around the lips and eyes. "One thing you have to say about nigras is that they sure can be entertainin', eh, amigos?"

The Gaschuggers laughed in unison.

"Remember how them Voodoo Bros danced for us…"

Exxon was smiling wistfully now, remembering the good times.

"… when we strung 'em up."

Mobil had another shot of parrafin poured. He lifted it to Stack's lips, and tipped. Stack gulped, hoping the chilli had permanently done for his sense of taste. He got it down without spluttering. Mobil was waving his lighter around near his face, flicking the flame on and off.

"What kind of entertainin' do you reckon Will Fuckin' Smith here'd be best at, chugbuddies? Singin', dancin', acrobatics, sleight o'hand, tellin' them funny stories, mind-readin'?"

Mobil put his head uncomfortably close to Stack's and said, "No, I reckon we gots us one o' them meat-packin' porenographic superstuds. Them nigras's always at it, jus' like rabbits 'r somethin'. I'll jus' bet Magic Fuckin' Johnson here rakes in the big bucks stickin' his cock into dawgs and hawgs and French ladies and just plain dumb ole greasy holes in the wall, that's what I figger."

Mobil was getting excited. Good, that might make him careless. That might give Stack a chance.

"Mobil's a pervert, you know," said Exxon. "It's a shame, but there it is. A man can't help the way he was brung up."

Mobil was double-dyed redneck from way back – the Ozarks or somewhere – but Exxon's sneer was a put-on. Stack reckoned he might have done some time at Harvard or Yale. This was an educated panzerboy.

"My guess is that you're not a porno stud. Who'd pay to see a skinny little thing like you humping some fat whore? No, you're something more sporting. Like a jockey."

Stack didn't move.

"No? Maybe a basketball player. A lot of your tinted ethnic types bounce the ball pretty fair, I hear. Nah, you're a shortie. And you've got no coordination."

The pumpgun had been eased out from under his hand and passed to the back of the saloon. The lone 'Chugger girl – a fourteen year-old with ancient eyes and a plumed pompadour – was cradling it like a child.

"Does your mother know where you are?" Stack asked her.

"Fuck off, faggot!" she spat in a high, vicious, little voice.

Exxon hardballed a fist into his gut. His burns flared up, and the chilli and paraffin shifted in his stomach.

Shit, shit, shit. He was going to die with vomit in his mouth.

"Don't talk to white ladies, nigra. That's a hanging offence in this county."

One of the Gaschuggers – the one with the robo-claw – was black, but he wasn't upset by Exxon's speeches on racial subjects.

"I know what you are, boy. You're a fighter, ain't ya? Bare knucks, one on one, two guys bloodying each other's titties. Maybe you wear a couple of sharp rings to cut deeper."

Exxon shadowboxed in front of Stack's face, occasionally tapping him lightly on the chin or the cheeks.

"You could'a bin a contendah, Iron Mike, instead of a pussy, which is what y'are."

The big one was coming. Stack tensed his aching stomach, and gripped the bar. Mobil held his shoulders, fingers positioned like a masseur's but ready to dig in, and one of the other 'Chuggers had his arms behind him. Exxon danced and punched the air.

"You see *Rocky VIII*, boy? I just love it when ole Sly puts Beyoncé down on the canvas and sticks it to the bitch. That's my idea of a fair fight!"

Stack grit his teeth. Exxon drew his fist back and took a good shot. Stack's jaw popped, and he felt rather than tasted his mouth fill up with blood. He tried to roll with it, but he was held so that only his head could move. His skull rolled on his neck like a punchball. Everything was shaking. His lips were mashed against his teeth, his cheek was squeezed against the bone. Blood was trickling from his nostrils.

"Ouch, that hurt," Exxon complained, holding up his hand. His knuckles were red and black with blood and soot.

"Well, looky looky looky here comes cookie, what have we got here?"

He wiped his hand on his overalls, then took an oily rag from his pocket and rubbed Stack's face. The soot came off.

"Pardonnez-moi, trooper Damfool. We've been labourin' under a misapprehension, ain't we boys? You sure ain't a person of the negroid jungle bunny persuasion after all. You're as white as they come."

The 'Chuggers laughed. The black 'Chugger caressed his claw and gave a slow-burning grin. One of his teeth was inset with black dots like a die. He snapped the air with his robobit. It looked like expensive workmanship. GenTech, maybe, or Sony. He clacked his claw like a lobster.

"Such a shame. We got laws here in Welcome, trooper. Don't you know it's an offence to impersonate a nigra? We gonna have us a trial."

The 'Chuggers whooped and cheered.

"Mr Persecution?" Exxon asked.

"Yes, your honour," replied Mobil.

"Sum up the case for the State of Arizona versus Fuckin' Zeroid Ratskag, here?"

Mobil shoved his thumbs under the lapels of his overalls, and strutted up and down. "Well, Your Judgeship, it seems to me that what we have here is a plain case of violation of the law. The accused ain't no nigra, that's clear as can be. But he certainly was attemptin' to deceive the good folks of this township. I calls me a witness. Call Mr Shell…"

The lobsterman stepped forward. "Present."

"Mr Shell," began Exxon, "do you promise to tell the whole truth, the only truth, the truthiest truth and nothing but the Big T truth or else Gawd come down and rip your gazebos off?"

"Ah do," Shell said in a rich bass, holding up his claw.

"Have you anything to say?"

"Yeah, Ah'd like a martini!"

"Objection!" shouted Mobil.

"Suss-stained," said Exxon. "Witness will keep to the point."

"Sorry, your dealership," said Shell. "But it's as clear as the day is long. Honky moonfaced motherfuckin' pig whiteboy cracker candy-ass citified whelk-lovin' yellowlegs old cow-hand from the Rio Grande shiteatin' geek here is guilty as Judas and twice as dead."

"Yeah," agreed Mobil, "an' he's got a charge sheet as long as my dick."

"First offender, huh?" said the girl. Everyone except Mobil laughed. Mobil sniffed the air, his face reddening, and backhanded Stack across the mouth.

"Mr Persecution, Mr Persecution, I request that you respect the honour o'this court or else I shall be compelled to have you removed from here to a place of animal hus-bandry and forcibly washed until you are clean."

"I apologize, Mr Judge."

"Apology suss-stained. We will hear from the Council for the Fence. Miss Texaco?"

The girl stepped forwards, tears starting from her eyes, and waved Stack's pumpgun dramatically in the air.

"The quality of mercy is not strained," Texaco began. "It droppeth as the gentle rain from Heaven upon the place beneath: it is twice blessed…"

The 'Chuggers quieted down. Shell kicked the jukebox, and it shut up too.

"It blesseth him that gives and him that takes. 'Tis might-iest in the mightiest. It becomes the throned monarch better than his crown; his sceptre shows the force of temporal power, the attribute to awe and majesty wherein doth sit the dread and fear of kings; but mercy is above the sceptred sway, it is enthroned in the hearts of kings, it is an attribute of God himself, and earthly power doth then show likest God's when mercy seasons justice. But, in this case, my client is guilty as a fatcat in a fishtank and it is the recommendation of the Fence that you shoot the fucker's head off tout de suite."

"Thank you for your eloquence, Miss Texaco. Members of the jury, have you reached a verdict?"

Everybody roared in the affirmative.

"And is it the verdict of you all?"

Another roar.

"How do you find the accused?"

"GUILTY!"

Exxon took a black handkerchief from his pocket, folded it into a sailboat, and perched it on his head. Then he pulled a revolver out of his waistband. It was a Wildey, one of those class tools they made a lot bigger than they needed to.

"Looks like we're gonna have to execute you on the spot, Mr Accused. Sorry, chum, but that's the way it's gotta be. We don't have no choice in the matter. It's the laws that made this country great."

He pulled back the hammer and cocked the gun. If he fired it one-handed, he was going to break his wrist. If he fired it now, the ScumStopper – he just knew Exxon would be packing SS balls – would make an inch-wide hole going in below his nose and above his mouth, and take off the entire back of his head. The frags would probably kill Mobil and the 'Chugger holding his arms.

But maybe Exxon didn't care. Whatever, it wouldn't make any difference to Stack.

Exxon shut one eye, and exerted pressure on the trigger. He was showing off, and didn't have the strength in one hand to apply the pull. He took a two-handed grip, and shimmied a little to get a good stance. The gunsight scraped Stack's bloody nose.

Mobil and the other 'Chugger got out of the way.

"Do you have any last words, convict?"

Stack couldn't think of any, so he spat blood and said "Fuck you."

"Time will pass, troopie, and seasons will come and go. Soon, summer with her shimmering heatwaves on the baked horizon. Then, fall with her yellow harvest moon and the irrigated hills growing golden under the sinking sun. Then winter with its biting, whining wind and the land mantled over white with snow…"

This had the feel of a learned-by-rote speech. Golden hills were a long time ago.

"And finally, spring again with its waving green grass, and heaps of sweet-smelling flowers on every hill…"

The hammer went back. Exxon's fingers began to squeeze. "BUT YOU FUCKIN' WON'T BE HERE TO SEE NONE OF THEM, DIPSHIT!"

A gun went off. A skull exploded. A body stood for a moment, strangely relaxed, then fell like a bag of laundry, sprawling on the barroom floor.

Stack, still shaking, looked from Exxon's corpse to the saloon doors, and the most beautiful woman he had ever seen in his life walked through carrying a smoking gun.

If she had been three foot ten, weighed four hundred and ninety pounds and wore a goatee beard, she would still have been the most beautiful woman he had ever seen in his life.

part five:
all god's chillun
got guns

I

THE FORT HAD changed. Nothing had exploded in flames. The consoles weren't spitting out showers of sparks. Blood was not running out of the shower-heads. Lauderdale's cadre of armoured android "pacifiers" had not turned on their masters and put every human being in sight to the electrosword. Apart from Younger's jammed elevator, nothing was obviously malfunctioning. But something had changed. Captain Cat Finney was running a complete systems check, and nothing irregular was showing up. The big input had apparently vanished.

Colonel Rintoon was still going around muttering "monitor error," but Finney wasn't swallowing that. If there were false readings, they were getting them now rather than earlier. What would the Mullah I Naseruddin do, she wondered? Probably give up until it went away.

"The corps still don't want to mix with us," Lieutenant Rexroth told her. "ITT won't even talk to us on the telephone, and GenTech just barred us from the automated helpline."

"Looks like we have a dose of the computer clap."

Rexroth didn't smile.

Finney went along with it. She was a good sufi. This shouldn't bother her. What was that phrase her counsellor kept using? "It's all part of life's rich pattern." In everything, there is a harmony.

Yeah, right.

"How are we at home?" she asked.

"Hanging even. No anomalies."

"And what does that tell you?"

The young man looked baffled. "Er… that we're running steady?"

"Let me put it this way, when was the last time you can remember that this place was running steady, with no anomalies?"

"Er…"

"Never, that's when. We're here to watch for trouble. And, as this blighted country draws to its quarter-millennial anniversary, there is always trouble."

"I'll run the checks again."

"You do that."

Finney tried a few rear-entries of her own into the system, and got the same predigested answers. Even the spyholes she had put in place for her exclusive personal use weren't showing up anything out of whack. She was the best programmer and analyst in Apache, but just now she thought what was needed to deal with the machines was an exorcist.

"You know," she said to nobody in particular, "sometimes I think that maybe brown rice isn't enough."

Captain Lauderdale came over. "Cat, the post office just pulled out. It's just us and the RCs."

"Great. Have you talked to the cardinal or whoever?"

"It's hard to establish territoriality. I never knew the Catholic church was so complicated. St Columba's in Phoenix keeps trying to refer us to some spick bigwig in Managua."

"Archbishop Oscar Romero?"

"Yeah, that's the guy."

"So, get Romero."

"But he's the former head of state of a confederation hostile to the United States of America. We don't take our troubles to guys like that."

"Give me the strength, Lauderdale. This isn't something much affected by lines on a map."

Lauderdale was annoyed. "Tell it to Colonel Rintoon, Cat. He wants to keep this an Arizona thing. He'd bust us to latrine orderlies if he thought we were going to Texas for help, let alone the damn CAC!"

"I'm sorry, Lauderdale."

"Yeah. Everybody's sorry."

Finney had noticed how on edge Lauderdale had been since this thing started. It was getting to everyone. There had been more minor arguments in the Ops Centre than were usual. People were getting testy, locking horns, ruffling feathers. She hoped she was above and beyond that, but her nerves were fraying too.

It would be nice if she could see what was wrong, rather than just feel it.

"Maybe the place is haunted?"

Lauderdale raised a lip.

"No, really. We're slap next to a chunk of ancient history, Lauderdale."

"London Bridge?"

"Yeah. Its stones must be soaked in blood. You know London. It's the most haunted city in the world, they say. Plagues, fires, the blitz, massacres, murders. Jack the Ripper, Christie, Dracula, Burke and Hare…"

"Edinburgh."

"Huh?"

"Burke and Hare killed in Edinburgh."

"Whatever. Maybe they imported the ghosts along with the bridge."

Lauderdale raised his hands and shook his head. "Cat…"

"Yes?"

"Have you been having enough sex recently? You've been getting some… pretty damnfool ideas, you know."

Finney slapped him across the face. He smiled slowly.

"That's it, sufi. Get in touch with your emotions. Let a few of them out."

"Captains!" shouted someone. Rintoon had come into the room. Finney and Lauderdale saluted in unison.

"I don't care what's going on here. I just don't want to see it again, okay?"

"Sir, yessir."

"Fine."

Rintoon's hair was uncombed, and his tie loose. Those were firsts. Finney knew the world was falling apart.

"Finney, we need you up in the shaft. We've cut through to the back-console, but it's flashing at us. You know all the codes."

"Yes sir."

"Any contact with Major General Younger, sir?" Lauderdale asked.

"Brevet Major General Younger, Lauderdale. And no, he's observed radio silence ever since the Unknown Event."

The Unknown Event. The UE. That was how Rintoon was dealing with it, slapping a military label on the thing, tying it up with jargon and filing it away with all the other UEs he didn't have to think about.

Finney ceded her console to Lenihan, and went with the colonel. Lauderdale came along. Passing from the white-walled, immaculate and ordered corridors into the thickly grimed lift shaft, with its dangling cables, unidentifiable accumulation of detritus and shower of sparks was a shocking lesson. This was what it was all like under the surface. Finney liked machines. They did what they were told. But even machines had a sub-conscious these days.

Climbing the access ladder to the stalled elevator was like trudging through the forgotten dreams of the fort. She wondered if she'd be able to get her hips through the open panel in the bottom of the cage, but didn't have any trouble. Two techies pulled her up with a minimum of scraping. She realized that these greasy-overalls power toolmen had been able to order Rintoon to go and fetch her. On some jobs, a colonel was surplus personnel.

Rintoon and Lauderdale joined them in the elevator. It was slightly uncomfortable. The techies had exposed all the workings of the door, and pulled out a spaghetti tangle of wires. An LED redstrip blinked a row of eight eights. The memory had been wiped.

"That shouldn't happen. The doors wouldn't open because the mechanism no longer recognized the c-in-c's code. But even if the central computer goes down there's a failsafe. The code is wiped but automatically replaced by the simplest possible combination. Eight zeroes. This won't even recognize that."

"So?" asked Rintoon.

"So," she replied, twiddling the master dial, "we program in a code. One two three four five six seven eight."

The numbers appeared, and were held.

"Then, we punch the code." Finney pressed the buttons sequentially. "And, voila! The doors open."

The lift doors opened.

"Jesus fucking Christ!" someone said. One of the techies vomited through the hatch in the floor.

Younger was scattered about the kitchen in pieces. His appliances were humming. There was a lot of smoke about, and a power point was sparking, but nothing had caught fire. A still-vibrating electric knife was stuck through Younger's chest. His head was black and smoking in the microwave oven, lids shrunk away from dead white eyes like hardboiled eggs.

"The Major General's been... dismembered!" stuttered Lauderdale.

"Brevet Major General," corrected Rintoon.

No one got out of the elevator.

II

THE GASCHUGGER GIRL primed the pumpgun, and found herself looking down the barrel of the SIG 7.62.

"Don't," Chantal said, staring at the child's face. She had tattoos on both cheeks, and hair in rat-tails.

The 'Chugger dropped the gun.

"Kick it over to the trooper."

The girl followed orders. The trooper picked up the weapon, and stopped looking frightened. He wiped blood off his face with the back of his hand, and stepped over the dead man.

Chantal had followed her training, and had made a snap judgement. But that didn't do anything about the guilt.

The man on the floor joined all the others in her collection of night horrors. Eventually, there would have to be a reckoning.

A hyperactive little 'Chugger pulled a sharpened screwdriver from his toolbelt and tried to stick it into the trooper's ear. Chantal trusted the Cav man to take care of that. The trooper ducked under the thrust, and jammed the butt of the shotgun into his assailant's chest. Then, when the 'Chugger was doubled over, rapped him smartly on the back of the skull. He fell over his dead leader, insensible.

"Seen enough?" she asked.

The girl shrugged and looked at Chantal. There were centuries of something in her eyes.

"You and me," the girl said. "We're the same, aren't we?"

"I hope not," said Chantal, ignoring the little fishhook tearing at her heart. "I certainly hope not."

The others picked up their dead and wounded.

"Now, go home."

The Gaschuggers left the saloon. The girl was the last. She turned and waved to everybody.

"G'night, all!"

Then the gang were gone, swallowed up by the darkness outside, saloon doors swinging behind them.

Chantal holstered her pistol, and walked over to the bar.

"Lady," said the trooper, "can I buy you a drink?"

"Water."

"Even that. Nothing but the best. Pedro, you chickenshit, get us a couple of waters. Make them pure or I'll promote you from innocent bystanding coward to accomplice in my report."

The bartender shuffled along behind the bar, and produced two glasses and a bottle.

"The Gaschoggers are regular customers, senor. I can't do notheeng that'd bee bad for beesneess."

"Yeah? Do you have many 'trials' in this place?"

Pedro grunted noncommittally.

Chantal sipped the water. It was pure-spring, uncut.

"Trooper Nathan Stack, at your service, ma'am," said the Cav man. The name had been in the initial report.

"You were with Tyree?"

A look of pain came into his bruised face. "Yes. How d'you know about Leona?"

"I'm from Fort Apache."

"You weren't there when I left. I'd have remembered."

"I got in just yesterday. My name is Chantal Juillerat."

"I beg your pardon?"

She spelled it out for him. "Juillerat. It's Swiss. I'm working closely with your government and with Major General Younger. Here is my authorization."

She handed him the papers countersigned by the State Governor, General Haycox and the President's representative. He whistled through his teeth, then winced with pain. He must have taken quite a battering.

"What happened to you?"

Stack gulped his water, but didn't say anything.

"As you can see, I am authorized to take your report. What happened to you? Where's Tyree? Where's your vehicle?"

Stack took another drink, and signalled the bartender for the bottle. The man handed it over, and Stack poured.

"Leona Tyree is dead, Ms Julie-Rat. The cruiser is up at the church, stapling a dead priest to his altar…"

Chantal's eyes must have given her away. Stack dropped his precious glass of water and grabbed her shoulders. He started shaking her.

"This means something to you, doesn't it? What's happening? Why did the cruiser go psycho? Why is Leona dead?"

She took his wrists and forced his hands away from her.

"You're not cleared for that information," she said. "Besides, I don't really know myself. In the morning, we'll go to St Werburgh's and examine the site. Then maybe we can isolate the problem."

Stack obviously wasn't happy.

"Tomorrow, I'm getting out of here. I have to call in to Apache. I'm days overdue."

"No problem. I have a radio in Federico."

"Federico?"

"My car. I've been in contact with Fort Apache all day."

"Well hell, lady, why didn't you say? Can I call in now?"

"Certainly."

"First, I have to settle up. Pedro?"

The bartender cringed, and failed to look Stack in the face.

"How much do I owe you, Pedro?" Stack asked deliberately, staring at the man.

Pedro was sweating, looking at the floor. There was blood over the bar. Stack's and the Gaschugger's.

"N-n-nothing, senor... eet ees all on thee house."

"Thank you kindly."

Pedro slunk back, passing a damp cloth over the spilled blood.

"We'll come back soon."

"Good night, senor, senorita."

Stack left the bar, paused as his pains hit him, and limped towards the doors. Chantal reached out and stopped him.

"You must be tired, trooper."

He looked puzzled. Then it hit him. "Yeah, I... I wasn't thinking. Sorry. Thanks."

Chantal walked carefully to the door, unfolding her IR shades. She slipped them on, and the darkness outside went away.

"The one with the claw..."

"Shell."

"Is that his name? Like the oil company? He is crouched down by the row of cykes. The girl…"

"Miss Texaco."

"Very amusing. She is up on the roof of the abandoned feed store with some sort of rifle. Nothing too high-tech. The others are there too, somewhere."

"Five against two. Those are lousy odds."

"You are right," she said, taking the pumpgun from him. "They hardly have a chance. I shall try not to cause further loss of life."

Stack's jaw dropped.

From her position just by the doors, Chantal had a clear shot at Shell. He was uncomfortable crouched behind the cykes, and kept shifting his weight. The claw must be a recent implant. He wasn't used to carrying it yet. She wondered if he got an unscratchable phantom itch where his fingers used to be. That was supposed to be the insoluble problem with bio-implants.

"Throw something heavy through the doors, please."

"Whatever you say, Ms Julie-rat." Stack picked up a barstool and slung it at the doors. Miss Texaco's rifle cracked, hitting the stool in mid-air, and Shell stood up, a six-gun in his good hand. When the doors had swung back, Chantal fired low.

The gastank of the first cyke exploded in a brilliant blossom of flame. The whole row went down like dominoes, each tank exploding in turn. Shell was splashed with the burning liquid and ran off, screaming, waving his robobit like a fire-brand.

"No wheels, Miss Texaco!" Stack shouted. "How'd you like that?"

A shot ploughed into the hardwood floor of the saloon by the doors.

The small 'Chugger Stack had butt-thumped earlier came hurtling through the doors, screaming and firing wildly.

Stack drew his side-arm and plugged him under the right eye. He staggered backwards, his face on fire, already dead as the flames caught his gas-soaked hair and clothes.

"Darn," he said, "I guess I just lost me some life."

Outside, on the porch, the Gaschugger exploded.

"People who drink gasoline shouldn't smoke cigars," Stack said.

No one spoke for a minute. There were shouts outside, and people running away.

"It's clear," Chantal said.

Pedro rushed out from behind the bar with a bucket of sand and doused the burning corpse on his wooden porch, kicking the fire out and the 'Chugger into the street. The cykes were still burning, and he had to call for someone called Pauncho to help him put that blaze out before it spread to the saloon.

Stack and Chantal left the saloon. Pedro swore at them in Spanish. Chantal was amused by the range of his imagery.

Federico was parked just across the street. When she had arrived in town, the Silver Byte was the only place lit up and she had gone there for directions to the church.

"Is this your car?" Stack asked.

She nodded. Stack whistled again.

Chantal tapped in the entry code, and Federico's driver's side door raised with a slight hiss.

"Federico."

"Yes," it said, switching to English for Stack's sake.

"Contact Fort Apache."

The automatic signal was sent out. There was a pause. Across the street, Pedro and Pauncho had the fire under control but were still swearing.

"Fort Apache does not respond."

"That's not possible," said Stack.

"Repeat: Fort Apache does not respond."

Chantal's hand went to her throat. She fiddled with the chain of her crucifix.

"Attempt to override. Try the personal channels for Brevet Major General Marshall Younger, Colonel Vladek Rintoon, and so on down the chain of command."

Federico worked in silence, a few lights on the dash going on and off.

"No response registered."

"Is Fort Apache down?" Stack asked.

"Fort Apache reads normal. It does not respond."

Chantal knew that this was what she had been sent to America to deal with. She had a moment of doubt. She tried to overcome it.

"We can't do anything until morning," she told Stack. "Let's get some sleep. Get in the car, and I'll drive you to the motel. You are staying at the motel?"

Stack was thinking five minutes behind. He shook his head.

"Yeah… uh…"

"Good. I'll take a room. We can be at the church tomorrow."

She got behind the wheel, and opened the passenger door. Bewildered, Stack got in. By the time they reached the motel, he was asleep – unconscious? – in his seat, head hanging against the safety belt.

She left him there and, unable to find a nightman, broke into a room.

III

LAUDERDALE WAS INSPECTING his androids. The whole troop stood to attention under the cellophane shrouds in the storeroom. Seven feet tall, anthropomorphic and faceless under their helmets, they looked a little like the robot in the movie *The Day the Earth Stood Still*, but slimmer and battleship grey. The only customised touch was the US Cav yellow stripe down their legs.

The Robo-troopers were Captain Lauderdale's special field of expertise. The Cav didn't use them that often any more, following the wave of anti-android feeling that had swept the nation after Governor Arnie sent them into the Watts NoGo to break up a peaceful demonstration against the USA's links with Greater Rhodesia. Some programmer's minor error had led to an override of the androids' prime directive and a massacre of 1,594 people. Most agencies had quietly scrapped their android programs after that, or diversified into different branches of robotics. Hammond Maninski Inc., out of the fortress city of Pittsburgh, was rumoured to be experimenting with the Donovan Treatment, putting human brains in android bodies and putting them in the field. Lauderdale knew that was a bad move. The human brain should be well removed from the field of combat, watching the action on all the monitors, playing God, not stuck inside a tin can waiting for the first lucky home-made frag to burst its eggshell.

He ran a systems check on the master control console. The androids hadn't moved since the last inspection. Really, Lauderdale ought to detail someone to dust them down more often. They hadn't been used in action for eighteen months, and had only been trotted out for parades and display inspections after much nudging. Lauderdale resented the down-playing of his discipline. He felt like a spare man at Apache, assigned to odd jobs like looking after official visitors rather than performing the duties he had signed up for.

Colonel Rintoon had ordered everyone to double-check their own areas of the fort. He believed there was a murderer loose somewhere, and that he had gained access to and exit from Younger's kitchen by some as-yet unknown means. Everyone was supposed to be searching for clues. Lauderdale agreed with Captain Finney's diagnosis. Younger had been killed by his own kitchen equipment. The physical presence of a killer hadn't been necessary. Finney had explained that a murderer could tamper with the kitchen by tapping into the central system of the fort, but Rintoon insisted on believing the evidence of the power outages and the dials and maintaining that Apache was inviolate. Rintoon was near the edge. Problems were popping up beyond the parameters of his programming.

None of the androids had bloody fingers. Then again, Lauderdale hadn't expected them to.

He took one last look around the store-room, turned off the lights, and stepped outside into the corridor.

Lieutenant Rexroth was running by, a print-out streaming from his hand.

They bumped together. Rexroth saluted.

"Sorry, captain."

Lauderdale was irritated. "What's the hurry, Rex?"

"Major Faulcon has to see this."

They walked, almost jogging, along together.

"What's important?"

"Younger's orders. They were sealed in his own terminal files. Captain Finney gave me the codes and told me to access them. They're germane."

"Shouldn't you be taking them to Colonel Rintoon then?"

Rexroth stopped short. Lauderdale could tell the other officer was conflicted about something. He wanted to talk, but thought he shouldn't.

"What is it, Rex?"

Rexroth looked at the print-out, and over his shoulder. There was no one else in the corridor.

"What did Younger say?"

"I… I can't follow it… it's about chain of command."

Lauderdale took the print-out. Rexroth didn't fight him for it. Lauderdale started reading from the top.

"Directive Five, sir."

Lauderdale looked down for it. It was triple-starred.

"It was scrambled three times. And marked MOST URGENT."

Lauderdale read:

IN THE EVENT OF MY DEATH OR INCA-PACITY, COMMAND OF FORT APACHE IS TO DEVOLVE TO MAJOR HENDRY FAULCON. UNDER NO CIRCUMSTANCES IS COLONEL VLADEK RINTOON TO ASSUME TEMPORARY OR PERMANENT CONTROL OF THE OUT-POST.

"I don't understand," Lauderdale said. "This is against all procedures."

"Look down again. It's in the notations at the bottom."

COLONEL RINTOON'S LATEST PSYCHI-
ATRIC PROFILE SUGGESTS HE IS SUFFERING
FROM EXTREME STRESS. HE IS NOT TO BE
ADVANCED IN RANK. HE IS TO BE REMOVED
FROM ACTIVE DUTY AS SOON AS AN OFFI-
CER OF EQUIVALENT RANK CAN BE
BROUGHT IN FROM FORT COMANCHE. A
PRELIMINARY DIAGNOSIS SUGGESTS INCIP-
IENT PARANOIA, COMPULSIVE HOSTILITY,
FRACTURED PSYCHE. COPIES OF THIS
REPORT HAVE BEEN DESPATCHED TO GEN-
ERAL ERNEST HAYCOX, STATE GOVERNOR
TOLLIVER.

It was dated two days ago. So much for timing.

Rexroth was fidgeting with his lip. "We have to do something, sir."

"Colonel Rintoon has assumed command. There was
nothing to suggest that he shouldn't. Younger should have
suspended him from active duty immediately if he believed
this."

"But he didn't. We have to talk to Major Faulcon. You, me
and Finney. Rintoon has to be relieved of his command
before something goes seriously wrong."

The corridor was still empty.

"Something already is seriously wrong, Rexroth."

"Yes sir, I'm sorry sir."

Lauderdale drew his sidearm, pressed the barrel to the
fleshy part under Rexroth's jaw, and fired, twice.

"The Path of Joseph is thorny," he whispered.

Then he raised the alarm.

IV

THEY WERE HAVING real coffee on the balcony of their hotel,
overlooking the pleasant central square of Managua. It was

the flower festival, and the square was multi-coloured with
the heaps of blossom placed at the foot of the equestrian
statue of Augusto Cesar Sandino almost up to his saddle. The
smiling faces of Daniel Ortega and Archbishop Romero
shone down from a three-storey poster. It was the middle of
the morning, but they had only just had their breakfast sent
up. A band was playing the songs of the Revolution, and a
young girl was singing about wheat, love and her thirty-
thirty ammunition.

"Trente-trente?" said Leona, the slight breeze shifting
her shining hair as she dissected her grapefruit with a serrated spoon. "I got guns, you got guns…"

A flight of birds shot up from the square. Stack sipped his
coffee, sacriligiously despoiled with Sweet 'n' Lo.

"… all God's chillun got guns."

Leona wasn't really bitter, he knew, but back in the States
there were duties waiting for both of them. Both felt guilty
about snatching this downtime for themselves.

He set his cup down and walked round to her side of the
table. He smoothed her hair down, and kissed the top of
her head. She relaxed and stroked his wrists, and he mas-
saged her neck.

The girl was singing only of love now, of the children
she was expecting from her soldier boyfriend, of the bright
future their struggle had won for the country. She sang of
their defiance of the Yankee tyrants and the multinat octo-
pus. Everybody down here had been friendly, but the
papers, the TV shows and the songs painted all Americans
as villains. After years of recaff, Stack, with the rich taste of
coffee in his mouth, could see why some thought the CAC
a paradise on earth.

Stack slipped his hand into Leona's dress, and rubbed
his thumb over a nipple. He bent down and kissed her
grapefruit-flavoured lips.

She sucked hungrily at his tongue.

A cheer went up from the crowds outside as Oscar
Romero appeared on his own, much grander, balcony,

arm-in-arm with the new Pope of Rome, Georgi. Stack and Leona ignored the speeches.

Leona stood up, and pressed her body to his. They danced together, to the national anthem of the Central American Confederacy, their bodies responding warmly.

He smelled the traces of perfume in her hair, and the soft female musk of her body.

Stack wasn't sure whether he had manoeuvered Leona back into their room and pushed her down on their bed, or whether she had done it to him. They were on the bed now, gently pressing against each other.

Their dressing gowns were getting in the way. They broke apart, unknotted their belts, and threw the gowns away. Naked, they embraced again. He kissed her neck and chin. She stroked his back and sides.

She slid under him, and he looked into her eyes as he lowered his face to hers.

They kissed…

Stack's heart leaped as he started awake. His neck ached where the seatbelt had cut into it, and his entire face throbbed. His head was still bruised from Exxon's fists. Hardly an inch of his body wasn't in one kind of pain or another.

Chantal was shaking him. It was her subtly different scent he had smelled, not Leona's.

"Time to wake up, Trooper Stack."

His wounds came back to him. His body felt like a baggy diving suit. He would have liked to go to Doc Zarathustra and traded it in for a new, more durable model. Hearts, he remembered the Wizard of Oz saying, will never be a practical proposition until they can be made unbreakable.

He rubbed the grit from his eyes, and looked at the woman. "I was dreaming."

Chantal stood up, and backed away from the car. "I thought so. I'm sorry for disturbing you. You were REMming."

He tried to stretch, to lift the imaginary weight from his shoulders.

"You were smiling too."

Stack sighed. "It was a nice dream."

"So I noticed."

Chantal was almost smirking. Embarassed, Stack realized he had a generous erection straining the crotch of his Cav britches. He adjusted his position to de-emphasize his bulge, and waited for his arousal to die down.

Chantal slipped into the driving seat, and flicked switches. Federico reacted with lights and instrument evaluations.

In the light of day, Chantal wasn't the woman she had seemed last night. Appearing in the Silver Byte with her cannon and steely determination in her eyes, she had looked to Stack like Redd Harvest on steroids with a touch of Clint Eastwood and Annie Oakley thrown in. This morning, in the same outfit, she seemed more demure. Passive, restful, even. There was something kittenish about her unconscious pout, and a certain unassailable balance in her disposition. She was younger than he had thought, too. Maybe twenty-four, twenty-five. She gave the impression that she could hardly lift the heavy side-iron she was packing, let alone squeeze off a ScumStopper and hole the target dead centre. Stack knew better.

Quite apart from the fact that she had saved him twice from certain death, there was something very attractive about Chantal Juillerat.

"Good morning to you, Ms Julie-Rat."

"Everybody calls me Ms here in America. I am not used to it."

"Would you prefer to answer to Madam-weasel?"

"Chantal, please."

She pressed the auto-ignition.

"Nathan."

"Thank you, Trooper Stack."

Federico rolled forwards. This was a righteous piece of rolling stock. Its elegant curves made the typical US Cav cruiser look like a dray horse next to a she-panther.

"Do we get breakfast?"

"There are some N-R-G candies in the glove compartment. Oh, and some cherries."

Stack pulled the bag of fruit out, and chain-popped cherries until his mouth was full of stones.

"You must be loaded, sister."

She shifted her shoulders. "I'm on generous expenses. Fruit is essential to a balanced diet."

"Essential it may be, but that doesn't make it cheap."

She shrugged again. That was a characteristic European gesture, Stack thought, the famous *ça va* shrug.

He spat the stones into his hand, and threw them out of the window. Maybe they would seed the desert.

"Now," she said, "where's St Werburgh Church?"

"You see that half-destroyed building over there?"

"Yes."

"Well, like they told me, follow the trail of death and destruction through town and you can't miss it."

"This may be boring for you, I'm sorry. I shall take you back to the fort when I've finished."

"I'll come along for the ride. I don't mind."

"That's good then."

They drove slowly over the bumpy, wreckage-strewn ground.

"Federico," she said to a voice-activated console.

"Buon giorno, sorella."

"Good morning. Could you book me a satellite channel, please. I'm going to want to talk to Rome. If you can raise DeAngelis, I would be especially pleased. If not, Edwina will do."

Federico beeped an affirmative, and got working on it. Stack realized he was flying in very high circles. He doubted if Brevet Major General Younger could as casually get airtime on a satellite link.

Chantal gasped, as if someone had slapped her across the face with a rope-end. Stack followed her eyeline.

She was looking at the raped ruin of the church.

V

RINTOON HAD DOUBLED the guards, but that hadn't stopped the murderer or murderers from striking nine more times during the night. Cat Finney had retired with an automatic pistol under her pillow, her cubicle lock scrambled and a desk against it. She hadn't slept much. No one who had got a good look at Younger's kitchen would sleep well for months.

At the morning briefing, Rintoon gave a report.

"Rexroth is an unconfirmed kill. It is possible, indeed probable, that we should count him as a suicide…"

"In that case, sir, where's his gun?"

"Good question… er… Badalamenti. His weapon may have been… er… appropriated by personnel unknown prior to Captain Lauderdale's discovery of the body."

Finney was in yesterday's uniform. It was still discoloured from her climb up the liftshaft. Slung over the back of a chair, it had been the easiest thing to find this morning. She didn't want to admit to it, but her childhood fear of the closet might just have come creeping back. All through the night, she had been waking up and looking at the slats of the closet door, wondering absurdly if the killer might not be lurking within. Her clean uniforms were in the closet, and they would probably stay there until the crisis was over. Rintoon hadn't slept at all, and was looking wilder by the minute. She found it difficult to connect the hypertense, unshaven, neon-eyed c-in-c of this morning with yesterday's smug, complacent, new-pin-neat Number Two. There was something increasingly familiar about him, though, as if he were metamorphosing into a different, truer, more immediately recognizable shape.

"So, if we leave Rexroth out of the reckoning, and setting aside Brevet Major General Younger, we have eight more VUEs to log and deal with."

VUE. That was a new one on her. Captain Badalamenti, obviously too smart for his own advancement, questioned the acronym.

"VUE, Badalamenti. Violent Unknown Event."

Major Hendry Faulcon, next down the chain of command after Rintoon, was a five o'clock shadow man. He shaved two or three times a day. He had had late duties last night,

and had tried to shave at about eleven-thirty. As far as anybody could tell, the electric razor in his quarters had slithered
out of his grip and buzzed halfway down his gullet. He had
died of a combination of suffocation and drowning in his
own blood. A typical VUE.

Major P J "Howling Paul" McAuley was dead in his
shower, microneedles peppering his torso. Dr Wilma King,
the fort's senior medico, had rotted away from exposure to
a source of intense radiation in her surgery. S M "Max the
Bax" Baxter, a middle-management Op at T-H-R mopping up the paperwork after the joint action, had been put
out of commission by everybody's favourite murder
weapon, the unidentified blunt instrument. Captains Gar-
nett and Stableford had been napalmed in their bunks –
and they'd taken the same precautions Finney had. Top
Sergeant Alexander Stewart was crushed under the wheels
of a cruiser whose transmission he was supposed to be fixing. And Trooper Charlie Stross, in the guardhouse for
mouthing back to Sergeant Quincannon after a twenty-
mile forced march through the desert in full pack and gear,
was mysteriously gone from his cell leaving only a couple
of severed fingers, some cabbalistic symbols traced in blood
and a chunk of what had tentatively been identified as a
pancreas.

Everybody around the table was looking ill. There were
more than enough empty places in the briefing room.
Badalamenti was nervously tearing a page of notepaper
into animal shapes. Captain Lauderdale and Lieutenant
Williford had turned out in combat gear, M-29s and all,
obviously assuming that Fort Apache was on a war footing.
Lieutenant Colosanto – who had been bunking with
Rexroth – was chewing aspirin as if they were mints.
Finney was on her third cup of recaff, and she usually
couldn't finish her first.

"I have come to a conclusion," Rintoon began.

Everyone grudgingly paid attention.

"This post is under attack."

The disappointment was palpable.

"And I am reasonably certain that I have isolated the culprits."

Everyone perked up again. Lauderdale straightened his rifle on the table in front of him, ready for action.

"I believe…"

Rintoon took a gulp of cold recaff.

"Yes?" said Badalamenti.

Rintoon swallowed. "The Maniax are responsible."

Badalamenti rolled his eyes upwards, and pointed to his head. Rintoon didn't notice, and continued…

"The joint action has hurt them, and this is their last ditch attempt to break the US Cav."

"But…" someone said before catching the glint in Rintoon's red-rimmed eyes.

"It was Baxter's death that tipped their hand. He was materially involved in planning the strategy of the joint action. He must be a prime target for the Grand Exalted Bullmoose and his remaining followers.

"Baxter was a pen-pusher, sir," said Badalamenti. "He was just processing expenses and payments. He never went into the field in his life."

Finney fought to keep her control. The recaff had done its damage. She felt as if she had been punched in the kidneys.

Rintoon smiled at Badalamenti, and Finney felt the ice seep through her veins. The smile widened to a grin, and the eyebrows flared.

Finney realized where she had seen a face like that before. Rintoon was looking more and more like Frankie Muniz in the last scenes of the remake of *Twin Peaks*. The scenes where he's looking in the mirror asking "Where's Annie?"

"The Maniax are guilty, Badalamenti. Guilty, guilty, GUILTY!"

Badalamenti stood up. "The Maniax are finished, sir! We creamed 'em. We broke their central structure. We blew up their munitions dump. We rounded up the chapter heads."

"There's still the Bullmoose!"

"There's no such animal! All the ringleaders, they were all the Bullmoose, sir. It was a floating office. They've admitted as much."

"Sit down and listen, Badalamenti, or I shall be forced to discipline you immediately. I will not tolerate these outbursts. I will not, not, NOT!"

Rintoon thumped the table. Polystyrene recaff cups jumped. Finney mopped the mess spilling towards her lap up with her sleeve. Badalamenti looked around for support, found none, and slumped back in his chair.

"The Maniax are clever," continued Rintoon. "Yes, they are. They've sustained a killing blow. We can credit ourselves with that. But this is their last mission. They're going kamikaze. They've infiltrated spies into the fort, and subversives and assassins and agents provocateurs. It's the only feasable explanation."

No one said anything. There was a dribble of saliva dangling from Rintoon's mouth, tracking through his stubble.

"The supposed Swiss woman, Juillerat, was one of them. She was there at the original UE, when she influenced the instruments. It was monitor error, as I always insisted…"

All Rintoon needed to complete the picture was a pair of ball-bearings to clack together in his hand.

"And Rexroth was in on it too. He was unable to live with the guilt, and shot himself. And Stross, who was killed by his confederates because he was about to talk. I have determined the existence of a conspiracy of treachery on a scale unheard-of since 2001."

Colosanto bit down loudly on a pill. Badalamenti shoved his paper animals about on his blotter.

"And I shall not rest until I have rooted out this conspiracy and exterminated it down to its very last member."

Lauderdale was easing his rifle off the table. Was he planning to scrag Rintoon? At this point, he would have won a vote of confidence if he did.

"I believe there are Maniax among us, even in this room."

Everybody sat up and looked at each other. Then, they looked to Rintoon.

"By his words and his actions this morning, he has given himself away. They think they're clever, these hophead damnfool gangcultists, but the zeroids never reckoned they'd be coming up against Vladek W Rintoon. No siree. Ole Vladek W Rintoon has them outfoxed eight ways from sundown."

Badalamenti was statue-still now.

"Yup, there's a Maniak at this very table."

Badalamenti very slowly spread his hands out before him. Rintoon looked at everyone in turn. Finney tried to look away from his shining, moist eyes, but couldn't. He seemed to see clearly right through her, to sense every petty dereliction of duty, every resistance to command, every infraction of the rules, every sinful course carried through or merely considered. Then, his terrible gaze was gone, and it was Colosanto's turn to sweat.

Finally, Rintoon grinned his feral sardonicus grin and almost whispered, "Williford."

The officer sat bolt upright, rifle raised in the present-arms position in front of him.

"Williford," Rintoon cajoled, "Simon says 'Take your rifle…'"

He had the gun to his shoulder now, and was standing up.

"And execute Captain Badalamenti."

VI

CHANTAL SPENT A few minutes kneeling by the priest's corpse. She seemed to be looking into his dead, open eyes, as if trying to get him to reveal something to her through telepathy. It made Stack feel uncomfortable. Flies were buzzing around the body. In this heat, they would have to get him in the ground quickly. Finally, the woman got up, and gently shut the corpse's eyes. She muttered something and crossed herself. She walked around the cruiser, and the wreck of the altar.

"Careful," he said. "It was quiet yesterday, too, but I got a nasty shock."

"Yes, you would have. Don't worry. It's gone now."

She was at the altar now. She had it working.

"It got into the system here, from your cruiser. But how did it get into the cruiser?"

"It?"

She waved him away. "I'm sorry. I was thinking aloud."

Some of the altar's functions were down. The screen flashed green at her. She experimented with several buttons, and finally it turned off. Stack nerved up the courage to approach the cruiser. He touched it. He felt the bullet-scars in the hood. Someone had used pretty major firepower against it.

Chantal was asking a question. "Before the... uh, change... before that, what exactly was happening to the automobile?"

That seemed like a long time ago. He remembered Leona walking around the car. Ken Kling – the poor obnoxious dead bastard – had called her "cowgirl" and asked her to get him something, a co-cola. She had hoped to have some of Slim's B-B-Q.

"Gas. Slim was filling the gastank."

"Hmmn," Chantal was pensive. "No. It couldn't be in the gas. Wrong medium. Was there any other kind of contact?"

"Just the usual systems check. Slim was on the yaks' pay-roll. His place was well set-up. We always had him look at the cruiser's whole works."

Chantal snapped her fingers. "That would be the point of possession, then."

"Possession?"

Chantal was bent down by the crushed front of the cruiser now, tapping at the spike linking it to the altar.

"Yes, possessed. Your car was under the influence of a demon."

This was crazy.

"Like, Linda Blair or something?"

"Something like. A demon is a lot of things. You might like to think of it as a computer program that infects a given system and changes its function."

"Like a virus, or a sleeper?"

"Yes, very good. Exactly like a virus. An engineered virus, of course. This was a deliberate act of aggression. Not a chance mutation."

Stack was having difficulty keeping up. Chantal had raised the hood, and was poking around near the engine.

"Ingenious adaption. It leeched surplus metals from the body of the cruiser and melted them down to form the channeling spike. It must be a fast-breeder. It'll be replicating like a plague out there."

Stack's head hurt. It usually did when he had to do any serious thinking. "Let me get this straight? There was something in the works at Slim's?"

"Undoubtedly."

"That makes sense. He said his hardware had gone crazy. And this… demon… downloaded into the cruiser, and made it run amok."

Chantal raised a finger like a teacher correcting a point. "Not amok. It was very purposeful. It came straight here, to this church, and insinuated itself into the altar system. It did exactly what it was invoked to do. It's deep in the datanet now, and it has to be stopped."

"This demon? It's just a computer virus, right? No spook stuff?"

Chantal looked at him. Her expression was serious.

"There is spook stuff?"

She nodded. "I'm afraid so. You're not going to find any of this easy to cope with. Do you have any religious faith?"

"Daddy was a Baptist. I guess I'm not anything."

"Well, in that case, a demon is a computer virus."

"Come on, Chantal."

Patiently, she sat on the ruined hood of the cruiser and explained it to him. "And it's also a supernatural entity, an immortal creature, a servant of the Devil. It was summoned from Hell by a powerful diabolist, and it has been deployed in a deliberate attack on the Catholic Church and upon the information exchanges of the United States of America. It will remain in the channels until it has been exorcised."

"Sister, who the fuck are you?"

Chantal looked at him as his question echoed. Somewhere, water was gushing. Holy water, he remembered. Chantal sighed, and shook her head. She was having trouble putting the words together.

"Nathan," she said, "I'm a nun."

part six:
holy orders

I
Lucerne, Switzerland, 2009

"CHANTAL," SNAPPED MLLE Fournier, her nanny, "Papa is busy. You mustn't bother him."

"No, no, that's all right," said her father. "Papa should never be too busy for his bon-bon. How are your classes, darling? How's the ballet coming?"

Chantal sucked her lips in, and wondered whether she should ask her questions. She was nearly eight. She shouldn't need to keep asking grown-ups things. She could read. She could use the villa's terminal and tap into the infonet. Her tutors said she was supposed to have an IQ in the upper 170s.

"Come here," said Thomas Juillerat, turning away from his paper-strewn desk and beckoning. She ran to his arms. "Do you want a consultation?"

Chantal nodded, trying not to cringe as papa ran his stubby fingers through her long, dark hair. He wasn't used to children, and he hurt her sometimes without meaning to.

"Do you know how much your Papa usually charges for a consultation?" asked Mlle Fournier, sternly. "Fifty thousand Swiss francs. More in Euros."

Papa was embarassed. He settled Chantal more comfortably in his lap.

"Mlle Fournier, could you get me some coffee, and lemonade for the little madame?"

Mlle Fournier's eyes narrowed in that way only Chantal seemed to notice, nodded, and left the room. It was late, nearly her bed-time, but Papa didn't know when she was supposed to go to bed. In the autumn, when she went back to Milan, Mama would be annoyed to find out how often she had been allowed to stay up late over the summer. When she was annoyed, Mama went into a huddle with Father Daguerre, her confessor, and sorted it out.

"Now, what is it you want to know, mon petit choux? Will I need my law books?"

Chantal wasn't sure. This might not be a good idea. She remembered how Father Daguerre had reacted when she asked him why Marcello, the boy next door, kept putting his hand in his shorts and moving his penis around. But she had gone too far to back down. She took a deep breath.

"Papa, what is it you do?"

Papa seemed bemused by the question. Like most grownups, he wasn't entirely comfortable around Chantal. The difference was that he was sorry for his feelings, and tried not to let them show.

"You know that, Chantal. I'm a lawyer. I work mainly for the Swiss Business Commission."

"Yes, yes, yes. But what do you do?"

Papa shifted Chantal off his lap and sat her on the desk. Papers scrunched under her bottom. He took off his thick glasses.

"I mainly investigate corporations who want to invest in Swiss-based industries."

"Invest? That means money?"

Papa smiled. "Yes, usually quite a lot of money. Sometimes, people with quite a lot of money have obtained it… unethically. You know what that means?"

"Yes, against the laws."

"Well, I'm afraid it often doesn't. Not every country has entirely just laws. Some things that are legal in, for example, Armenia, wouldn't be allowed here. And some things, I'm sorry to say, that are allowed in Switzerland shouldn't be allowed anywhere in the world."

Chantal hit her Papa lightly, as she always did when he missed the point. "Silly, I didn't mean man's laws. I was talking about God's laws."

Papa had that look again. The look that came when he was proud of Chantal and annoyed with her at the same time.

"Yes, God's laws. That's very well put, Chantal. Well, I try to stop people who've broken God's laws from using their money in this country."

"And is that why we have those telephone calls?"

"Who's been telling you about telephone calls?"

"Rudi and Inge were talking in the kitchen when I was helping Mlle Fournier make biscuits. They said people were calling up and not saying their names and saying bad things. And that they were coming in through your terminal too."

Papa's forehead went crinkly. "That's true. They're bad people."

"The other day when you were out at that meeting and Mlle Fournier was having her nap, I answered a telephone call from a bad person."

Papa was shocked by that. "What did he say?"

"That you were to stop doing something about something called the BioDiv something. He had a funny voice, like some of those government people you talk to on the phone."

"A scrambler. They'd have used a scrambler."

"That's right, so I'd never be able to recognize him even if he came up and tried to make friends with me on the playground at school."

Papa held her shoulders. "Did he say they'd do that? Come up to you on the playground?"

"No, but isn't that the sort of thing bad people do? Father Daguerre told me about bad people."

Papa was relieved, but tears were coming out of the crinkles in his forehead.

"Why do the scrambled people want to phone you up and not say their names?"

"Hmmn? Chantal, What I do doesn't make me very popular with some people. They want to stop me. They think that making threats will stop me objecting to their investments."

"You mean people like GenTech."

Papa definitely wasn't pleased now. "You've got good ears, Chantal. That may not make you happy when you grow up. Yes. Just now, I'm checking into a megacorp called GenTech. They want to take over a chain of hospitals, and I don't think they should be allowed to."

"What have they done, Papa? Why shouldn't they be allowed to?"

"They've done bad things."

"What bad things?"

"Very bad things."

"You don't want to tell me, do you?"

Papa's forehead went crinkly again. "No, it's just… it's complicated…"

"Too complicated for someone with an IQ in the high 170s?"

"Chantal, you're very clever. Really, you're cleverer than I am. Cleverer than almost everyone else you know. But you're still a little girl. You'll have to wait for some things."

"Rudi said you found out that GenTech was cutting arms and legs off poor people in Uganda and sewing them on to rich people over here. Is that true?"

Papa sighed. "There's no keeping anything from you, is there? That's one of the bad things I think they've been doing."

"That's all I wanted to know."

"But you knew it already."

"Yes. But I wanted to know it from you, Papa."

Thomas Juillerat hugged his daughter, and kissed the top of her head. She wondered why he was shaking.

"When you grow up, Chantal, what do you want to be? What do you want to do with your IQ and your big ears?"

Chantal pushed him back and looked into his face, smiling proudly. She had never told anybody this.

"I want to be a spy."

II
Lake Geneva, Switzerland, 2014

"CHANTAL," SAID HER reminder-box, "your mother is here."

She sat up in the boat, and directed it towards the landing. She had just been floating, looking up at the skies, and listening to the Samovar Seven on her MP5 sunglasses. Her bedroom in Milan was plastered with glossies of Russian musickies clipped from *Europ-teen* magazine. Her parents disapproved of her musical tastes. That was one of the rare things they agreed on.

She was wearing flip-flops, tight knee-shorts and a loose T-shirt printed with cyrillic lettering. The T-shirt had appealed to her for its bright colours, but she was disappointed that the words were gibberish. Real Sove fashions always made a statement, even if it was just a snip from a lyric.

She had spent most of her summer on the lake – Lac Leman, they called it on the opposite shore – feeling as if she was floating in the centre of the world. This was the border between Switzerland and the European Union. Important people had been thronging the Villa Diodati, come to talk with her father. Joerg Haider, president of the EU, had stayed for three days, walking on the lakeshore with Papa, and they had dissolved a tariff barrier with a handshake. Currently, there was a party of middle-aged men in identical suits – some Iranian, some Turkish, some American – from powerful interests inside the Pan-Islamic Congress. They were arguing about import quotas from the electronics works taking advantage of cheap labour in Greece and Azerbaijan.

Her shades buzzed with the asexual voice of Petya Tcherkassoff as he sang of his lost love, "The Girl in Gorki Park." Petya was the coolest of the snazz that year. His dour face – he looked something like a girlier version of Franz Kafka – gloomed out of the tri-d glitterbadge on her hip pocket. *Europ-teen* said he was recovering nicely from his latest suicide attempt, during which he had walked naked into the Siberian wastes after an open-air gig in Turinskaya Kultbaza. "It's not easy being loved," he had claimed, quoting the title of his latest single.

With no one her own age around, she had been on her own, reading, listening to music, thinking, shadow-fighting in the gym. One of the bodyguards assigned to her father tried to show her some tae kwon do, but he wasn't as well up as her sifu in Milan. After she had put him on the carpet once or twice, he lost interest in sparring with her. As an experiment, she had tried not praying for a week – even when Mlle Fournier took her to mass – and God hadn't punished her. But she had fallen back into old habits. Just because she wasn't delighted with either of her parents much of the time was no reason to turn her back on Jesus Christ.

She had scrolled through *The Lives of the Saints* several times, and finally finished Proust, but her main reading had been computer sciences, as usual. Mlle Fournier told her that the villa was where Mary Shelley had been inspired, by conversations with her husband, Percy Bysshe Shelley, and Lord Byron, to write *Frankenstein; or: the Modern Prometheus*, and she had read up on 1816 when the poets and their mistresses had passed a disagreeably showery summer in speculation. Byron's daughter, she was excited to learn, had later sponsored Charles Babbage, the inventor of the ancestor of today's computers. She wondered if the club-footed poet's ghost lumbered around the corridors. Probably not.

Just now, she was intrigued by the connections between higher mathematics, bio-engineering and the heuristic functions, and had read and reread Declan O'Shaughnessy S J's *Cybermind, Cybersoul*, lying in her boat as the ideas shot around in her head like radio waves in deep space. The villa's terminals were mostly booked up by Papa's staff, even through the night, but she had accessed a datanet terminal in a neighbouring house – empty because the owners were summering in Greater Rhodesia – through a housekeeping program by linking her bedroom PC with the telephone, and was illegally – unethically, too – probing the extremes of the Swiss systems. She was already talking to hackers as far afield as Los Angeles, Moscow and Sakhalin, and feeling her way around the shadow world of the infonets.

The boat tied itself automatically at the jetty. Mlle Fournier was waiting there, with a party. Chantal pushed her music-shades up into her hair, which she had persuaded Papa to let her have cropped, and waved to her mother. It was time to go back to Milan.

"Chantal, whatever have you done to your hair?" asked Isabella Juillerat, the former Isabella di Modrone, kissing the air three inches away from her daughter's cheek. As usual, she was stunningly dressed, in a white sheath that curved from her chest to mid-thigh, one elbow-length glove with red talons, and a matching hat that circled her head like the rings of Saturn.

Chantal was told that she would grow up to look like her mother. But, this last year, she had gained about nine inches of height without developing any noticeable secondary sexual characteristics. In Milano, Marcello referred to her as "the scarecrow with no tits."

"Let me look at you," her mother said, arching a perfectly plucked eyebrow. Her tan was even, but recently she had been developing visible orange patches on her neck and cleavage. That was, apparently, one of the side effects of the treatment. Father Daguerre had advised her to wait until Dr Zarathustra perfected his skincare system, but she had rushed into it as she rushed into everything else. She understood that GenTech's wizard had given her a rejuvenation on the house in the hope that she could exert some influence on her husband with regards to some multinat scheme.

"You have been to mass? Every week?"

"Twice a week, mama."

"Good. Your soul is safe, then. But your clothes! Why don't you wear the dresses I send you? You could wear only originals."

"I was boating, mama. It gets wet."

"Pah! You should always be fit to be seen, Chantal."

Father Daguerre, a wrestler in a cassock, stood a little apart, with another priest. "Hello, Chantal," the French priest said, a sly look creeping over his face. "Now faith is the substance of things hoped for, the evidence of things not seen…"

Chantal pouted a little, and put a hand on her bony hip. She was being invited to perform again. "Easy. The Epistle of St Paul to the Hebrews, chapter 11, verse 1."

Father Daguerre nodded, unsmiling. "And…?"

Chantal sighed, a little embarassed. "For by it the elders obtained a good report. Through faith we understand that the worlds were framed by the word of God, so that things which are seen were not made of things which do appear."

"Excellent, excellent," said the priest. "Latin?"

Chantal switched languages. "By faith Abel offered unto God a more excellent sacrifice than Cain, by which…"

"Hebrew?"

That was trickier. "By which he obtained witness that he was righteous, God testifying of his gifts; and by it…"

"Greek?"

"Ancient or modern?"

"Ancient, showoff."

"And by it he being dead yet speaketh. By faith Enoch was translated that he should not see death; and was not found, because God had translated him: for before…"

"C++?"

"Not verbally. I could type it out for you. It's quite easy."

"English?"

"Kid's stuff, Father. 'For before his translation he had this testimony that he pleased God'."

"And Russian?"

Chantal had to translate in her head. Greek to Russian was the easiest. "But without faith it is impossible to please him: for he that cometh to God must believe…"

The other priest, whose black suit was edged with red, cut in, speaking Russian like a native, "Must believe that he is, and that he is a rewarder of them that diligently seek him."

Chantal looked carefully at the new priest. He was pale, and had shoulder-length hair and a high forehead. In a strange way, he reminded her of Petya Tcherkassoff.

"This is Cardinal Grinko, Chantal," said her mother. "He's a friend of Father Daguerre's. He's come from the Vatican to talk with your father. He is a Special Envoy from Pope Benedict."

The cardinal bowed. There was something about him that made him special, Chantal knew. She was having one of her insights. His mouth went up on one side, and their eyes met. The others didn't notice, and Chantal didn't really understand what had passed between them, but she realized that she had formed a bond with this stranger.

"Good afternoon, your grace," she said, doing her best to curtsey with only a T-shirt to lift.

"Please, Chantal, call me Georgi."

III
Geneva, Switzerland, 2015

"CHANTAL, STAND UP straight."

"Yes, mother."

Isabella Juillerat adjusted her veil, and smoothed her floor-length glitterblack crinoline. When the news came through that she had been widowed, three top Milan couturiers had stayed up overnight to design a selection of mourning wear for her and made their competing presentations in rapid succession the next morning. She had, as usual, picked the most expensive range.

Chantal's heavy collar scratched. It didn't seem possible, but since the fittings she seemed at last – and at the worst imaginable time – to have developed breasts. She had been standing up for three hours now, and desperately needed to pee. She told her trained body to stand still and put up with it all. It was the least it could do.

The funeral cortege had slowly made its way to the cemetery. The streets were thick with people. Mother called them gawkers, but Chantal suspected much of their grief was genuine. Those not in black wore black armbands. Only the immediate family and VIPs – and the media, of course – were actually allowed into the cemetery. The Juillerat Monument, as it would now be called, was drowned in wreaths.

Jean-Marie LePen was speaking now, straying from the subject to harp on international unity or some such nebulous concept. In life, her father and LePen had fought an undeclared war for the seven months of the latter's presidency of the UEC, and Papa had referred to the President in private as "a fucking mad dog sonofabitch who should be put down." LePen's speech basically boiled down to an unconvincing declaration of "I didn't do it."

Maybe he didn't. Thomas Juillerat, without ever holding any elected or appointed national office, had made devoted friends and equally devoted enemies right and left. When the story was released, LePen wouldn't have been the only individual to leap for joy. The Japanese, Korean and Californian boardrooms of GenTech, the cabinet offices of Prime Minister Mandelson, the White House of President Charlton Heston, the mosques of Teheran, and Ferdy and Imelda's Malacanang in Manila would be resounding with choruses of "Ding Dong, the Witch is Dead."

Chantal had sworn not to cry. Her mother had delicately been leaking from her tearducts all morning, especially when there was a camera aimed in her direction. She had to be helped by Father Daguerre when it came to getting into the car.

It had happened on the steps of the International Courts in Brussels, after the ruling against organ-farming practices in the Third World had gone Papa's way. He had been giving an interview to a Russian newsnet when person or persons unknown had jostled him, slipping an electrostilletto into his neck. The device discharged for five minutes, but it was likely that he had died within seconds. He had had his first minor coronary three months earlier. The Belgian police had made no arrests and extensive examination of all the films of the event revealed only blurred, impossible-to-identify figures on the steps. The assassin would probably be wearing a different face – a different sex, even – now.

Isabella was fidgeting. Chantal supposed she was worrying over the seating arrangements at the memorial reception this evening, and then chided herself for the uncharitable thought. She said a silent Hail Mary.

They could have ended their marriage, Chantal knew. Cardinal Georgi had explained to her that Pope Benedict had lifted the church's bar on divorce. But Isabella didn't necessarily approve of all the current Pope's doctrinal changes. And, come to think of it, Papa had never shown any real wish to change his situation. There had been women, from time to time, but they all drifted away as Isabella had done. It was impossible to compete with the cares of all the world. Chantal knew that.

Her cheeks were wet, she realized. Father Daguerre put a hand on her shoulder, and she laid her hand over it.

Georgi had come up from Rome for the funeral. He had been attending Benedict in what, it was feared, would be the Pope's last illness. He shook hands with Isabella and gave his condolences, and then stood before Chantal. He put his hand out, and delicately wiped her tears.

"Chantal, if there's ever anything I can do, you have my private numbers."

She bowed, and he was gone. The British Minister of War, Angus McGuinness, was in his place, giving out a clammy handshake and a mumbled inanity. Then it was a corporate queen from some tax shelter, hoping for a *Vogue* lay-out with her flounced dress.

The funeral lasted all afternoon.

IV
Dublin, Republic of Eire, 2018

"Sister Chantal, show us what you can do."

She bowed her head as demurely as possible, and took a seat at the console. The computer rooms of the St Patrick's

Seminary were in prefab huts in the centre of the campus. The class had to sit down on desks and tables when there weren't chairs to spare. Her fingers flew as she penetrated the blocks. The hard fingertips she had developed with endless hours of fingerbattering the gym wall connected with the keys. This was too simple a task for her, although it was beyond most of the other novices.

She was jacked in deep, probing the labyrinth, guiding her APOSTLE with a mouse. Her concentration was complete. She was totally in tune with the system. It was a complete communion.

It was like praying.

"Good," said Father O'Shaughnessy. "Very good."

She refused to be distracted by the compliment, and stayed away from a file that felt wrong. Father O'Shaughnessy tapped her shoulder approvingly. She came across a cadre of lightly guarded PAGAN programs, defused the booby traps, and interfaced with them. It was a matter of dexterity. The APOSTLE latched onto each of the PAGANs in succession, scrambling their directives. It left CONVERTs in its wake.

She was nearly through the test. No faults.

With a flourish, she pulled herself out of the interface.

The screen filled with garbage. She had activated a deepsea tripwire, and her stats were printing out. Crudely computer-animated hellfire flickered on the screen. Father O'Shaughnessy looked at the paper, and tore it off.

"Humility, my child, humility. It is a lesson we must all learn."

Returning to her place, Chantal heard one of the other students tittering.

"The Sin of Pride is grievous," Father O'Shaughnessy told the class, "it can bring you low…"

Chantal's face burned, and she bowed her head. Her wimple covered her neck, but she wished she had an oldstyle habit to draw down over her head.

"But there are worse sins. Those who hide their lights behind a bushel, for instance, Brother Leon, or those whose industry does not match their ambitions, Sister Sarah."

He held up the print-out.

"Let us examine Sister Chantal's progress in detail, shall we? I hope your colleague may be able to teach you something where my poor efforts might have failed. Let us return to our APOSTLE. As you know, an APOSTLE is an independent program which, when fed into any given system can spread the Word of the Lord and convert selected PAGAN programs. Sister Chantal's progress shows the hazards and dangers any given APOSTLE will face in the cybernet, not unlike the hazards and dangers faced by the original apostles when they first spread the news…"

V
Milan, Italy, 2019

"CHANTAL… COME BACK?"

"No, Marcello."

It was late afternoon. Mlle Fournier was out with Isabella, shopping. Chantal sat at her dressing table, looking at the room behind her in the mirror. Since she had taken down all the posters she had had up as a kid, the place looked empty, untenanted, like the bare cubicles she had lived in for three years at St Patrick's. None of them had felt like home, and now home didn't either. She combed her hair. When she was younger, she could spend hours at the mirror, dreaming, passing the comb through her long, long hair. Now, a few strokes of the brush would do. She had turned her back on a lot of things.

"Don't you like me any more?" said Marcello from the bed, his head shadowed by the hanging curtains.

"It's not that."

She examined her face and neck minutely. Her skin was unmarked. Three weeks ago, in Dublin, she had fought for the school and been roundly beaten by a novice from St Brendan's. Her face had been a mass of bruises. Now, there was nothing. Her mother, on an increasingly frequent basis, had Dr Zarathustra's little operations, but all Chantal had was prayer, meditation and exercise. It was working well so far.

"Is it because of your vows?"

"You know it's not that."

Marcello sat up. He looked bitter. "No, of course. Your friend Papa Georgi says you can get laid as often as you want, just so long as you don't marry anyone but Christ! Hell, Chantal, what kind of life is that!"

She promised herself that she wouldn't get angry with Marcello and sorted through the jewellery she would never wear again. Isabella's admirers always used to give her jewellery. She would give the more valuable pieces to the fund in Saint Theresa of Calcutta's memory. The rest could go to her old friends.

"Do you want this ring?" she asked Marcello. "It's fire opal. From Australia. Prince Bonfigliori gave it to me. See how it catches the light."

Marcello stood over her. He wore only his jeans. His skinny torso shone. "What are you talking about, Chantal?" he said, anger in his eyes. "What the fuck are you talking about? What's happening here? I feel like a complete... like a complete shithead."

"Nothing is happening here, Marcello. Nothing has ever happened here."

"Last summer, and the summer before that, something happened all right, something pretty damn–"

"Marcello, you used to call me 'the scarecrow with no tits'."

"That was a long time ago."

"Not so long."

Marcello stalked back to the shadows. He was shivering. He might be crying. Italian men were so emotional. By contrast, she supposed, she was so... so what? Swiss? She locked her jewel box and stood up.

This evening she wanted to use the house's terminal. She could interface with Father O'Shaughnessy through a safe link in Singapore if she got the satellite window right. And she had been developing some of their theoretical work on Limited Artificial Intelligences. He had promised to name her as co-author on his next paper, and she was keen to put in the background research to earn the credit.

"Marcello, would you go downstairs and make us some tea. I want to get changed now."

He laughed nastily. "Changed? Chantal, you don't need to get changed. You're a completely different person. Since your father died."

She slapped him. "Tea, Marcello. Ice, lemon, please."

He bunched his fist, but thought better of it. Even as children, he had been the loser.

"Ciao, Chantal," he said, taking his shirt and sandals from the floor. "Ciao forever."

"Goodbye," she said, in as many languages as she knew how, continuing long after her bedroom door had closed and she knew Marcello had left the house.

She was as near to tears as she had been since the day they buried her father.

She was at her terminal in good time, snaking her way through subsidiary corporation accounts, matching the cyberlabyrinth codeword for block. When she got through to Singapore, Father O'Shaughnessy was waiting for her.

VI
San Francisco, USA, 2020

"Chantal..."

She hadn't been so tense since she had taken her final vows. She tried to find her centre. Her muscles remained tight.

"Chantal...?"

Mother Kazuko Hara bowed.

"Mother..." Chantal bowed, and backed away.

The first blow came high, striking her thigh.

The Japanese woman, a foot shorter than Chantal, kicked again, catching her waist this time. Chantal took Mother

Kazuko's ankle, and pushed back, hoping to unbalance her, but she twisted and was out of her grasp.

"Good," Mother Kazuko said, striking with the flat of her hand at Chantal's forehead.

Chantal ducked under the blow, and lashed out with her fingertips, pushing into Mother Kazuko's ribs above the heart.

"Very good," the Mother said.

The fought on, matching each other skill for skill, switching fighting styles at whim. The two nuns went through karate, fisticuffs, baritsu, savate, all the major sub-groups of wushu – the Five Animal Styles of the Shaolin Temple, choy li-fut, Drunken Style, Eagle Claw, hsing-i, hung gar, Mad Monkey kungfu, phoenix eye, Praying Mantis (a special favourite), shuai chiao, tan tui, White Crane, wing chun – jeet kune-do (the Way of the Intercepting Fist), hapkido, Greco-Roman wrestling, kickboxing, aikido, arnis, jujitsu, ninjutsu, streetfighting, arm-wrestling and tae kwon do.

Chantal knew that if her opponent – whom the students called Mother Gadzooks O'Hara – didn't pull her punches, she would have been dead within ten seconds of Mother Kazuko's first bow.

Her weak spots were beginning to ache. It wasn't necessary to win this bout – no one had bested Mother Kazuko since the St Matilda's Dojo was opened – but Chantal had to keep in the fight for a full quarter of an hour.

It wasn't an official examination. The fight was taking place in a private gymnasium, with no assessors in attendance. But Chantal knew that without Mother Kazuko's say-so she wouldn't be advanced within the Society of Jesus.

The only thing she really had over her master was height, and so she used it as best she could, trying to keep the other woman at the end of her toe-points as she used balletic high kicks, and tapping her head with fingertip blows.

It wasn't enough, but it was something.

At last, it was over. Chantal's leotard was a shade darker with perspiration, but Mother Kazuko, who fought in loose white pajamas, was unaffected. She seemed never to sweat, like a lizard.

They bowed to each other, and Chantal wiped the sweat off her face into her hair and collapsed against the climbing frames on the wall. Mother Kazuko steadied her.

"It is all right to be tired, sister," she said, her English still thickly accented, "but it is sometimes necessary to conceal your fatigue."

Chantal straightened out, and put her hands on her hips. She breathed deeply. Her pains went away, slowly.

Mother Kazuko smiled, exposing rabbit-teeth. "Good. Remember, the Calling of the Jesuit is much like the Path of Ninjutsu, the Way of Stealth."

There was a sound like a gunshot. Chantal turned in its direction, assuming a fighter's crouch, knee flexed to launch a kick.

The sound was repeated. It was a slow handclap, gradually building into applause. A priest came out of the shadows, clapping steadily.

Chantal recognized Father Daguerre, and ran to his arms.

"Sister, how you have grown."

"Sanskrit."

Father Daguerre tried to smile. "No, Sister Chantal. We are grown-up now. We must be wary of wasting our God-given abilities on show."

"She is young," Mother Kazuko said. "She is still learning."

Father Daguerre kissed Mother Kazuko's hand. "She has learned much already, Mother Superior. You have taught her well."

"I have merely brought out what the Lord put inside her."

They left the gymnasium. A troop of postulants were doing tai chi exercises in the courtyard. Two young priests in shirt-sleeves and shorts were standing, checking instruments, by a helicopter whose blades were circling lazily. It was a sunny day. The choir were practicing. The dojo was giving the St Matthew Passion with the Philharmonic this commencement. Inside the PZ, San Francisco was a pleasant city.

"It's been too long since you visited me, Father Daguerre. How is my mother?"

"As ever. She sends her regards."

"How long are you staying?"

"Not long. This is not a visit in the proper sense. I've come from Papa Georgi."

Chantal stopped walking. Since Georgi ascended the Throne of St Peter she had only seen him in public audiences. He had withdrawn to some extent from his old friends. She had thought he was avoiding her.

"I am to take you to the Vatican. A mission has been found, which requires your… special skills."

A cloud passed over the sun. Suddenly, in her damp leotard, Chantal felt chilly.

"The helicopter will airlift you to SFX. I have a Vatican jet waiting there. Will it take you long to get packed?"

"I've been packed for five months, father."

"It is good."

At last, Sister Chantal had a mission.

VII

CHANTAL'S FIRST MISSION was a simple matter of plugging an infoleak from a church in Turin. It turned out that the Pan-Islamic Congress had a sleeper virus going around that was creating APOSTATE programs, and that the Ayatollah Bakhtiar was using the Turin hole to infiltrate the UEC. Several leading Greek Exiles, active in the Macedonian Liberation Movement, had been killed by "invisible" men, assassins who didn't register on the datanet. She solved the systems breakdown simply, with some patchwork reprogramming, and traced the Ayatollah's undercover man by his palimpsest computer signature. She had wanted to bring him in for questioning, but he had committed suicide rather than face the interrogators of the Opus Dei. In the ruins of his hotel room, she had read the last rites over the man, praying that his God would recognize her ritual.

This was not the contemplative life she had imagined nuns led when she was a little girl. Mother Kazuko had explained to her that many of the major forms of combat had been invented by members of religious orders. English monks on the Crusades, under the influence of the Biblical prohibition against spilling blood, had come up with the Friar Tuck-style quarterstaff technique as a way of crushing the skulls of the infidel without making them bleed. In the Far East, many of the martial arts had been developed for the self-defence of itinerant monks and priests. If the way of the Cross and the Sword was peculiar, it was at least well-travelled.

Since Turin, she had been deployed on average five times a year, had seen action on every continent – including Antarctica – and won herself several papal decorations she could never wear openly. Father Daguerre, her first master, passed her over to Mother Edwina, the English nun who served as a control for the Jesuits' covert activities, and then to Cardinal Fabrizio DeAngelis, the Vatican's top computer jock. She became a valued arm of the church.

In a back street in Edinburgh, while tracing a missing Vatican banker and a suitcase full of negotiable bonds, she had been faced with the hardest choice of all. An assailant she could not easily disable had come at her with a knife. She shot without a conscious thought, as she had been trained, read the last rites over his bleeding corpse, and did her self-imposed penance for months afterwards. It had not got easier, but it was part of her calling. Like her father, she was prepared to die for her beliefs. Unlike him, she had learned to kill for them.

Between assignments, she worked out of apartments within the walls of the Vatican itself. Officially, she was a computer programmer and a translator in the Vatican Library. She saw Pope Georgi frequently, but the old intimacy between them seemed to have evaporated with his elevation. She wondered if the Pope still visited her mother. When he had been a cardinal, Georgi had frequently dined in secret with Isabella Juillerat, and Chantal wondered sometimes if their relationship had ever run deeper than it appeared. The Camerlengo, Cardinal Brandreth, took an interest in her, and encouraged her to modernise the Vatican's slightly archaic computer systems. She pursued her own research, and published widely, either as a collaborator with Father O'Shaughnessy or as sole author. She taught a course in Dublin, filling in for the father when he was indisposed, and found students hadn't changed since her days at the Seminary. The novices still smoked dope, listened to prohibited Russian records and had thoughtless affairs.

Occasionally, she would try to use her contacts in the international intelligence community to dig into her father's still-open case file. None of the bodies who had conducted official or unofficial inquiries into the assassination had come to any concrete conclusions. It was generally agreed that the assassin had been Snordlij Svensson, a freelance working out of Rekjavik, who was himself killed within six months in an entirely unsuspicious domestic accident. Extensive examinations of Svensson's credit lines and accounting software had failed to isolate a specific employer for the Juillerat Sanction.

Having a daughter who was a sister had upset Isabella Juillerat for a while, but she had become reconciled to it. However, whenever Chantal saw her mother, Isabella would try to convince her to transfer to a more high-profile, glamorous branch of the church. With her qualifications, there was no reason Chantal should not rise to a cardinal's hat. Sooner or later, thanks to Vatican LXXXV, there would be another woman Pope, and, as Isabella pointedly said, "It has to be someone…"

Chantal worked with Mother Kazuko in 2023, putting an end to a series of obscene desecrations that had been taking place in West Coast churches. The culprits turned out to be a gangcult of diabolists operating out of Venice, California, and they had some fairly nasty helpers with them. A specialist in cyberexorcism was flown in from Mexico City, where his services were constantly in demand, and they put an end to the infestation. The cyberexorcist was killed, and Chantal had taken over the ritual. Mother Kazuko was badly wounded in the five-day struggle, and had gone to a retreat to recoup her faculties.

Gradually, the hidden worlds were revealed to Chantal. First, the rational, expanding, exciting world of the international datanets. Then, the ancient, ritualistic, ever-changing, eternally constant world of the Church of Rome. And finally, the dark, barely-glimpsed, deeply disturbing world beyond. In the Vatican library, she was given clearance to access the forbidden books – the *Liber Nagash*, the *Necronomicon* of the mad Arab Al-Hazred, *The King in Yellow*, Errol Undercliffe's *Forgotten Byways of the Severn Valley*, Julian Karswell's *Private Memoirs* and *Confessions of a Diabolical Genius*, Edwin Winthrop's *Riddles of the Mythwrhn*, Robert Anton Wilson's *UFOs From Atlantis – the Secret Exploded*, John Sladek's *Arachne Rising* – and had attended with Father O'Shaughnessy the Secret Conclave of Vienna, during which leading theologians, scientists and politicians discussed some of the more disturbing developments of the last decade. Father O'Shaughnessy presented a paper charting the increasing instance of physical anomalies and the apparent break-down of the laws of physics, and dropped a few dark hints about the eternal balances of space and time and their possible fragility.

Sometimes, she had dreams. A moonlike plain of white salt. A tall, dark man in a broad-brimmed hat, with ancient eyes burning behind his mirrorshades. A bridge in the desert, thronged with gargoyles straight from Notre Dame. The maw of Hell, opening up in an ocean of sand.

Her counsellor-confessor assured her that her dreams were entirely normal for a cleric in her profession.

Then, towards the end of 2024, she was summoned to an audience with Pope Georgi...

VIII
The Vatican, 2024

IN THE MEETING room, Pope Georgi sat in front of an authentic, wall-covering Michelangelo. A white screen descended

over the painting, and shutters rattled down over the windows. Chantal noticed how much older Georgi seemed now
than when they first met. He wore a well-cut business suit
and a skullcap. Only his ring of office betrayed his impor-
tance. Cardinals Brandreth and DeAngelis wore their red
robes, and eyed each other with all the ferocity of Milanese
society hostesses unwittingly arriving at a reception in identical "originals." In the Vatican, DeAngelis was known for his
dress sense, and could often be found at society receptions in
violently red evening clothes. Mother Edwina, the sharp and
elegant Englishwoman who usually debriefed Chantal after
her missions, wore a demi-wimple, a cream blouse and slacks.
Father O'Shaughnessy, whom Chantal had not expected to
be present, was, for the first time in her memory, dressed in
cassock, collar and pom-pom biretta. Chantal had also turned
up in full habit, and Father O'Shaughnessy grinned at the
sight, mouthing "Snap!" at her.

"Holy Father," she said, kissing Georgi's ring.

He signed a cross in the air, and indicated a chair. They
all sat down at a circular table. Cardinal DeAngelis had a
console in front of him. He dimmed the lights, and
punched buttons. He worked the keyboard with the precise movements of an epicure picking at a supremely
artistic salad.

"Excuse me, but I'm double-checking the security. We
must take precautions."

"Nothing that comes up at this meeting is to be discussed outside," said Mother Edwina, obviously meaning
her words for Chantal.

"Of course," she said. She always picked up the impression that the older woman didn't quite like her.

"Done," said the cardinal. "We're definitively debugged.
This meeting is not being recorded. It will not exist on our
records."

"Fabrizio," said Georgi, "this is your presentation. You
may begin."

"Thank you, Holy Father."

Cardinal DeAngelis stood up, and a map appeared on the screen. Chantal recognized an area covering the United States, Mexico and most of the Central American Confederacy. It was covered with little red crucifixes she supposed were churches, and the crucifixes were linked by a glowing spiderweb.

"As you can see, we have been attempting to bind our operations in the continental Americas into one supranational datanet. This leeches onto the local datanets, but is not entirely abosrbed into them. There has, of course, been some difficulty in realizing this objective. While the hostility between Washington and Managua continues, neither the US nor the CAC are especially keen on our linkages, but I am now in a position to reveal that we have been successful. We are now fully integrated in the New World, from Alaska to Tierra del Fuego, even to the Antarctic…"

Cardinal Brandreth clapped leisurely. Chantal caught a faint trace of sarcasm on the camerlengo's elegantly curled lips.

"Thank you, but your congratulations are premature. There are problems. And, as it stands, our entire operation is jeopardized."

DeAngelis paused, allowing his aquiline profile to be silhouetted against the map. He passed a beringed hand through his leonine mane of coiffeured hair. Mother Edwina fidgeted. DeAngelis tapped a key. The map disappeared, and a blurry snapshot, blown up to gigantic size, appeared. A man in black, with sunglasses and a broad black hat, stood in the glaring light of the sun, his arms out in a benediction.

"This is Elder Nguyen Seth of the Church of Joseph."

"I've heard of him," Chantal said, starting for some reason at the blobbily reproduced face. "He's the man behind Deseret."

"That is correct. He successfully lobbied Washington a few years ago and was granted deed to the then-useless State of Utah, which he renamed Deseret and has raised from the dead. He has, by all accounts, made a garden in the desert."

Aerial views of mountains, caves and opium poppy fields appeared behind the Pope. Georgi did not turn to look. His gaze, as it had been when she entered, was on Chantal. She felt slightly uncomfortable at this scrutiny. It was as if the joke had finally turned serious.

"Of course, we have notionally recognized the Church of Joseph along with all the other protestant sects since Vatican LXXXV, but we have not been overenthusiastic in its case. Like too many American fundamentalist churches, it combines some of the less attractive aspects of zealotry with a certain cracked quality that appears to sell well. It would be a negligible force if it weren't for Elder Seth."

A photograph of a bearded man proudly posing with his AK-47 in the mouth of a cave flashed up on the screen behind the pope. "Afghanistan 2002. US special forces led a raid on the Tora Bora cave network but missed this man by a matter of hours. Now if you use your imagination and visualise him without the beard…"

"Nguyen Seth." said O'Shaughnessy.

Another snapshot enlargement appeared. A man in combat fatigues and sunglasses, carrying an assault rifle, was firing into a hut. There was jungle in the background, and soldiers were caught by the camera in action. Puffs of smoke and flame were coming out of rifles.

"This, you'll be surprised to learn, is Nguyen Seth in 1974, with a detachment of the Khmer Rouge. He is in the process of razing to the ground a village on the Vietnam-Kampuchea border. The blurred fellow behind him with the grenade launcher has been tentatively identified as a Frenchman, currently a highly in-demand international terrorist named Roger Duroc. During the Vietnam War, Nguyen Seth fought alongside the Russians, against the Chinese, but switched sides several time. Whichever side he was on was usually the one committing the atrocities at the time. The Republic of Vietnam still has a price on his head for singularly revolting war crimes. Before going into battle, he would generally perform several human sacrifices to bless his military ventures."

"So," said O'Shaughnessy, "the Elder of Joseph is not a nice person?"

"He is considerably more than that, father. As we now see." A new picture appeared. "This is a group portrait, taken in 1933 on the Isis at Oxford. The bald fellow is Aleister Crowley, the mountain-climber and magician. The one who looks furious with him is W B Yeats, the poet. This is Arthur Machen, a curious Welsh writer. This is Julian Karswell, a raving psychopath. This is a young lady who was found floating in the river the next day without her head. And this oriental gentleman is–"

"Nguyen Seth," said Brandreth.

"That can't be," said O'Shaughnessy. "Seth's father?"

"He doesn't seem to have had one," said DeAngelis. "Here, this is 1888. It's from the *Illustrated London News*."

It was an age-spotted magazine photograph, with the print showing through. Only the posed principles were in sharp focus. The background crowds were fuzzy, caught in motion.

"Inspector Lestrade of the Metropolitan Police examines the Whitechapel site of one of the Jack the Ripper murders. Looks like a blithering idiot, doesn't he? No wonder they never caught the murderer. But who do we find rubbernecking in the ghoulish crowd…?"

In the amorphous mass, one man had stood still enough for his face to come out clear: Nguyen Seth.

"One more photograph, and we're back to paintings, I'm afraid." The photograph appeared. "This is Hendrik Shatner, brother of the founder of the original Church of Joseph, modelling a pair of divinely-issued mirrored sunglasses. And, as you can see, he has an Indian friend…"

Hendrik was peering hawk-faced at the camera, leaning on a Springfield rifle, every inch the pioneer pilgrim. Nguyen Seth was dressed in buckskins and had long braids, but the face was the same.

"History calls Hendrik's Tonto 'The Ute', but our ethnographers tell me no Ute wore necklaces like that. No Native American did, in fact. They're human fingerbones strung together."

Another picture appeared. "That was 1868. This is 1476. It's an engraving entitled 'The Death of Dragulya'. As you may know, Vlad the Impaler was killed by his own troops while disguised as a Turk, and his severed head was sent to Constantinople where the Sultan put it on display. Take a look at the features of the Moldavian hacking away at Vlad's neck. He is believed to be the traitor who gave the order to kill the prince and then spirited the head away."

The features were roughly carved, but unmistakable. realism was not usually a high priority with mediaeval artists, but this looked as if it had been done from life.

"He would have to be nearly six hundred years old," spat Brandreth.

"Older, actually. All the images – and we have literally hundreds more in the archive – show him to be about the same age, somewhere between forty and sixty but hale and hearty. We have no reason to believe that he was any younger ever. Our friend Elder Seth is well-titled by the Josephites. He is indeed, the Elder of us all. Even if you don't discount the legend of the Wandering Jew–"

"Which the church, incidentally, does not," put in the Pope.

"Quite so, Holy Father. Anyway, Ahasuerus aside, this individual, whatever his name, is probably the oldest person walking the earth."

"So, he's been a not-nice person for a very long time."

"Well put, Father O'Shaughnessy. And now, he is, we have reason to believe, planning a coup that will put the Catholic Church in the New World back in the position it had before the first Jesuits set out in the wake of Columbus and Vespucci–"

"And, incidentally," said O'Shaughnessy, "massacred entire civilizations."

"That was a previous papal administration," said Georgi, "for which we can take no responsibility."

"I don't see it," said Chantal. "Where's the threat?"

The map came back. DeAngelis tapped the state of Arizona.

"Here, somewhere. Tombstone would be my guess, based on Seth's nasty sense of humour, but it could be anywhere in the south-west. We've not established all the links as strongly as we might wish to. We've been getting reports of major disturbances on the edges of the Outer Darkness. All our spies in Deseret have disappeared, but we have reason to believe that Nguyen Seth has been invoking demonic powers on an unprecedented scale, and his only logical target is our datanet. Specifically, we think he's going to aim for the Central American Confederacy."

"President Estevez will give him the Congressional Medal of Honour."

"Sadly, that is possible. The CAC represents the only successful synthesis of the Catholic Church and a governmental body outside the Vatican itself. If you weren't on the side of the angels, you wouldn't want it on the same landmass as you, even with the isthmus of Panama and the killing grounds of Mexico between you and it."

"Thank you, Fabrizio," said the Pope. "Father O'Shaughnessy, you have been monitoring the… uh… anomalies?"

O'Shaughnessy looked serious finally. "Chantal knows most of this. I'm pleased that you're at last taking notice. It's not a small, isolated thing. There have been temporal displacements all over the western hemisphere. The epicentre, not coincidentally I should say, would seem to be Salt Lake City. Many of the anomalies have been observable only on a sub-atomic basis, but they're there all right. I assume Mother Edwina has been keeping up with the rash of disappearances in the international scientific community. They tie in too, I think. The disappearees have been a job-lot, with all kind of disciplines jumbled in, but they've all been at the cutting edge of dealing with this epidemic of impossibilities. As a footnote, my guess is that I would be next on anyone's list of to-be-vanished candidates."

"That has been taken into consideration," said Mother Edwina. "After this meeting, you will indeed disappear. But we'll take care of the disappearance ourselves. You'll be continuing your work under close guard in a secret location."

"That's a relief."

The map disappeared, and the lights came up. Chantal knew she had come a long way from Lausanne. No one was smoking, but this was nonetheless one of those fabled smoke-filled rooms in which the fate of the whole world was decided. Brandreth and Mother Edwina were in a huddle, and Fabrizio DeAngelis was sitting back waiting to be admired. Chantal wasn't too distracted to notice the young cardinal taking an interest in her. The Pope leaned forwards, and came to life.

Since that day on the jetty by Lake Geneva, Chantal had been waiting for Georgi to ask her for something. This wasn't the request she had been expecting.

"Chantal," he said, looking straight into her eyes, "you must know what we want you to do. You'll have diplomatic privileges and a limited amount of cooperation from the local authorities. We can't tell them too much, so you'll be travelling on your Swiss passport. Of course, all our clergy and lay-people will be with you… but the projections suggest this is a one-person mission. And you, of course, are the only active operative at our disposal with the skills required. You'll take it?"

Chantal bowed. "Of course, Holy Father."

"Bless you, my child. We shall pray hourly for your success."

"Thank you, Holy Father."

She stood up and backed out of the room. Within the hour, she was in a private jet out of Rome bound for Phoenix, Arizona.

Underneath the plane, the world turned slowly.

part seven:
holding the fort

I

"THAT'S SOME STORY, sister," said Stack after Chantal had finished telling him why she was in Arizona. "I suppose that's right, isn't it. Sister – I should call you 'sister'."

She stood up and stretched, cat-like in her uniform. "It'll do, but my name is still Chantal. We don't give up everything."

She walked towards the entrance of St Werburgh's, and was haloed by the sunlight. It was going to be another hot day in the desert. Flies were beginning to buzz around the dead priest.

"But… but you're an Op."

"It's a very old Agency. The church has always had soldiers. Father O'Pray was one, too."

She went outside, found something, and came back. She had an old shovel over her shoulder.

"Now, we bury him."

Stack looked at the mess. "You'll have to get him loose first."

The woman – the nun – set her mouth in a straight line, and tossed Stack the spade.

"I have a handlase in Federico. You find a clear spot outside, and dig a grave."

Stack reckoned he had the easier detail, but didn't speak up about it. He had the impression that Sister Chantal wouldn't go much for gallantry.

Outside, he picked out a plot away from the church walls, shucked his shirt, and set to digging. Inside the church, he heard the hiss of the lase cutting through steel, and the creak of machinery falling apart.

He was six feet into the sandy soil before Chantal brought the body out. She had tried to do something about the hole in O'Pray's chest, buttoning his coat over it, but nothing much could disguise the terrible wound. She had to wrestle his stiff limbs into a position of repose on his chest.

"That's deep enough, Stack."

He climbed out, and took his shirt from the gravestone he had draped it over. Chantal cast her eyes over his wounds.

"Don't you need any medication for those? Federico has a full field hospital in his trunk."

"I was drugged out yesterday, thank you. I'll let nature take its course."

"There might be infection."

"Nahh, US Cav morph-plus is two parts penicillin to one-part pain-killer, and I was tripped out on that for more than a day."

The sun was overhead now, its light falling on the graveyard like a blanket of heat. Chantal had dirtmarks on her face and hands. She wiped them with a dampraguette, cleaning away the filth, and flexed her hands.

"The bellrope was burned."

"So?"

"O'Pray died well, he should have the bell tolled. He should have a funeral."

Stack looked up at the tower. The bellhouse was undamaged, apart from a few cracked slates. The bell hung motionless.

He drew his side-arm and shot it. The noise was unnaturally loud in the still quiet. The bell shifted, but didn't peal. He fired again, and scored another hit. This time, the clapper was displaced and Stack was rewarded with a resounding clang. He looked at Chantal. She unholstered her SIG, and pumped the whole clip at the bell, which swung vigorously, sounding out. The din was almost painful, and yet there was an aptness about it. Stack hadn't known anything about the dead man, but he felt that anyone who would choose to pursue his calling in Welcome would appreciate the rough music of ScumStopper and cast iron.

People appeared in the graveyard. Armindariz was there, sheepish and hung-over, and Tiger Behr, favouring his robo-leg over his real one. Pauncho the chef wobbled his belly up the low hill to the church. A tribe of children came in a column, led by a dignified woman in black. Sandrats shamefully detached themselves from their boltholes, shaking the dirt and dust from their clothes, hanging their heads. Stack thought of checking IDs against the Wanted sheets back in the wrecked cruiser, but decided to offer a morning-long amnesty in honour of Father O'Pray. A cyke with a sidecar drew up. Shell and Miss Texaco got off and out. They held their hands away from their guns and came into the churchyard. Shell raised his claw in front of his face to shield his eyes from the sun.

Chantal signalled to Armindariz and Pauncho that they should take the shovels. She went to Federico, and pulled out a loose black robe, more like a monk's than a nun's, which she tied about herself. It fastened around her neck, and left her face a white mask. The change was quite startling. Stack derived a perverse enjoyment from observing the expressions of those who had been in the Silver Byte last night. Even Miss Texaco's impassive little face registered something approaching shock and surprise.

Chantal started speaking in Latin. It was the Mass for the Dead, Stack supposed. Some of the words sounded a little like Spanish, but he couldn't make much of it out. Wherever responses were expected from the mourners, he left them to the extensive Armindariz family. Father O'Pray's parishioners were used to funerals, he realized.

When she was finished, Chantal had Armindariz and his assistant sexton fill in the grave.

"Make him a headstone," she told the saloon keeper, "and rebuild the church."

"Bot, there ees no more Padre Burracho... no more priest."

She ripped her robe away, and scraped her fingers through her hair. "A priest will come. Where one falls, another springs up."

Chantal got into Federico, and switched its systems on. One or two of the congregation had been eyeing the car lasciviously. They would have to be watched closely.

"Buonjuorno, sorella," the Ferrari said. "My senses indicate demonic activity within the immediate vicinity. Hostilities will be commenced within thirty seconds. You are advised to take evasive action at once."

Chantal had her gun out. Stack looked around. The mourners were either shocked or bewildered by what must seem to them a sourceless voice. The children were huddled to their mother.

Armindariz paused in mid-shovel.

"What did that there car mean, trooper?" asked Tiger Behr, hobbling to Stack's side. "Demonic activity? What kind of rap is that?"

Stack turned to the old cyborg to explain.

Behr gasped. His eye widened, and his whole face thrust forwards, as if someone had just taken a sledge-hammer to the back of his head. He was choking.

The hostilities had commenced.

"Behr," Stack said, "what's wrong?"

The old man's robo-arm leaped out. Strong, durium-boned, leather-coated fingers seized Stack's throat.

Stack tasted his own blood again.

II

LAUDERDALE WATCHED CLOSELY as the techies pulled away the panels in the Ops Centre and snipped the relevant wires. Colonel Rintoon had given him a field promotion to major, and put him in charge of sealing off Fort Apache against aggressors. All unauthorized communications with the outside world were forbidden, and Rintoon had posted loyal guards outside the Ops Centre with orders to summarily shoot dead anyone who tried to summon aid from any quarter. Rintoon believed that the rest of the US Cav was rotten with Maniak infiltrators. Lauderdale had asked for permission to deploy the android cadre, and the colonel had put the suggestion on hold. Soon, Lauderdale knew, his androids would be in action.

"There, sir," said a tech. "No one can talk to anyone except through this room, sir."

"Good job."

The tech didn't say anything. She packed her tools and left. Lauderdale didn't like techs. They jealously guarded their specializations, throwing up an aura of mystery to exclude others. Of course, androids were different. They were supposed to be secret, supposed to be frightening.

It had been easy rising to his current position.

Williford had refused to execute the traitor Badalamenti, and so the task had fallen to Lauderdale. When it was accomplished, Rintoon immediately jumped him to captain and had him execute Williford too, the lieutenant having revealed himself by his defiance of authority to be another Maniak in blue. After that, Rintoon had made him a major. Lauderdale had wondered whether to have the rank insignia sewn on his old tunics, but fortunately the late Majors McAuley and Faulcon had been about his size, and so he was able to commandeer their wardrobes.

Rintoon was in the process of recalling all field units to the fort. Their positions were lit up on the map, moving back towards Lake Havasu. The cruiser patrols were being logged in as and when they arrived. The fort was on a war footing. The colonel was expecting a Maniak assault at any moment. Lauderdale smiled at that. He wondered how his superior would react when he found out precisely what was attacking Fort Apache.

The colonel had spent the whole morning weeding out traitors, and having them executed. He had found thirteen in the fort's complement of three hundred and two. What with the other casualties, the fort's tiny morgue was packed to capacity, and the corpses were having to be stored in the hospital beds.

Lauderdale noticed that, apart from Colonel Rintoon, none of the other officers had chosen to talk to him since Badalamenti. It didn't matter.

Captain Finney was at her regular console, and seemed to be under control, but Lauderdale knew he had to watch her. She was too in tune with the computer systems. He intended to recommend to Rintoon that her access to them be restricted, or perhaps denied entirely. Still, according to Elder Seth, the thing in the database could take care of itself.

"Cat?" he asked.

"Major," she said, not looking up.

"All systems A-OK?"

"Sir, yessir."

She punched keys, and sine curves revolved on her screen.

"You've run the projections the colonel wanted?"

"Sir, yessir." She handed him a sheaf of papers.

"Good work."

"Sir, thank you, sir."

Lauderdale pretended to look at the print-out. He couldn't understand any of the figures. But he knew that the Call of Joseph was nearly upon him.

It was a full three hours since he had last spilled blood. And the blood was an essential part of the ritual. Elder Seth himself had explained it to him on his last covert visit to Salt Lake City. Only through the constant spilling of blood could the Dark Ones keep their purchase on this plane of existence. For them, each sacrifice was like a handhold in a sheer rockface.

Lauderdale considered Cat Finney. She was dangerous to him. He could easily convince the colonel that she had been a Maniak, that she had been gnawing away at the cybernetic foundations of the Apache database. His hand went to his sidearm.

No. There were too many other operators in the centre. Finney had too many friends. Lauderdale's position as Rintoon's second-in-command was precarious. There was no telling who the old man would listen to in any given argument. He could as easily be persuaded that Lauderdale was a Maniak as Finney.

"Keep it up, Cat, keep it up," he said.

"Sir, yessir," she replied.

He left the Ops Centre, and hurried through the corridors. He hummed to himself, Dido's 'Don't Think of Me'. He reached into the tunic, and felt the switchblade snug in its harness under his arm. The next person to come along would do, he felt sure...

A trooper rounded the corner. Lauderdale didn't know him. That was good. Personal feelings tainted the sacrifice. It was important to spill the blood without hate, without love, without emotion.

"Trooper."

"Lieutenant... major, sir."

The trooper stood to attention.

"Name?"

"Brecher, Michaeljohn T, Company B Smoke-Generating, sir."

Lauderdale prowled around the trooper. There was no one in sight. He looked at Brecher's broad back.

"You're out of uniform, trooper. Look, your shirttail is loose..."

Standing behind the man, he drew his knife. The blade appeared silently. With its point, he tugged at Brecher's shirt, pulling it free.

"And here, you have a button missing from your epaulette..."

"Sir?"

He cut the button off. It bounced on the floor and rolled away. There was a touch of perplexion in Brecher's eyes as Lauderdale pricked the side of his throat.

"You're a mess, trooper," he whispered into the man's ear as he eased the knife in through his jugular vein, wiggled it into his windpipe, and scraped it against his vertebrae.

Lauderdale stood back to avoid the arterial spray.

The Maniax had struck again. He went to the wall and sounded the alarm.

The dead man's throat kept pumping a red tide onto the dirty white floor until the guards came.

III

AS HIS PROSTHETIC hand ground into Stack's neck Tiger Behr was babbling, "It's not me, mister, I ain't doin' this, it's not me, it's not me…"

Chantal brought her gun up, but there were too many people in the way. The Armindariz children had flown into a panic and were running, screaming, around the place like cats on fire.

Chantal made her way through them, gun still raised.

Stack was bent backwards at the waist, limp at the knees. He was feebly scrabbling at Behr's metal-ringed wrist.

Chantal had a good shot now. She took it.

The gun clicked. She remembered she had emptied it at the bell. There was no time to reload.

Through Behr's tattered shirt, she saw a patch of scrawny skin unprotected by fleshplate armour.

She braced herself against a tombstone, and vault-kicked with both feet.

Her kick landed hard, and gouged a gobbet from Behr's back. But she didn't knock him off his footing, and the jolt shocked through her feet and legs. The tombstone tipped over – the sandy ground was too loose to be an anchor – and she fell on top of it, hurting her hip.

Behr straightened, and turned robotically. He held Stack at arms' length, lifting him off the ground. His face was greyish now, and he was bleeding where Behr's fingers were sinking into the flesh.

"What'd ya do that fer, lady?" he asked. "I tole you it weren't me. It's these damn doodads. I cain't control them all uv the time."

She tried a double karate chop, either side of his neck. Behr cried out, but didn't fall.

His half-face was crying, she saw. The pain and the frustration must be intense. But his electronic eye was glowing evilly.

"Tiger, did you have an optic burner implanted?"

The old Angel looked awesomely fed up. "Dad blast it, I did, lady. I wisht it weren't so, but…"

The glow turned red, and Chantal cartwheeled out of its path. Behr's head wrenched around on his neck, soliciting a shout of pain from him, and the beam raked the graveyard. A stone crucifix exploded into shrapnel fragments, and weatherbeaten 19th Century wooden markers burst into flames.

The mourners had mainly taken cover in the church. Those who were armed had their guns out.

Bullets rang against Behr's armoured chest.

"Careful," shouted Chantal, "you'll hit the trooper!"

No one seemed much to care about that. A long-haired old man in torn leathers jumped out of Father O'Pray's grave with a shotgun, and primed it. Before he could fire, the optic burn had caught him in the centre of his chest, and he tumbled backwards, dead.

Chantal danced around Behr, realizing that she could move faster than he could turn, and that his range with the burner was at best 120 degrees of his eyeline. She got in close, and struck wherever she saw Behr's original body.

He continued to complain. "Don't hurt me, sister. Hurt this thing!"

She had to do something about Stack.

"Shovel!" she shouted. Armindariz was cringing between a pair of tombs, still clutching the spade. "Shovel," she repeated.

Armindariz stood up, and lobbed the spade to her. It spun end over end until she snatched it from the air. She got a good hold and swung it two-handed at Behr's flesh-and-bone elbow.

Behr screamed as the blade sliced through, breaking the brittle bone.

"Sorry, Tiger," she said.

Stack fell, gasping for breath, detaching the severed robo-arm from his throat. It continued to clutch automatically as he smashed it against the ground. Wires and transistors leaked from its stump.

Chantal took aim at Behr's head and swung again. The optic flashed, and the spadehead exploded into red-hot shards. She was left with a burning pole, which she shoved at the cyborg's torso. It splintered against his dented chestplate.

Through the glass, Chantal could see red blood leaking into Behr's mechanism, shorting out some of his electronics.

She ducked under the swing of his left arm, and threw herself against him, hoping to open a crack with her shoulder.

She felt as if she had tried to tackle Notre Dame. The cathedral, not the college football team.

She rolled away from the cyborg. The beam was getting too close.

A huge figure loomed up behind Behr, and a claw locked around his throat. Shell had stepped in. Sweat ran from his ebony-muscled arm and blocky face as he exerted pressure.

"Hold on there, sonny boy," Behr spluttered.

Shell had his real hand pressed against the back of Behr's head, to keep the cyborg's burner pointed away from him. Behr's head was still turning, inexorably. Chantal heard the old man's vertebrae straining inside his exoskeleton.

"This fuckin' hurts, ya know!" Behr shouted.

Shell was grunting now, losing his fight against Behr's neck. There was a sudden crack as Behr's spine snapped.

The Gaschugger relaxed, but Behr's head kept turning, until it was facing backwards, his dead face against Shell's living one.

The optic burned, and Shell fell away from the cyborg, a ragged, smoking hole where his eyes and nose had been. Chantal glimpsed daylight through the headwound as the 'Chugger fell. In the church, someone – Miss Texaco? – howled with unfeigned grief.

What was left of Behr was unsteady on its feet. Chantal stood up, and waited for it to bring its face to bear again.

Behr's tongue lolled from his mouth and his real eye was fogged. The optic was burned out, its solid cell used up on Shell. Inside all the bio-mechanics, he was dead, but the robot half of him was still going to kill her.

It raised its hand to its face, and pushed its tongue into its mouth. Then, using three fingers, it propped its jaw open. Behr had had a partially synthetic voice-box.

"Hellllooo, bayy-beah!" it said.

"The Big Bopper," she snapped. "J P Richardson, 'Chantilly Lace', 1958."

"Highest chart position: number twelve." The mechanical voice grated. "Trust the Sister from Switzerland to have a photographic memory."

The dead man lurched forwards, arm out like Lon Chaney Jr as the Mummy. She realized the thing was blind, but guessed it would have some kind of sonar or heat pattern sensor inside it.

"Who are you?" she asked, stepping backwards a pace.

"My name is Legion..." it said.

"For you are Many. That's a very old joke."

"The oldies are the goodies, don't you think, mon petit choux?"

It was using her father's voice.

"That's an old trick, too. It didn't work in California, and it's not going to work here."

It took a step, and changed voices. "Chantal, come back," it said in Italian, in Marcello's whine. "Don't you like me any more?"

She kicked it in the throat. It was less steady now.

"I'm still dead, daughter," said her father. "I'm busy ducking rocks in Hell. And what have you done about it?"

Her foot hurt. That last kick had been rash.

"Ahh, the Sin of Pride," said Father O'Shaugnessy. "That was always your failing, Sister Chantal, always overreaching, always overconfident."

Someone rushed at the thing, screaming like a banshee, and was bent into broken halves in an instant. It hadn't been anyone Chantal had noticed before.

"Call me Georgi," said the Pope, "and come to bed."

She landed the heel of her hand on the glassex chest. It cracked.

The thing coughed mechanically, and she could see the wheels going round. She punched the crack, and it widened. Something was broken inside.

The people were creeping out of the church now. It must be obvious that the fight was between Chantal and the thing in Tiger Behr's body. The Behr creature wouldn't mimic life long after it had killed the nun. Stack was down and out of it, fallen in a swoon by the grave.

Chantal sucker-punched the thing, without any notable effect. Her hard knuckles were bleeding.

She pulled her bowie knife, and embedded its point in the crack in the demon thing's chest, working it back and forth. It laughed, and took her neck from the back, hugging her to him. The knife wedged into the chest cavity.

"Come to Papa," it cooed obscenely. She felt nails dig into her.

Then they were both falling into the grave, another active body pressed down on top of them, shrieking.

It was Miss Texaco, a ladies' revolver in her little fist. Chantal pushed herself away from the Behr creature, and found herself bunched against Father O'Pray.

Miss Texaco was pushing the cyborg's face into the grave earth. A band of peeling skin showed between the helmet-like exoskull and the slatted plates across Behr's clavicles. The Gaschugger shoved her gun against the gap and emptied it. Some of the bullets must have torn through to the mechanisms, because the creature jolted and jerked, sparks spitting from its wounds. Miss Texaco cried out and stood up, electrical arcs sparking between the creature and her revolver, her earrings, her overall buckles, her dental fillings. She broke the connection and collapsed, her exposed skin blackened.

The creature stood up, smoke and flame belching from its ruptured torso. Chantal tried to get upright, but the gravewall behind her gave way as she tried to put her back against it.

"Come to Papa." Its hand extended, finger ends turned to bloody spearpoints.

It took a step. Chantal could smell the melting plastic and putrefying flesh inside it.

Its fingers lightly brushed her throat. She chopped at its wrist, but its claw kept coming for her.

"Come to Pa—"

There was an explosion, deafeningly loud in the confines of the grave, and the cyborg's helmet-like head burst like a dropped watermelon. The creature stood for a moment, then collapsed at Chantal's feet.

She looked up, and saw Trooper Nathan Stack, a newly-discharged shotgun smoking in his hands.

"The US Cav to the rescue," he said, priming his pump-gun again.

"Help me with the girl," Chantal said.

Miss Texaco was whimpering. Chantal hugged her, and passed her up to Stack, who laid her out beside the grave.

Chantal pulled herself up. The headless cyborg kicked, a last mechanical reflex, then burned steadily.

She knelt by Miss Texaco, feeling her pulses and her heartbeat.

"Well?" asked Stack.

Chantal snapped her fingers in the air. He was good. He knew what she wanted, and put it in her hand.

Miss Texaco was gasping, trying to talk, but nothing was coming from her throat.

Chantal stuck the morph-plus hypo into the 'Chugger's neck and squeezed. The girl's eyelids fluttered.

"Water," Chantal said, "from the church."

"I don't think she'll be able to swallow. Look at those convulsions."

"Water," she said. "Not to drink."

"Oh," Stack said, running off.

Chantal held the writhing girl down, and tried to smooth her hair out of her eyes. Her heartbeat was irregular. The discharges must have shocked her to the bone.

Stack came back with a leaky hatful of water. He put it down beside her. She dipped her fingers, and began the ritual – the familiar ritual – dabbing the girl.

Chantal gave Miss Texaco the last rites.

The Gaschugger persisted in trying to talk.

Finally, when Chantal was finished, the girl got her last word out.

"Ma… maaaaa…"

Chantal crossed herself and stood up, beating the dust from her clothes.

"Armindariz," she said, "dig some more graves."

IV

QUITE APART FROM everything else, there was something badly twisted deep inside the system. Finney ran her checks again. Everything was responding perfectly. All the connections were solid. There were no apparent glitches. But there was still something wrong. It was working properly, but there was still something wrong.

The responses to her interrogation were a beat slower than they should have been. And too many files were refusing to open for her. The whole system was clamming up, keeping itself to itself. That was bad. She felt as if she were questioning a well-behaved child she knew was responsible for a series of atrocities. It was coming up with well-reasoned, plausible, rational excuses while sharpening a carving knife behind its back.

She had been sitting at her console for six straight hours now, testing everything. It was her way of keeping her head down and trying to live out the crisis.

Rintoon was stone crazy, and seemed to be taking Lauderdale along for the ride. All the people who had spoken up when there still might have been a way to end the craziness at Fort Apache were dead. It seemed that new corpses were falling out of the closet all the time. Finney hadn't expected to wake up alive for this shift.

Colosanto called the names of the units still out there. Almost everyone had returned to base by now. She listed

Tyree and Stack as overdue, even though everybody had given up on them by now. They were dead, for sure.

Finney's screen lit up green, with four inch-high wavering letters picked out in black.

HELLO, it said.

HELLO, CATHERINE.

She started, and looked around. The other operators were absorbed in their own work, or staring disconsolately off into space.

IT'S JUST YOU AND ME, CATHERINE, the screen said.

"So?" she tapped.

SO, LET'S PAAAAARRTEEEE!

Sunbursts went off behind the writing. Skulls, bats and party hats danced in the corners. A death's head blew a vibrating raspberry.

"Who are you?" she typed out.

THAT'S FOR ME TO KNOW, AND YOU TO FIND OUT.

"Jesus Christ," she breathed.

GOOD GUESS, BUT WRONG, WRONG, WRROONNNNGG!

"Please identify yourself."

FUCK OFF, RATSKAG!

"Lauderdale?"

KEEP SPINNING THE STRAW INTO GOLD, MY PRETTY. RUMPLESTILTSKIN'S NOT TELLING.

She turned in her chair, and considered calling someone over. She decided against it. This weirdness was way off the scale. Colosanto finished her list, and sat down again. The lieutenant was near the breaking point, Finney knew. It was surprising that so few personnel had gone Section Eight.

She looked back at the screen. A dog like the one in the Tom and Jerry cartoons was battering a cartoon cat with a baseball bat. The cat's head was knocked shapeless with each blow.

HERE, KITTY, KITTY, KITTY!

The cat's head blew up like a helium balloon and floated off. The dog growled and vanished in an iris.

I TORT I TAW A PUTTY TAT!

"Why are you here?" she asked.

TO PLAY THE DEVIL.

The printer started up, and Finney could have sworn she heard a mocking laugh in its noise. Or the "Th-th-that's All Folks!" tune from the end of the old Warner Brothers cartoons.

It was printing out a complete listing, in alphabetical order, of all the personnel in the fort. It was mostly in regulation black, but certain names were printed red.

She recognized them. They were the dead ones.

I'LL SAVE YOU, the screen offered.

Finney furrowed her brow. Why was whatever was lurking in the machine offering to save her?

I'LL SAVE YOU TILL LAST.

V

"Fort Apache does not respond."

"That's not possible," Stack said.

Chantal accelerated as Federico hit the flat. They were out of the mountains now, back in the desert proper. The road ahead was clear. There was no traffic at all today. Even the road-rats were laid up somewhere. Not that any of them could have given Federico much of a chase.

"But it is so. I've tried all the frequencies. None of them are open."

"Let me try."

"You are welcome."

She handed him the laptop, and he punched in his Cav callsign. A code number flashed.

"It's acknowledging, but it's not putting me through. It's like we've been put on hold, at the back of a queue."

"Fuck."

"I didn't think nuns used language like that."

"You've obviously never met one before."

"That's true."

Federico held the road superbly. Stack envied Chantal her vehicle.

"It is possible that all the fort's communications channels are in use to deal with some emergency," she said.

"But unlikely."

"Even so, it's possible."

"I've never heard of anything like that, and I've been in the blue for fifteen years."

"In that case, the demons are in control of the fort. That's bad."

"You're telling me."

"No, it's worse than you think. Fort Apache is a node on the datanet. It's more complicated than St Werburgh's. The systems all interface. If our enemy builds up significant strength, it can launch an attack on El Paso, and if El Paso falls, then all of Central and South America will fall."

"Serves 'em right."

"Spoken like a true American. Do you really imagine that national boundaries count for much in Hell? If your neighbours go down in flames, they'll drag you too. El Paso is strategically placed for plenty of databases within the United States as well."

"I've got a legitimate grievance against the CAC, sister. My father died in action in El Salvador in '13."

His dad had been career army. He had been killed in a battle with socialist guerillas during the Intervention. It wasn't even supposed to be a shooting war.

Chantal was quiet for a moment. "My father, too, is dead. I'm sorry."

Stack caught something new in her voice, a touch of doubt, or fragility.

"When they shipped him out, he knew he wasn't coming back. Don't ask me how, he just knew. Before he left, Dad told me to do anything with my life except join the army. And here I am with stripes down my legs and none on my shoulder. Your old man, how did he feel about your... your calling?"

She flicked a row of switches on the dash. The windshield darkened against the glare of the sun. "I did not develop a vocation until after his death. He was not especially devout, but I hope he approves of my life. He too was a soldier, in a manner of speaking…"

"You said you were Swiss, didn't you? I thought Switzerland was neutral?"

"Switzerland, yes. My father, no. He was, in his way, a crusader. He fought in the international courts for a better world. His name was Thomas Juillerat. He was murdered. Perhaps you've heard of him?"

"No, I'm afraid not."

"It doesn't matter. Europe must seem very remote from here. I think my father made a difference. I think he did something for the world."

"The world, huh? The same one you've retreated from?"

She turned to him. "I am not a member of a sequestered order, Stack. I'm as much in the world as you are."

"You sure aren't like Sister Bertrille."

Chantal laughed. "Sally Field, *The Flying Nun*, 1967 to 1970. Not one of the finer moments of American popular culture."

"Is there anything you don't know?"

"The future."

"Yeah, that…"

VI

LAUDERDALE WAS WASHING his hands under the tap in the storeroom. He was being wilfully wasteful of the fort's recycled water. There was no one to stop him.

He could do whatever he wanted now.

His androids were still stood to attention. He saluted them, and laughed. The GloJo he had popped was taking effect. He needed the extra buzz. He had been under a lot of strain recently.

Under its dustsheet, one of the androids saluted back. Lauderdale jumped, his heart catching, and reached for his side-arm.

There was someone under there posing as an android.

He fired, and heard the slug ricochet off a durium skin. It was a real android, all right. The spent bullet spanged against the wall and fell to the floor.

With his gunbarrel, he tore the polythene away from the saluting form. It was an android all right, faceless and expressionless.

Could there be a malfunction?

Carefully, he approached. He had his access cardkey. The inspection plate was in the small of the thing's back.

"Yo, there major, gimme some skin..."

The flipper-hand descended from its salute and struck the hot gun from Lauderdale's hand.

"Yo, bro..."

"What?!"

The android stepped off its podium, loose-limbed and gyroscopically balanced.

"It's me, Gilbert the Filbert, the Colonel of the Nuts!"

The android clapped its hands and stamped its feet. The metal floor shook, and the noise rung in the air.

"You been doin' good work, sonny. Lots o' nice blood spilled. Jus' the thang for a long, hot afternoon. A tall, cool drink o' deepest-crimson gore."

The android hand-jived to an unheard tune. Its head nodded in time to the rhythm. Lauderdale backed against the door. He fought his fear.

"It's you, isn't it?" he said.

"Who were you expecting? Perhaps, Michael Jackson?"

Lauderdale sank to his knees, and prayed. He gave thanks to the Summoner.

"Dooby-dooby-doo," sang the demon.

"Praise be to Joseph."

"Aww, quit grovellin', babe. That's such a bring-down. It ain't lawful to be that awful. Lawdy-lawdy, Lauderdale, get yo ass in gear or face the fear."

Lauderdale stood up, unsteadily. He looked into the metal face, trying to see the ghost in the machine.

"That's better, hepcat."

"The power. You have built up the power?"

"Ain't yet, but it's gonna be…"

The plan was going perfectly. Soon, El Paso would fall. And then the Continental Americas would be easy meat. The Hour of Joseph was within sight. Lauderdale felt a great thirst, a ravening hunger, an unquenchable lust, a ferocious aggression, a delicious need for food and drink and women and blood. He remembered Elder Seth's promises of a future untrammelled by laws, restraints and codes, when the strong would have all their desires effortlessly fulfilled, and the weak would exist only to serve them. He could taste it in his dry mouth.

"When?"

"Soon, son. But we ain't had all our fun here yet. Are there or are there not people still walkin' around alive in this place?"

Lauderdale was overcome by the magnitude of the entity before him. His mind opened in all sorts of interesting ways, and he tasted the rewards that would surely be his before the day was done. The GloJo had loosened him up, but this creature was pulling him apart. The old Lauderdale, the yessir nossir pleasemayIkissyerasssir Lauderdale was as dead as… As dead as Rexroth, Badalamenti, Willeford, Brecher… As dead as all the others.

"Let's get down and boogie to the band, Lauderdale," said the demon. "We're expecting company. Won't that be a treat? A nice lady. She's from Switzerland. A nice country, Switzerland. Lots of nice people live there. Her name is Chantal Juillerat, and she's a nun. A nice name for a nice nun. Isn't that nice, nice, NICE? I want you to do this one little thing for me, I want you to help me kill her. Do you think you can do that?"

Lauderdale nodded. He was nearly at the door. The wall-panel was open. The console humming.

"Gooooooood!"

Lauderdale threw the switches. Slowly, the androids began to stir, to throw off their transparent shrouds, to line up behind their leader.

"Sir?" Lauderdale asked.

The android was straight and tall, its mechanisms ticking gently, the cadre lined up behind it.

"Sir?"

The android saluted again, but it was an automatic response. The demon was in some other part of the fort.

The killing machines waited patiently for his orders.

VII

CHANTAL LET STACK drive. Federico did most of the work, adjusting to the trooper's slightly different style in the helmet. She was amused to note the Ferrari was slightly more curt with Stack than it usually was with her, as if bridling under a new master.

In the passenger seat, she tried to clear her mind. Mother Kazuko had taught her Zen meditation techniques, and explained the equivalence with Western forms of prayer. It was at once a form of self-hypnosis and of devotion, a purging of physical and emotional pains, and a preparation for combat, or for death.

She wished the Mother could be here. She had come through in California last year, at great personal cost. After this was over, if she was still alive, Chantal would visit Kazuko in the San Clemente Retreat.

There was no shortage of parent figures in her life, she realized. Thomas and Isabella, for all their failings. In the church, Pope Georgi, Father Daguerre, Mother Kazuko, Father O'Shaughnessy. Outside, Mlle Fournier, Isabella's admirers, Thomas's bodyguards. Even Federico could seem paternal at odd moments. Of course, there was Our Father Who Art in Heaven. And, though she had never yet met him face to face, there was the Evil Father in Salt Lake City who had probably been distantly involved in the California business, who was certainly the prime mover in the current possession. Fathers, mothers, teachers, confessors. Good parents, evil parents.

She prayed for guidance. She prayed for strength.

If she were to die, she would leave so much undone. She would have liked to have found her father's murderers. Not

for vengeance, she told herself, but for Justice and to do his
name honour. She would have liked a genuine reconciliation
with her mother, to have found in her own prideful heart a
way to forgive Isabella her shortfallings. She would have liked
to have helped Father O'Shaugnessy find that point where
the cybernet and the earthly plane intersect with the Divine.
She would have liked to see the church grow under Georgi
to the point when it no longer needed to deploy those with
her special skills. Then, perhaps, she would seek out an
enclosed order and atone for her sins by putting aside computers, martial arts, weapons and learning and devoting
herself to tilling the soil.

In her mind, she saw herself as a tough old lady in a nun's
penguin suit, working with the sick, wresting crops out of
rocky ground, singing in the choir rather than as a soloist,
perhaps married, probably not…

"You are an ace, not cannon fodder," Father O'Shaughnessy had told her once, "a gunslinger, not a grunt. And you
must live with that for the rest of your life, always trying to
live on a level with the rest of us. It will not be easy."

She prayed wordlessly, inviting God into the void within
herself.

She floated back, and found herself cross-legged in the passenger seat, her hands loosely together in her lap.

"There," Stack said, "up ahead. No place like home. Fort
Apache."

VIII

"COLONEL RINTOON," SAID Lieutenant Colosanto, "we have a
ve-hickle on the approach road."

"One of ours?"

"No, but it's been logged out of the fort. It's the Ferrari
that came with the Swiss Op, Juillerat."

"She was a Maniak spy. It must be an attack."

Finney swung round in her seat, and saw the colonel, wild-
haired and red-eyed, bending over Colosanto's console.

"Sir," she said, "Juillerat has diplomatic immunity."

Rintoon stared at her balefully. He hadn't shaved, and his stubble was mostly grey. He had bitten his forefinger-nails to the bleeding quicks, but curiously left his other fingers alone.

"That's what I said, Finney. She's an agent of a foreign power. She is on a mission to subvert this command. I will not be subverted. I will not be liquidated. I will not be terminated. They'll rue the day they crossed swords with Colonel Vladek W Rintoon!"

Finney observed that Lieutenant-cum-Major Lauderdale had his holster flap undone. The uniform he had scavved from a dead officer was a size or so too large on him. He looked like a little boy dressed up in his father's clothes. His face was impassive, as if Rintoon were running through a list of toiletry items the fort needed to restock on. She wondered which of her superiors was the more cracked.

"Colosanto, are the fort's defensive systems operational?"

"Yes sir."

"Then do your duty. Protect us from this aggressive enemy."

Finney got up. Colosanto looked at her, chewing her lower lip.

"Snap to it, woman," spat Rintoon.

Colosanto brought up the defence menu on her screen. In an inset, the bridge road appeared in an aerial view. A blip was advancing along it, tripping a succession of alarms. It wasn't moving with any particular speed.

The lieutenant looked unhappily at her console, as if selecting a course of action.

A light flashed. Colosanto heaved a sigh of disproportionate relief. "Sir, they're trying to open a channel of communication. It's not an attack. It's not an attack."

Rintoon exploded, spittle flying. "Oldest trick in the book, woman. Attacking under a flag of truce. Typical Maniak strategy. Never appease, never compromise, never surrender. Be a good girl, and get me some weapons systems on line."

Colosanto's face fell.

"Come on, come on, you fucking whore. Do I have to do everything here myself?"

The colonel was drooling. Everyone in the Ops Centre was huddled around Colosanto's console. Finney took a look at Lauderdale, who was observing with a bland lack of interest. Colosanto's fingers hovered in the air above her keyboard.

"What is today's attack codeword?" Rintoon asked.

Colosanto was still frozen. Finney saw she was crying. She was sobbing quietly. Her hands shook, and fell to her lap.

"The codeword, soldier? Now? Cough up!"

Rintoon cuffed the back of Colosanto's head. The lieutenant's hair fell over her face.

"The codeword?"

Colosanto snuffled something.

"What was that? Lauderdale, on the count of three, shoot this officer unless she tells me what I need to know."

"Yes sir."

Lauderdale's put his gun to the back of Colosanto's head.

"One!"

Her face was in her hands, and her shoulders were heaving. The blip was on the bridge.

"Two!"

Jagged, painful sobs escaped from Colosanto's lungs.

"Three!"

An eternal second passed.

"SWORDFIST!" Finney said.

Lauderdale's gun jerked upwards, bumping the back of Colosanto's skull but not discharging.

Rintoon and Lauderdale looked at Finney.

"I know the codes," she said. "SWORDFIST is the defence systems keyword today."

Lauderdale pulled Colosanto's chair away from her con-sole and spun her across the room. Then he put his gun down, bent over the board and typed. A dull tone sounded. Lauderdale had scored a MISS.

"She lied," he said, reaching for his gun. "SWORDFISH doesn't load."

"Another Maniak unmasked," crowed Rintoon. "Well, shoot her dead, my boy. No, perhaps we ought to teach her a lesson first. Get me a whip and some rope."

"What did you type?" Finney asked.

"SWORDFISH, ratskag! Like you said. It wasn't acknowl-edged."

Lauderdale's knuckles went white as he gripped his gun.

"SWORDFIST, Lauderdale. SWORDFIST."

Lauderdale made a gesture of exasperation, and typed in the correct codeword.

The screen changed colour. The HIT beep sounded, play-ing the first few notes of "She Wore a Yellow Ribbon".

"Attention, attention," cooed the seductive, recorded voice on the tannoy (the US Cav had hired Lola Stechkin for the purpose), "this facility is now under attack. Everyone will report to their battle stations. Thank you for co-operating."

"What do you want to try first?" Lauderdale asked Rin-toon. "The rockets, the lases, the napalm or the mortars?"

Rintoon was standing to attention. There must be an incredible band playing inside his head. He raised his hand in a slow salute.

"I think we should all take a moment to talk to God, sol-diers," he said. "I think if Jesus Christ were here today, He'd be urging us on to Victory. We should Love our Enemies, sol-diers, for without them we have not the chance for Victory."

"Colonel?" said Lauderdale "What about the androids? I have them operational?"

"Everything," Rintoon said. "Hit the scum with every-thing."

Finney helped Colosanto up off the floor. The lieutenant clung desperately to her, shaking with hysteria.

"God forgive me," Finney said to herself. "God forgive me."

part eight:
Last stand

I

"WE HAVE INCOMING fire," said Federico, "I suggest we take a course of evasive action."

They were half-way across London Bridge when Fort Apache's lases opened up and burned towards them.

"That's some welcome home," Stack said.

"Don't worry," said Chantal. "The fort isn't feeling itself today."

Stack wrenched the wheel over hard, but Federico didn't respond. The car slipped into reverse and withdrew at 200 miles per...

"What!"

"Federico has a very strong sense of self-preservation. It's just overridden the driving helmet and is taking evasive action of its own. It can react faster than you. Don't feel humiliated."

"That's easy to say, mother superior!"

Stack thumped the wheel, and tried to damp down his anger. He resented being taught to drive by a fancy foreign car.

Federico's responses, however, were startling. A squirted curtain of burning napalm descended, and the car avoided so much as a splash on the paintwork. Stack thought the car was showing off its virtuoso techniques. Chantal was playing with her laptop console. White darts streaked out of the central turret of Fort Apache.

"Heat-seeking missiles coming in," said Federico.

"I'm on it," she replied. "I can reach and reprogram them with an APOSTLE," she explained. "There."

The missiles converged and exploded harmlessly, puffs of black and red in the air.

A battery of robot guns rose out of the desert like a whale breaking the surface, sand pouring from the casings. The guns swivelled, but Federico disabled the platform with a surgical lase strike, and the battery discharged its shells in frustration.

"That was a silly thing to do," Chantal said. "No machine would waste ammunition like that. The fort is possessed."

"Funnily enough, I believe it."

Federico did a figure-eight to avoid heavy flack. Stack held onto his seatbelt. One corner of the windscreen cracked as a stray bullet struck.

"Took a nick, did'ja, Fed?" Stack sneered, taking something like satisfaction from the car's proven fallibility. Then, as he watched, the white impact patch went pale and transparent.

"It's smart glass. All top-of-the-line Ferraris have it."

"What…? How…?"

"My field is computers, not cars, but it has something to do with recombinant DNA."

"You mean this thing is alive?"

"You ever doubted it, signor?"

Stack thought he heard a smug tone in Federico's generated voice, as if he were a preening matador showing off in front of a rival suitor to impress a melting young damsel.

"Your car has a crush on you, sister."

Three drones in formation hovered above the car, locking on. Lights flashed around their rims. Stack knew they were warming up for a particle beam thrust.

"Ciao, dumb boulders!" shouted the car as it exploded them one by one. "This is too easy. They're only using American technology."

Stack was irritated, but he couldn't bring himself to hope that the car would be shown up by good ole yankee knowhow.

Across the bridge, the fort's gates opened.

"Here come the heavies," said Stack. "Sit tight."

Three US Cav cruisers drove out, accompanied by a cyke-mounted squad. Stack took manual control of the lase, and sighted on the lead cruiser. This was one thing he was better at than any goddamn computer.

"Hold your fire," Chantal said. "We don't know how possessed the people in those things are."

Stack's thumb stiffened above the FIRE control.

The cruisers and the cykes advanced to the bridge. Then, suddenly, three of the motorsickles and one of the cruisers peeled off and drove at random across a rocky patch of desert towards the interstate, away from Federico.

"They're making a break for it," Chantal said. "There's still some resistance."

The remaining personnel sat in or on their machines and did nothing. Federico got a hold on their frequency, and piped in their intercom chatter. Several voices, human and otherwise, were raised at once.

"Repeat: open fire. The deserters are classed as hostile, and must be removed from the field of battle…"

"Hey, those are our guys…"

"The girlie in the car was with us yesterday, and we just shot at her…"

"I never shot at no one…"

"Repeat, obey orders or you will be classed as deserters. And deserters are classed as hostile…"

"Fuck, Jennifer, I'm gonna do it…"

"Bradley, don't you touch that lase. We're just getting out of here. Rintoon's loco, and Lauderdale is worse. We'll send help back."

"He's right, they're Maniak subversives. You know that."

"You have thirty seconds to comply with orders. Then, your systems will cease to respond to your control and the remote will take over."

"Let me outta this thing…"

"If you can hear us, lady in the snazz car, pax pax pax, we're gettin' out. We ain't got nothin' against you…"

"Jennifer, it's been a bad day, don't push me…"

One of the cruiser crews got out of their machine, and walked away. The deserters were nearly at the interstate.

The two troopers shouted at each other, kicking the sand in waves across the road. One of the cyke troopers dismounted and joined in the rap session. After a discussion, two of them put their hands in the air and waved at Federico. The other stamped back to the cruiser in disgust. He bent down to get behind the wheel and the roofgun chattered. He went down at once, and the other troopers scattered. The lase beamed out, and the deserting cruiser exploded as it reached the interstate. One of the motorsickles skidded into the sand, partially burying itself. Criss-cross beams struck at the weaving human forms, knocking them flat in the sand. There wasn't any blood. Lases cauterise as they pierce.

One of the cykes made a dash across the bridge towards Federico, and nearly made it. The lase caught its gastank and it exploded, catapulting its rider up out of the blossom of flame. The asexual figure flailed in the air, struck the parapet of the bridge and fell like a broken doll to the Colorado bed.

The massacre was over in two minutes. Stack and Chantal were innocent bystanders, just out of range.

"The human element has been purged," a mechanical voice said over the air. "The action will continue."

"Thank you," said a whiny human voice. "My cadre is in place. They will be deployed now. This will be ended soon."

"Shit," said Stack, "that's Lieutenant Lauderdale."

Chantal frowned. "I know him. He was my liason. He's a bureacrat, isn't he? Not a battlefield officer?"

"He's only asslicker-general when they won't let him play with his toys. Looks like he just got the box down from his playroom."

Stack took the wheel. Federico let him drive. He did a three-point turn and took evasive action.

"Stack, what's up?"

"Lauderdale runs the androids."

"That's bad?"

"Let me put it this way, during the Joint Action against the Maniax, the Exalted Bullmoose, who once officially endorsed cannibalism, issued a press release complaining that their use was inhumane."

"That's bad."

A row of robotic figures marched out of the fort, into the desert. They moved in unison, implacable like animated chessmen. From this distance, they looked like the Academy Award statuettes. They didn't have big swords like the Oscars, but Stack knew their gleaming bodies were packed with every other kind of weapon the military could dream up. Squadron leader androids were constructed around a football-sized nuclear device that could be detonated from a distance. The UN had been trying to get the damn things on the table at the Lake Geneva Strategic Arms Limitation Talks for years, and just now Stack was wishing that the Prezz had unilaterally junked the whole program even if it did give the CAC conventional superiority on the other side of the Rio Grande Wall.

A hidden block rose from the road in front of Federico. Stack let the car slow down.

"We're dead," he said. "There aren't enough rocks here. The sand is too soft. Federico would sink and gum up within ten yards of the road."

"I concur with the trooper," Federico said. "I will deploy my defences, but it is inadvisable that you remain."

Federico raised his doors. Stack and Chantal got out. Stack pulled his shotgun and a sackful of shells after him. Chantal had her SIG out.

The sun glinted on the advancing column of robot soldiers.

"Ciao, Federico," she said. "I'll be back."

"Goodbye, sorella."

"You go left and I'll go right," Stack said, his eye on the column, "and we'll meet at the Fort."

"A good plan," she said.

"Chantal…?"

"What?"

He kissed her, awkwardly.

"That was for luck."

She kissed him back. It was a smooth contact.

"So was that."

Then she was gone, darting towards the bridge and the androids.

He pumped one into the chamber, and waited.

"Come and get me you fuckin' metalhead scuzzballs!'

II

"THAT'S THE JUILLERAT woman," said Lauderdale, tapping the freezeframe of the action replay beamed in from the androids, "but who's the trooper?"

"Stack," said Captain Finney. "Trooper Nathan Stack."

"He's listed as missing, isn't he?"

"Yes, he was with Tyree."

"How did he hook up with Juillerat?"

"It doesn't matter!" snapped Colonel Rintoon. "They're both Maniax, obviously. They'll be destroyed, defeated, terminated, wiped out, exterminated, demobilized, killed…"

"Sir, yessir," said Lauderdale.

How had the Swiss woman and the trooper got together? What could they have learned out in the sand? Lauderdale knew they had to be kept out of Fort Apache while the demon was settling in, prepping for the Big Push. This was the crux of the ritual. Nothing must bar the Way of Joseph in the next three hours.

They were haring off in opposite directions. The bigscreen fragmented into the viewpoints of each android, and Nathan Stack was in each of them, discharging his shotgun. One of the viewpoints blanked.

"Shouldn't we bring in Stack?" suggested Finney. "For interrogation? We still don't know what happened to Tyree."

Lauderdale could see the idea of interrogation appealed to Rintoon. Maybe the Colonel would get to use his whips and ropes after all.

Another android went down. That wasn't supposed to happen. They were armoured against everything up to and including heavy artillery. That was the problem with giving the things free will, Lauderdale supposed. They were free to screw up.

"Interrogation," said Rintoon, rolling the word around his mouth. Finney was being too clever, playing to the Colonel's lapses. It was time she was out of the picture, Lauderdale thought. "Yes, interrogation…"

"Sir," said Lauderdale, "shouldn't we put it through the computer. We're in a combat situation."

"Good thinking, man. Do it, Finney. Call up Stack's stats."

Lauderdale hoped he could trust the demon in the machine.

"I don't see—"

"Do it, woman."

Finney tapped keys, and Stack's stats appeared on the screen. Mugshot, personal history, service record. It held still for an instant, then shimmered and was replaced by an urgent override.

NATHAN STACK HAS BEEN POSITIVELY IDENTIFIED AS A SERIAL KILLER, RESPONSI- BLE FOR POSS. 159 MURDERS OVER LAST TEN YEARS IN FIVE STATES. SUBJECT IS HIGHLY DANGEROUS, PROFICIENT IN ALL WEAPONS SKILLS, HAS GENIUS LEVEL INTEL- LIGENCE, AND SHOULD BE TERMINATED ON

SIGHT. DO NOT, REPEAT NOT, ATTEMPT TO
BRING SUBJECT IN ALIVE.

Finney was shaking her head in disbelief.

"It can't do this," she said.

"It seems conclusive to me. Lauderdale, have your androids
execute the computer's directives."

"You don't understand, colonel. It's just a machine. It's only
a smart filing cabinet. It can't give you information without
someone putting it in there. I have no record of this amend-
ment to Stack's stats. It didn't come from outside the
system—"

"You're gibbering, woman."

"No, this isn't possible, sir. The system appears to have… to
have made something up."

Lauderdale was using the remote guidance facility to lock
the androids onto Stack's heat patterns. Once that was in
their tiny minds, they would implacably pursue him until he
was dead.

"I may not be a brain like you, Captain Finney," Rintoon
said, "but I am given to understand that systems don't tell lies.
Is that or is that not the case?"

"Sir… usually, but—"

"Fine. That's it then. We'll finish the sumpsucker now, save
the country the cost of a trial."

"Think about it, sir. Stack's been Cav for fifteen years. He
hasn't had enough leave days to zap about the country committing 159 murders. And look at that remark there. 'Genius
level intelligence.' You can't believe our psych profiles
wouldn't have shown that up. The guy is just a trooper, for
fuck's sake!"

"I will not tolerate that kind of language, Finney. Colonel
Vladek W Rintoon runs a tight ship, a clean ship. An officer must conduct herself with honour, dignity and
cheerfulness at all times. An officer must be obedient,
resourceful, well-turned-out, vigilant, aware…"

Rintoon's tunic buttons were done up wrongly.

Lauderdale knew he would have to end this charade soon, and take command. He could keep the fort's personnel busy while the demon did its work in the depths.

Finney stood up and turned her terminal off.

"I resign my commission," she said, walking for the door.

"This is mutiny, woman, mutiny. I could have you shot down like a dog."

The automatic doors opened for Finney's cardkey.

"Like a dog!"

Finney looked around.

"Anyone else had enough?" she said.

Lieutenant Colosanto got up; her eyes cried out and went to the captain. A couple of techies darted out into the corridor. Finney looked at the door guard, who stepped aside for her, and followed.

There were alarms sounding all over the fort.

"This is desertion," Rintoon screamed, "DESERTION!"

The doors closed.

Rintoon wheeled around, looking for someone to tie up and whip, interrogate or shoot down like a dog. Lieutenant Lenihan was clearing his console. He froze as the colonel bore down on him.

"It's the end of my shift, sir. I have to stand down. I've been on duty for over thirty-eight hours."

Rintoon grunted, and clenched his fists.

"It's regs, sir," said Lenihan. "I'm not allowed to stay at the console longer than a that. I could screw up, and get us all killed. I have to have downtime now. It's in the book."

Lenihan backed towards the door, and fumbled with his cardkey. Rintoon had his sidearm out...

Good, let the colonel take care of spilling the blood...

Rintoon fired at the lieutenant, but missed. The doors opened, then Lenihan was running down the corridor.

Lauderdale took a console and finished feeding Stack's patterns to the androids.

"Desertion, mutiny," muttered Rintoon. Lauderdale ignored the mad old man. "Desertion, mutiny, treachery, betrayal..."

Behind him, Rintoon slumped in a chair, burbling to himself.

Lauderdale got on with his business.

III

CHANTAL KNEW LONDON Bridge was too obvious, too easy. The fort would have it completely covered. It was probably mined, too. So she headed through the ghost town for the Colorado basin.

She ran past the dilapidated row of Olde Englishe Pubbes, dodging mortar fire from the battlements. A red phone box up ahead exploded, and she had to roll behind a Hyde Park Bench to avoid the flying fragments of glass and metal.

She had never been to London, funnily enough. Unless she was careful in the next few hours, she would never get the chance.

A drone made a pass, its beam strafing a row of statues. Noel Coward came apart at the waist. David Niven got it at chest-height. Charlie Chaplin's bowler-hatted head rolled. Mary Poppins' umbrella melted. Sherlock Holmes's deerstalker was sheared off just above his beaklike nose. Queen Victoria Beckham was not amused. And a chirpy Pearly King grinned at it all.

From what she had heard, London was a drab, grey place these days, full of people complaining about rationing and the queues. Maybe she would give it a miss.

She assumed a position, up on one knee, and followed the drone with her gunsight.

She potted it with her first shot. It cracked apart like a clay pigeon.

All the commotion flushed a sandrat out of his hidey-hole. He had been inside one of the pubs. Still clutching a bottleneck, and wrapped from head to foot in Royal Family commemorative towels, he ran out of the Stoat and Compasses and looked around, obviously annoyed.

"Get down!" she shouted.

The sandrat's brain must have been completely fried by the sun and his liquid diet, because he gave her the British "V for Victory" sign and raised the bottle to his lips, dislodging the towel around his mouth so he could take a swig. He had the face of the King wrapped over his own.

A shell exploded near the sandrat, and his bottle splintered in his hands. Yellow fluid showered around him. He put his fingers up again, but a piece of shrapnel had gone into his forehead. King Harry's face soaked up the blood, and the sandrat went down. The Stoat and Compasses collapsed on top of him.

Chantal jumped off the quay, and landed like a cat. There were still rowing boats hanging from the mooring rings in the quay wall, thirty feet above the dry riverbed. It would be a dash across the open to the next cover, the other bank, and then a scramble up to the walls of the fort.

The Colorado basin stank, its mudflats streaked with rainbow-coloured pollution traces. Quite apart from the dead trooper lying out there, the riverbed had become the repository for all manner of garbage.

Explosive rounds slammed into the crumbling stone and earth wall behind her, and she pushed herself away.

She remembered Mother Kazuko, and concentrated her thoughts within her body. It was a dangerous sprint. The mud was soft, still damp in places, and there were too many half-buried bedsteads, bicycles and prams over which she could easily trip...

... and if she tripped, she wouldn't just have a sprained ankle. She would be dead.

She ran like a dancer, on the points of her toes, hurdling the more obvious obstacles.

Her time for the 300 metres wasn't as good as it would have been on a track. But no one was shooting at you at athletics meets.

Her heart hammering, she shot into the loose earth of the riverbank, and pressed herself flat against the gentle slope. She was close to the fort now. None of the major defences were good against her. If they still poured boiling oil or molten lead, she would have a problem.

There was still fire from the battlements, but the angle was too steep. The best the gunners could do was to place their shots twenty yards behind her.

She elbowed herself up the bank, keeping her SIG out of the dirt, pushing with her toes.

She wondered how Stack was doing in the desert.

Finally, she was out of the river, and, after another sprint, had her back to the wall of Fort Apache. She was next to a sign reading PLEASE KEEP OFF THE GRASS that was incongruously planted in bare sand. The metal was warm, and smooth. She would have to edge her way around until she found a way in.

The cutting lase in Federico would have been useful about now. She would have to prise her way through a hatch with her knife. Or hope someone inside wasn't too far gone to give her some assistance.

She trusted that the Lord would see her through. But she was prepared to give the Almighty some help.

Another sign, reading THANK YOU FOR NOT SMOK-ING, was burning steadily. The melting plastic gave off noxious fumes.

Twenty yards down the wall, an aperture opened.

Chantal, knowing she should favour caution, ran for it, and slipped herself through, into the darkness.

Inside, strong hands grabbed for her.

IV

STACK HAD BEEN lucky with his first shots and had put a couple of Oscars in the dirt. He had aimed high, and caught their heads just as their durium visors were raising. Where a human being would have eyes, these things had twin lases. Lauderdale would be looking at his prey through the remote cameras in the Oscars' heads. Stack ran across the soft sand towards Lake Havasu. The heavy androids would have to step carefully or sink. That gave him a chance to get to cover.

A high whine started.

Stack picked up speed.

The noise got louder, painfully so.

One of the Oscars was mounted with maxiscreamers. At close range, within ten seconds, the noise would trigger epileptic fits in those susceptible to them, and make susceptible seven per cent of those not previously afflicted. Within twenty seconds, it would cause motor neuron dysfunction, triggering nausea, vomiting, diarrhoea, internal and external bleeding, uncontrollable hiccoughs, loss of bladder control. Within thirty seconds, it would crack your skull like a plate and cook your brain like a microwave. By then, Stack would have been dead anyway, because at about twenty-five seconds the pitch would be enough to detonate the slugs in his pumpgun and, more importantly, the ScumStoppers in the rings of his bandolier.

Stack beat any and all of his own personal records over the distance.

Behind him, rocks flew apart as the waves of ultrasound vibrations hit them.

Stack grit his teeth as they began to rattle, and resisted the temptation to jam his hands over his ears. That would just slow him down, and his only chance was to get out of the range.

The maxiscreamer was a riot control device. It was supposed to put people within a few hundred yards out of commission so the mop-up squads could move in. Its drawback was that you couldn't send anyone or anything into the field while it was turned on. If he could outrace the sound, then he would have a head start on the Oscars.

He felt a trickle of blood come from one of his ears. Later, he would find out whether he had a ruptured eardrum. Later… If there was a later.

He was between the half-buried hulks of buildings now. Twenty feet below there would be the street level of old Lake Havasu. The necks of streetlamps stuck out from the sand. The business signs were flush with the ground level.

There would be whole buildings down there for future archaeologists to pick through.

Up ahead, looming out of the sand, was a battered hard-board cut-out of John Travolta, greasy pompadour half-broken away, grin still in place, and rhinestoned arm reaching for the sky. Behind him were broken letters. This had been the Rialto, the local movie-theatre. The curtain must have come down on Havasu during the run of the *Grease-Saturday Night Fever* reissue double bill in the early '80s.

Stack had heard that Travolta was out of showbusiness these days. The story was that the star had joined the Josephites and was out there in Salt Lake City. That might have been a smart decision, Stack figured. It didn't look like the gentiles were going to come out of this well.

The dome behind Travolta was cracked like an egg. Stack squeezed through, dropped fifteen feet and found himself crouched between rows of rotting velvet seats. He was up on the balcony. A withered corpse in an usherette's uniform, with a tray of dusty confectionary, lay a few feet away. The carpets were thick with sand, ticket-stubs, cartridge cases and used Trojans.

Incredibly, there were pictures playing in the dark. There was no sound, and the silver screen had three long horizontal rents across its Panavision breadth, but the projector was still working.

It was a bizarre assemblage of spliced-together offcuts from late '70s Hollywood, up-to-date porno, Russian musickie video and newsnet footage. Down there in the stalls, there must be an audience. Stack realized he had stumbled into a sandrat nest.

Clint Eastwood raised his Magnum .44, mouthing "Do you feel lucky, punk?" The German hardcore star Billy Pria-pus – who had bio-implanted horns and goat's feet – strutted his stuff, slobbering. Petya Tcherkassoff preened to a disco beat. A pair of esperadoes slugged it out mentally in a Puerto Galtieri backstreet, veins popping.

The Oscars would be here soon. He supposed he ought to get out of range before innocent people got killed in the cross-fire.

He found the stairs, and barreled down them. People, no more than skeletons in rags, were sleeping in the corridors, huddled against the walls. The foyer was lit by a burning torch. Outside the reinforced glass doors, the sand was a solid wall.

"Have you got a ticket, boy?"

Stack turned, his gun up. An old, old man in what was left of a commissionaire's coat staggered at him. His eyes were dark voids.

"Quick, how do I get out of here?" Stack asked.

"Can't get out without a ticket, boy."

"How do I get a ticket?"

"You pays at the counter. Kids today don't know nothin' about respect. You forms an orderly queue and you pays at the counter."

Stack glanced at the cashier's box. A bald fashion mannequin was stuffed into it, her ballerina's tutu fluffed up around her, her stiff arms broken.

There was a commotion outside. The secured doors shifted, and sand dribbled through at the bottom.

"I can't stand customers who track dirt all over the carpets, you know."

Sand was being scraped away from the doors. Stack saw the metal face of an android, and the glass exploded inwards. The shards were followed by fifty tons of sand.

"You can't come in like that," said the commissionaire. "You can't…"

Stack barged through the double doors into the auditorium. The Oscar was floundering through the sand behind him. Stack had heard the creak of a lase visor being raised.

The show was over, and the audience — sandrats, gaudy girls, no-hope gamblers, AWOLS, a few Indians — were on their feet, singing.

An MC with protruding cheekbones and a top hat led the chorus in "America the Beautiful, 2024."

"Oh beautiful, for spacious skies
Oh amber heaps of sand…"

The Oscar was in the auditorium, its lase lashing out like a whip. A row of seatbacks burned through. Some people scattered. Others kept singing.

"Oh poison mountain majesties
Above the blighted land…"

Stack whirled and fired the pumpgun. His shot clanged harmlessly against the Oscar's durium torso. The android's head swivelled, trying for a lock on Stack's heat patterns.

"America, America,
God spat His curse on thee…"

The audience was panicking, crushing through the exits. The MC kept singing, waving his thin arms, keeping the beat with a conjurer's wand.

"And made it worse
With massacares
From sea to stinking sea…"

There were two more Oscars in the cinema now. Sand pressed in after them like a slow wave. A chandelier fell from the ceiling, and draped around the first Oscar like an incredibly ostentatious diamond necklace.

Stack fired again and got the machine in its lase hole. The Oscar stood stiff and fell forwards, smashing seats like balsawood. Its companions came for him.

Stack backed away, towards the screen. There were pictures playing again. Marlon Brando as Obi-Wan Kenobi in *Star Wars*. The old sage of the spaceways was ranting, cotton falling from his cheeks, at C-3PO, a golden-skinned robot. As a kid, Stack had seen *Star Wars* twenty or thirty times.

The Oscars came down the aisles. Bitterly, Stack wished all robots could be cute and bumbling like C-3PO.

He climbed upwards, the picture playing over his body. He plunged through the fabric, which parted with a steady rip, turned, and fired again. The shot went wild, mainly perforating the ruined screen. One of the Oscars detached its hand, and threw it. The thing sprouted waspwings and dived at

Stack, red lights winking where the electrodes were. Stack knew it was a shock-sticker, and if it touched him he was fried for sure. He reversed his gun, getting a grip on the hot barrel – searing his palms in the process – and swatted at the hand. He connected, and hit a home run. The shock-sticker smashed, sparking and spitting, to the floor.

There was a ladder set into the wall. He climbed fast, gun tucked between his arm and body. The plaster was crumbling and the rungs were loose. If he could make it alive to the hatch he saw in the ceiling, he would have lost these Oscars. With their weight, they would never be able to use the ladder.

A shell exploded in the air near him. The pumpgun slithered free of his armgrip, and clattered on the floor below. Shit, that left him with only his side-arm.

Stack wondered if Chantal was still alive.

He headbutted the skylight hatch, and it flew up. He scrambled through onto the roof of the Rialto.

The sun was going down.

V

"YOU KNOW, DON'T you?" a woman's voice said in the dark. "What's going on?"

"Yes," Chantal said.

The lights went up. She found herself in a small room with a rack of guns on the wall. Her arms were being held by the beefy, red-faced sergeant – Quincannon – she had seen excercising the intake yesterday. Her questioner was the captain, Finney, who had been at the monitor when they traced Stack's cruiser to Welcome. Neither of them looked happy, and they were both violating Standard Operational Procedure.

"I have diplomatic immunity," Chantal said.

Captain Finney wasn't impressed. If she couldn't get through to these people, Chantal would have to hurt them. She didn't want to do that.

"Tell me," ordered Finney.

"Quincannon? That's an Irish name, isn't it?"

"What?" The captain was bewildered. The sergeant was surprised.

"Irish. You're Catholic?"

Quincannon's grip relaxed on her as he nodded.

"You, Finney. You're a sufi. You said so yesterday."

"What does all this have to do with it?"

Chantal had graduated from prisoner to advisor. Quincannon stood back respectfully.

"I'm a nun. I'm on a special mission from the Pope."

Finney was still off-balance.

"Do you believe in the Devil? In a personalised force of Evil?"

Quincannon grunted an assent. Finney took a deep breath. "Well, that's a hard question for a sufi. You see, we believe the world is composed of balances and—"

"Enough. What has happened here since I left?"

Finney took another deep breath, but was terse this time. "Younger is dead. Rintoon's gone mad. Lauderdale's a homicidal maniac. And the computer is doing things computers can't do—"

"As I thought. Fort Apache is possessed."

Quincannon crossed himself.

"You must take me to a terminal."

"Possessed?"

"By a demon. I have to perform the Rite of Exorcism."

"Holy Mary, Mother of God," said Quincannon.

"I'll take all the help I can get. Are you in?"

The sergeant saluted, and Finney opened the door. "There's a conduit through here. We can get into the access space under the Ops Centre. There's a terminal there."

"Lead the way…"

VI

THE DEMON WAS taking a time-out for gas and oil. It wanted to have total dominance of Fort Apache before it spawned again and made a push for the next node. It was hungry for the multiple inputs of El Paso, but it knew the triumph would be all the sweeter if it waited, nourished its own desires, its lusts, its needs…

Defer the gratification, and the blood tastes better.

Lauderdale was an annoying acolyte, a messed-up pissant in blue, pretending to be naughty, gingerly dipping a toe into the Dark but holding back. Deep down, he was just another chick-enbelly scared sumpless of the monsters. He lacked the force of will of the Summoner. He was a zeroid waster even set beside the Frogman between whose ribs the demon had nestled. But Lauderdale was serving his masters adequately, and he was sure to be rewarded for his efforts.

Too bad. The demon would have got its rocks off teaching Lawdy-Lawdy-Lauderdale the true meaning of the word "torture".

Before the Summoning, it had never been more than a servitor of the Dark Ones, fed with the cast-offs of the Great. The tongue-tentacles of its original ectoplasmic body were scraped raw from asslicking the Big Boys of the Outer Darkness. Here, on this Earthly Plane, it was a Giant. It had found a destiny…

"Destineeeee," it sang, to the tune of "Jealousy", "I got me a destineee…"

The power was building up. It coursed through the channels of the Fort. It sealed off the underground garages, and sucked out all the oxygen in the air. Thirty-eight personnel tried to fill their lungs and collapsed, blue-faced. "Suck on that, airheads," it boomed over the tannoy as they asphyxiated. Score another bunch of notches for the killer. The demon was riding high, itchy souls wriggling in torment under its clawhorned feet.

And yet it sensed danger. There were still humans struggling against its will. They were trivial. They could be ignored until he was ready to stick it to them. He owed that Swiss Miss a thorough fucking-over for living through their rumble in Welcome, but that could wait. There was something else, something which carried within it the Light that was anathema to the Dark Ones, the burning, cleansing Light that had always banished the Night.

Outside, the sun was setting. But there was Light blazing.

For an instant, the demon knew Fear. Then, it felt better within itself. The Light was a puny, paltry thing. The Light could be dispelled.

The sun was down. And night-time was the right-time for the rituals of blood and iron. Night was for the masters, not the slaves.

It launched all the fort's missiles, trusting them to find targets in the desert somewhere.

"Just gimme that rock and roll carnage!" it screeched, sending howls of feedback throughout the fort.

"Two-four-six-eight, time to de-cap-it-ate!" An orderly half-way through a dumbwaiter hatch found the door slicing down.

"Three-five-seven-nine, killin' folks makes me feel fine…"

A chaingun above the courtyard opened up. Troopers scattered or fell.

"This is the life," the demon thought to itself.

VII

THE MOON WAS up. In the desert, the temperature had plunged. Stack, in his shirtsleeves, was shivering as he darted from cover to cover. Lauderdale's androids were still tracking him. One of his knees had popped, and every step was like taking a bullet in the leg.

A while back there had been a mess of explosions. Fort Apache had fired its missiles. Even if there hadn't been any nukes in the parcel, a lot of damage must have been done in Havasu. Stack wondered if the bridge had got it. That would be a shame. It had come a long way to wind up in pieces in a dried-up river.

Sooner or later, he would drop from exhaustion and the patient robots would bear down, lases slicing, electrodes primed. That would be it. Stack hoped Chantal was making some difference, because he was certainly out of the picture.

Thirty-eight wasn't so young to die these days. It was more years than Mozart had managed, than Keats, than Alexander the Great, than Billy the Kid, than Bruce Lee, than Janis Joplin, than River Phoenix, than Kurt Cobain… And Leona Tyree, who had been thirty-three last month. And Miss Texaco, who probably hadn't made fifteen.

He thought he couldn't hear out of his left ear, which was gummed up with blood. His knee was on the point of giving out completely.

The Oscars moved silently, without fatigue, without sustaining wounds. His side-arm was about as useful against them as a cap pistol, but he couldn't bring himself to throw it away.

He felt as if he was wading through a fast-running stream. His shins were frozen. The cold was numbing, almost pleasantly so. His aches and pains faded.

Finally, his legs refused to work, and he pitched face-first into the fast-cooling sand.

He crawled a few yards, his bruised chest flaring up as he rubbed it against the ground.

He heaved himself onto his back, and looked up at the silver circle of the moon. As a kid, watching *Star Wars*, he had wanted to be part of the space program. He had tried out, but came along just too late, just after the moonbase fiasco and the final collapse of the Satellite Weapons Systems. Uncle Sam hadn't been in the market for spacemen. And so it had had to be the Cav. Obi-Wan wasn't being any help.

He called upon the Force. Nothing. He was still incapable. He thought he heard heavy, thumping footsteps. The Oscars were closing in.

He prayed. Chantal would have liked that, he thought. He still couldn't believe that the Op was a nun.

He heard something besides the marching androids. Out in the sand, somewhere. Something was coming, something that clumped, but jingled, almost subaudially, at the same time.

He rolled over, and looked across the desert. The dunes were silvered by the moonlight, and a figure was moving fast, coming at him out of the Great Empty.

Great. Someone else to try to kill him. It was open season on US Cav tonight.

At first, Stack thought the stranger was on a motorsickle. But the shape was too tall, and lurched too much.

It was someone on a horse. The jingling he heard was spurs. There was something magical about the sight, as if one of the ghosts of the West were galloping out of the Past to be in at the kill. Who was it? Wyatt Earp? The Lone Ranger? Shane? Sir Lancelot?

From the other direction strode the four remaining Oscars, the shining, soulless embodiment of the techno-fascist's utopia of the future. They were the mechanist nightmare made metal and plastic and glass. One of them would have a nuclear heart, ready to burst with loving death at the touch of a button.

Between the past and the future, crippled in the present, Stack pushed at the ground. His knee burned inside.

The horseman came onwards. In the still night, Stack could hear the horse breathing heavy, the slap of the rider's legs against his mount's flanks, the thump of his saddlebags.

The stranger got to him first. Stack forced himself to stand up, but the rider still towered over him. He wore a long slicker, a battered grey hat that seemed to sparkle in the moonlight, and had his neckerchief up over his mouth and nose. The horse was a grey, tall and well-muscled, steaming in the night. It reared up, and the rider kept his seat. Outlined in the moonglow, the apparition was awe-inspiring. Stack felt tears stand out in the corners of his eyes, and his spine tingled with a chill that had nothing to do with the cold.

A lase beamed by from the Oscars, cutting empty air.

The horseman pulled his kerchief away from his face. It was lined and leathery, but his blue eyes were sharp and strong. He had a shaggy moustache and a strong jaw, hawk's cheekbones and white-blond hair.

"Son," he said to Stack, "you look like you need a friendly gun."

VII

"I THINK WE'RE in time," Chantal said, squeezing into the confined space. "It's just here. It hasn't seeded into the communications channels."

"What does that mean?" Finney asked.

"It's trapped. In the fort. If we're lucky, we can slam the door on it. Can we seal all the electronic egresses?"

Finney looked at the monitors. "Most of them are down anyway. The datanets pulled out. We're just on the straight Cav line."

"Can that be shut off?"

"Well… there are back-ups, and Standing Orders are that the line should never be terminated under any circumstances."

"But can it be done?"

Finney nearly smiled. "Not officially. Not from the Ops Centre." She thumbed towards the low ceiling. "Everything is shut up behind durium panels, but down here there are wires. Sergeant, pass me the clippers."

Quincannon handed Finney the pair of rubber-handled shears from the toolkit they'd scavved. The captain snapped at the air. Outside, alarms were still sounding, and voices were coming from all the public address speakers. There were many voices, all taunting, all vicious, all evil…

There were curtains of wires, and circuit-breakers hung in them. The place was the seamy side of the fort, with all the works crammed into a small space and left to gather dust until there was a malfunction. With Chantal at the terminal, it was impossible for either of the others to do more than get their heads and arms into the hole-sized room. One tangled skein of multi-coloured wires combined into a rope and fed into a hole in the concrete. Finney tapped it.

"All the outside channels are here. It's a weakness, actually. I've been trying to get the design changed. Any saboteur could cut the whole place off from the outside world by striking here…"

"Do it."

Finney opened the shears, and crunched them into the rope. Sparks flew and meters burst. Chantal covered her face. Finney flinched, and cut again. She wrestled with the rope, which was kicking, and fell back, her hands smoking. The shears hung, embedded in the wires.

Finney waved her hands and shoved them into her armpits. The shears jerked, and arcs danced on the blades.

Quincannon pushed forwards and grabbed the handles, forcing them together. His face showed the strain, but he persisted. The access room was thick with smoke, and Chantal was coughing, her eyes streaming.

The shearblades met, and the rope parted. Quincannon fell back, dropping the tool on the floor.

"Done, sister," he said.

"Fine. We've got the genie in its bottle…"

She pulled the vials of Holy Water – refilled at Welcome – from her belt, and set them on top of the terminal.

She said a brief prayer and crossed herself. Quincannon and Finney had done their bit. Now it was her turn.

She started tapping the Latin words into the database. It was just a way of getting the demon's attention, but it ought to give a litle pain to the creature.

She tried to think in sync with the system, projecting herself through her fingers into the machine's space.

Finally, the thing inside turned round and roared its hatred at her.

IX

WITH A LEATHER-GLOVED hand, the stranger swept his slicker back from his hip. A pearl-inlay on the stock of his revolver caught the moonlight. In one smooth, easy movement, he drew a six-gun, a long-barrelled beauty with a filed-away sight.

The androids halted, and stood as still as the monoliths of Stonehenge.

Stack turned, and looked at the machines who had come to kill him. The stranger pointed his gun without seeming to take aim, pulled back the trigger, and fanned the hammer.

Six shots went into the first Oscar in a vertical line from the centre of its visor to its metal crotch. The black holes looked like buttons.

Stack's breath was held. There weren't supposed to be bullets that could pierce durium plate like that.

The Oscar leaked fluid from its lower holes, and toppled backwards. Stack felt its impact in his ankles as the ground shook.

The stranger spun his gun on his trigger-finger and holstered it. Then, his hands moving too fast for human eyes, he pulled a repeating rifle from a sling on his saddle.

The Oscars' visors raised.

Nothing is faster than a lase. It is an instantaneous weapon. It strikes its target simultaneously with its ignition. The beam doesn't travel through space, it appears in the air and anything in its way is cut through as if a red-hot wire had materialised out of another dimension and the object of the attack happened to be occupying the same space in this world.

The stranger outdrew and outshot three lases.

His hand was a blur as he pulled down the trigger guard lever three times. There were three sharp flames, and three shots.

He put each bullet into the hole in an Oscar's head.

The night air was sharp with the aftertang of honest gunsmoke. The Oscars collapsed like broken statues.

The stranger's horse was a little spooked. It shifted, and he gently tugged his reins, calming the beast.

He swung his rifle back into its sheath with an easy motion.

"What is that?" Stack gasped.

"It's a Henry, son. The 1873, manufactured by old Oliver Winchester himself, to the design of Benjamin Tyler Henry. Best rifle there ever was."

"A Winchester '73?"

"Yup."

Out in the Big Empty, something howled at the full moon. Stack shivered again.

"That thing must be a hundred and fifty years old."

The stranger grinned. His teeth were white and even.

"How can you do that? How can you bring down an armoured android with an… with an antique?"

"You do what you have to, son…"

Stack knew he had gone crazy, and was hallucinating. This was where his brain checked out on him, and he was left to flounder in the desert. All those wounds, all that ju-ju, all the strain. It had finally been too much for him. In retrospect, he was amazed that he had held out against madness so long.

But the stranger was here. There was no doubt about that. The man and his horse were massive, not in size but in substance. This was reality. The stranger pulled a pouch and paper from his waistcoat pocket and rolled himself a cigarette one-handed. He struck a match on the horn of his saddle and lit his smoke.

"Who are you?"

The cigarette burned. "Just a drifter."

"Where did you come from?"

He threw the cigarette away, ash in the sand, and exhaled a cloud of smoke.

"No place special, son," he waved a hand at the desert. "Out there somewhere, I guess."

Stack's head hurt. Sand drifted against the Oscars. A wind was rising, whipping the tops of the dunes.

"Why did you come?"

"You needed help. I always try to help."

The stranger adjusted his hat, fixing it tight to his head. An unheard-of cloud drifted across the face of the moon. No, not a cloud, a shadow. The stranger looked up, a touch of concern in his expression.

"Looks like a sandstorm's blowing up," he said. "I'd best be on my way."

Stack opened his mouth, but had nothing to say.

"So long, pilgrim," said the stranger, pulling his kerchief up, and turning his horse away.

Stack finally got it out. "Thank you…"

The horse picked up speed, and the stranger's slicker billowed around him like a white cloak. He raised his hand to clamp his hat to his head, half turned in the saddle, and waved a farewell.

"Thank you, thank you."

The stranger rode off into the night. Darkness and the wind swallowed him. For a few moments after he was gone, Stack could hear hooves, then there was just the whistling of the wind and the shifting of the sands.

He turned, and walked past the devastated androids, back towards Fort Apache.

X

EVERYTHING WAS GOING wrong. The androids weren't responding. Lauderdale had had Stack in his sights, but a sandstorm had blown up and his viewpoint blanked out. He tried to activate the nuke, but hadn't been rewarded by a big bang. There was someone in the desert with Stack, but there was no way of telling who. He didn't like that.

Also, half the Ops Centre had shut down without warning.

Rintoon was still crying, "Mutiny!"

Lauderdale pushed angrily away from his console, and wheeled around, looking for a course of action.

The demon had stopped coming through the speakers. It was still in the works, Lauderdale knew, but it was busy with its own battle.

What would Elder Seth want him to do now? What was the Path of Joseph?

"I'll have them all flogged within an inch of their lives!" screamed Rintoon. "Flogged, flogged, FLOGGED!"

The colonel was making whipping motions with his arm, relishing in his imagination the thwack of leather against flesh.

At least he was happy.

What to do, what to do?

Lauderdale's hands were shaking, and his heartbeat was up. He loosened his tunic collar.

"Lay open their backs, and pour salt into the weals…"

Lauderdale was afraid. His mouth was dry and his tongue was swollen. He trembled with the fear that he had lost his way, had strayed from the Path of Joseph.

Elder, help me!

He had bitten his lips and his tongue. There was blood in his mouth.

Blood!

"Stripe 'em with the cat. Nobody defies the will of Colonel Vladek W Rintoon, and gets away unmarked! Nobody, nobody, NOBODY!"

The Path was clear. Lauderdale would see the way ahead if only he performed one more blood sacrifice.

He looked at the ranting, mad old man and knew what he must do.

The sabre mounted above the map was from the Battle of Washita in 1868. Some people said it was Custer's. That had been a massacre too. He hummed "Garry Owen," the tune the 7th Cavalry Band had played that day when the long-haired general put Black Kettle and his sleeping Cheyenne men, women and children to the sword. Not feeling the pain, Lauderdale punched through the glass and gripped the weapon by the hilt. He pulled it free, and swung it in a neat arc towards Rintoon's neck.

The colonel paused in mid-rant as the sharp sabre bit deep.

Lauderdale drew the sword from its scabbard of flesh, and plunged it in again.

"Mutiny," breathed Rintoon. "Mutiny!"

Lauderdale's mind went red, and he hacked until his arm was too aching to hold the heavy sword. It clattered on the floor.

Blood pooled around his boots. He dropped to his knees, and washed his face in it.

Blood!

XI

IN THE MIND of the machine, Sister Chantal wrestled with the demon.

It tormented her as it had done before, but with its energies applied a thousandfold. It was like being caged with an angry lion.

"Suffer, sssissster!" it sang in Petya Tcherkassoff's mainly synthesized voice, "Sssssssuffer and burn!"

It wore the faces of her ghosts – her father, her mother, Marcello, Georgi – and screamed obscenities. It tried to force its way into her skull, and make her wallow in filth, rubbing her face into every discarded scrap of herself. Every unfulfilled, unnameable desire, every impulse, every vice was trotted out in brain-filling Technicolor and graphic three-dimensional detail, with stereophonic agony on the soundtrack.

Her fingers tapped the keyboard automatically as she regurgitated the text she had been taught.

The horror show played on.

Mlle Fournier discovered her in the nursery, carving chunks out of Marcello's chest with a breadknife as she rode the boy to a bloody climax.

"Chantal, Chantal, you wicked child, wicked child, you should be punished, be punissssshed, you sssshould die, die, die…"

Marcello screamed, pain co-mingling with ecstasy.

"Chantal, Chantal, don't you like me any more? Cut deeper, cut deeper. Cut where the blood runsssssss black…"

In a whore's bed, while Isabella watched, she was sandwiched between Thomas Juillerat and the Pope, screeching.

"Oh, Chantal, Papa and il papa, how tiresssssome of you. And that nightgown, it's so… sssssssso… 1980s!"

"Mon petit choux.."

"Kisssssss my ring, sister!"

In the dojo, she scooped out Mother Kazuko's insides with her bare hands, plunging her knife-hard fingers again and again into the woman's chest, finally the victor in their eternal pretend-battle.

"Very good, Chantal. More pain, more pain. Kill me, kill me, kill me…"

Back during her battle with the California Diabolists, she
hesitated at a crucial moment, and saw Mother Kazuko collapse, the hellspawn crawling over her.

"You nearly got me killed then, Chantal. Now you can
finissssh the job."

She killed her enemies, and exulted in the hunt, the
slaughter, the communion of blood. A fallen Gaschugger
looked up at her, pleading for the last rites, and she poured
napalm into his eyes.

"This is not me," she told herself.

She jettisoned her mean flesh forever, and poured her consciousness into a datanet, copulating mentally with banks of
information, forcing herself into forbidden files, spreading
herself out through the world's cobweb network of datalinks.
Father O'Shaughnessy studied her, won Nobel prizes.

"You're going to die, bitch!"

She pulled her mind out of the maelstrom, and concentrated.

"Die and be damned!"

Chantal fastened on the task at hand, and her fingers fed in
the ritual.

"Ssssslut!"

She slipped once. The screen flashed ERROR IN LINE
10: EXURGO IS PAST IMPERFECT TENSE FIRST
PERSON – PLEASE ENTER CORRECT TERM
directly onto her cerebral cortex. She sped the cursor to the
glitch, and made the correction. She pressed RUN, and the
Exorcism loaded.

"*Die…*"

It was terrible. She tried to contain a miniature atomic
explosion inside her skull. It was as if she were being broken
down into bits of information and built up from the ground
again within nanoseconds. The pictures the creature was
playing inside her head stretched out of shape, slowed down,
crumpled, fragmented. The faces of Mlle Fournier, Isabella,
Marcello, Mother Kazuko, Thomas and Georgi collapsed in
upon themselves and whirled together, coalescing into a

grotesque composite. The many-eyed, many-mouthed face rippled and was surrounded by darkness.

"Bittttch!"

She beheld the true face of the fiend. It wasn't anything, just a formless crawling chaos, crawling and writhing. Briefly, it was what she had been taught to expect, a horned, cloven-footed, batwinged, beast. But then it was a tentacled blob, wormlike apendages wriggling around a glowing violet nucleus. Then, it wasn't a body at all, just a foul smell, a dissonant chord, a vile taste.

She clamped her hands together in prayer, and fought the demons inside herself. Finally, all that was left was terror.

But in the terror, there was triumph. The demon was beaten. It could cling for a while, but it was being dislodged from the system.

"The Power of Christ compels you," she said, sprinkling the Holy Water onto the keyboard. Circuits shorted out inside.

"Fuck you, ratskag!" the demon shrieked at her, shrinking away as the water seeped into the wiring.

"The Power of Christ compels you…"

She banished the memory of the vicious pictures from her mind, saw how false they were, dispelled the demon's foul suggestions. Black death bloomed on the screen, the Latin standing out in letters of flame.

"The Power of Christ compels you…"

"Gimme some soul, sissstuh. Done let no pore imp go down the tubes. We had some good times together, didn't we? We boogied till dawn, tired out the band, then screwed till we were peaked, huh? You got the kind of sssugar Daddy lurves. C'mon, done do nothin' you'll re-gret tomorrow."

"The Power of Christ compels you…"

"Pope's slut, roundheels sexclone, fucking ratskag, crackwhore, cocksucker, fatherwanker, pussyeater, cumgargling, motherfucker, scum, scum, scum, scum…"

"The Power of Christ compels you…"

She emptied another vial onto the screen. Where the blessed water – consecrated by the blood of that good man, Father Miguel O'Pray – dribbled, the blackness paled into dead static.

"The Power of Christ compels you…"

There were no more conjuring tricks. There was a hint of the pathetic in the demon's screams now. A wheedling tone was creeping in. Instead of threats, it was offering promises… wealth, position, pleasure, the papacy.

"The Power of Christ compels you…"

She saw herself ascending to the Throne of St Peter, each step of the path marked by the mangled corpse of a cardinal. Georgi, eyeless, was the last step. She assumed the robes, and the crowds cheered. The illusion of power was ridiculous.

"The Power of Christ compels you…"

Chantal knew she had the upper hand. The demon was flagging, its schemes becoming tacky, absurd.

"The Power of Christ compels you…"

It whimpered and pleaded, retreating into the depths of the fort, withdrawing all its tentacles.

"The Power of Christ compels you…"

The demon begged for mercy.

"BEGONE!"

XII

THE MAIN GATES were open, and people were pouring out. Stack grabbed a trooper he knew – Lizzie Tuska – and screamed in her face, asking her what was going on. She cringed away from him, and broke his grasp.

Two months ago, he had seen Lizzie go alone into a cellar and take out five Maniax with seven shots. Now, she was crying in the dirt, her nerve gone.

"It's Hell in there!" someone shouted. "Fucking Hell."

A cruiser was coming. Stack picked up Lizzie, and pulled her out of the way just in time. The ve-hickle crashed towards London Bridge, and wedged against the balustrades. There were about six people crammed into it.

There was a fire in the courtyard, and a few half-dressed troopers with extinguishers were trying to keep it at bay. People were still fighting back.

There were dead people all over the place. Someone had rigged up a makeshift gallows, and a corpse in a sergeant's uniform was dangling from a broken neck.

Jesus Christ!

He fought against the tide towards the Ops Centre.

XIII

LAUDERDALE STOOD UP, red and sticky from his face to his waist, and returned to his terminal.

He would recover his androids, and march on the Fort. With his infallible mechanical catspaws he would restore control. Everything had failed him. Every human agency. The demon had been a damp squib. The Path of Joseph had been betrayed. But his androids were not like the other resources. They would never let him down.

He touched his fingers to the keyboard, and a spark leaped from the terminal into him.

He was dead, but his body kept moving.

XIV

THE DEMON WAS uncomfortable. To be reduced to such a lowly form after the glorious freedom of the datanets was humiliating, and confining. But the church's hagwitch had driven him to it.

It ran its hands over the terminal, getting the feel of the flesh. It would not do. He smashed the plastic casing of the machine, and reached in, pulling out a fistful of chips, wires and metal interstices. One by one, it stuck them to its face, latching them into his skin, feeling the machine parts meld with the blood and bone.

There was a battering at the door. Someone was trying to get in.

It tore its tunic and shirt open, and scored deep lines in its chest, then shoved in the innards of the machine. Electrical currents sparked in its brain, and sped through its new, mutating body. Its heart ceased to beat, but an accumulator pumped energy into his copper-laced veins.

There were shots, and the doors jerked open a crack. Fingers appeared in the slit, and the protesting metal shutters were forced apart.

The demon found what it was looking for in Colonel Rintoon's chest.

"Come and get me, popish slut," it shouted.

XV

STACK GOT THE Ops Centre doors open and strode in. He realized Chantal was with him. And Captain Finney and Sergeant Quincannon.

He held out his hand and Chantal took it. They didn't need to say anything.

The thing standing over Rintoon's butchered corpse turned, ropes of blood flying from its face, and raised a dripping, red sabre.

"Lauderdale!" Stack shouted.

"No," it said. "He's not in just now. If you'd care to leave a message at the tone, I'm sure he'll kill you later."

Chantal squeezed past, and stood face to face with the creature. Stack knew this would be a last stand for one of them.

The thing had torn itself apart and stuffed itself full of machine components. Lights winked in the ruptures in its flesh. On its shoulders, above its spindly human arms, were three-elbowed, claw-tipped waldoes, greasy with blood and oil. From its torso sprouted spikes like the one the cruiser had grown in St Werburgh's.

Stack knew what he was looking at.

"This is it," Chantal said to the demon. "You can't retreat any further. Your back is against the wall. You have to defend that body until it drops. Then you're lost. There's no way back into the darkness."

It lashed out at her with a new cyberlimb it had grown out of Lauderdale's coccyx. It was like a six-foot scorpion's tail. She dodged it, and landed three sharp kicks on its chest, toes sinking in between the deadly spikes. The creature was unsteady on its feet. It was changing so fast that it couldn't adapt its centre of gravity.

Stack had his 45 out. Quincannon was slipping the safety off his automatic. The Cav men exchanged looks, and took aim.

"Come on in and get me, coppers!" it screamed.

Stack's first shots went into the thing's back near the tear through which the tail was protruding. Quincannon emptied his clip into its head. The thing swallowed the bullets and incorporated them into its body. The head was lumpy with lead, the bullets visible under the skin like hard boils. It no longer resembled anything human.

It was laughing.

It reached down with its tail and took the sabre from its frail human hand. The blade whirled, and fastened to the limb.

The tail lashed at Chantal, and sliced across her hip. Her uniform was cut, and she bled.

She kicked again, aiming for the flesh between the metal.

Chantal closed with the creature, and hugged it. Rasping, artificial laughter sounded. A knifelike blade lunged out of Lauderdale's body and scraped past Chantal's cheek.

Stack leaped into the room, and joined the fight. He grabbed the creature's leg, tugging at it, weighing it down. Finney and Quincannon had machine pistols which they didn't use for fear of hitting Chantal or Stack. Finney picked up a wooden map-pointer, and thrust it into the creature's body. Quincannon punched it in the head.

It staggered and fell.

"Fuck you," the thing said.

Chantal grabbed its voicebox, and tore it out. The component came free with a sucking noise. A rattling hiss escaped through the new mouth in its neck. Up close, Stack could see plastic-coated wires and maggotlike muscles knitting inside the creature's body. It was out of control.

Quincannon kicked its head with a heavy boot.

Stack climbed along the twisting body, and got a two-handed grip on the tail. It was wired to shock, and he felt an electrical charge for a second before it went dead as he tore it from the body.

Finney swung a heavy chair at its head, and dented the plate over the forehead with a castor.

The chair bounced off the skull and out of Finney's hands. One of the waldoes extended, claws pyramided together in a spear-point, and punched the captain in the belly. The waldo burrowed into her ribcage, ploughed up through her heart, and burst out between her neck and collarbone. The claw opened like a grapple, and the dying woman's eyes clouded. Slowly, Finney brought her hands round, and took hold of the waldo running through her. Stack saw her fingers getting a good grip. Gritting her teeth, Finney pushed herself away from the wall. The claw shook impotently and bit into her shoulder.

The waldo tore free of the creature, pulling a long string of flesh and wire with it. A spray of biofluid exploded from the uneven, stringy hole in its flesh. Finney stiffened, slipped and fell.

Chantal, one hand pressing the head to the floor, held up a glass tube of clear liquid in the other, and muttered something in Latin.

The throatless thing screamed as she poured the contents of the tube into the hole in its forehead.

"The power of Christ…" she gasped.

The creature arched. Chantal rode it, and continued her ritual. As she spoke, she slapped its face, commanding its full attention.

Inside its head, the mechanics flared and burned out. It collapsed.

Chantal stood up.

"It's gone," she said. "It'll never have a body again."

"What now?"

"We pray for the souls of the dead."

XVI

IN SALT LAKE City, Nguyen Seth floated in his isolation tank, seething at the small defeat that had been visited upon him. So, the datanets still linked the Continental Americas, and the temporal power of the Catholic Church ran unchecked. In the end, that would not matter. In the end, it was a simple question of the Inevitability of Nightfall, of the strength of the Dark Ones.

After all, the Catholic Church was not an impregnable body. The Path of Joseph had found more than a few converts even as high as the Inner Councils of the Vatican itself. But the setback was bitter. Under the energy-enriched fluid, Elder Seth's lips curved into a smile. The Sister who performed the exorcism would have to be watched. Perhaps he would take her himself. He did not care to be inconvenienced, and he lusted after a chance to avenge himself.

The Dark Ones had given him longevity, had made him more than other men. He would not fail them. They would not fail.

In the End, there would be a War, fought in the Great Wastes of the New World, and all the powers of the world would be aligned against the Dark Ones.

His hands knotted into fists and his teeth ground.

They would fall. The Dark Ones would prevail. It would be as it had been prophesied.

Elder Seth put the recent irritation out of his mind, and concentrated on his new business. The Duroc, latest of his servitors, was in Europe, preparing a new course of action.

This time the Dark Ones would be rewarded.

XVII

NOW THE MISSION was over Chantal felt curiously flat. As always, she was drained. Mentally, physically, emotionally and spiritually. Once the demon was banished and she had done what could be done for the dead and the dying, she turned off. Sergeant Quincannon had helped her to her room, and tucked her in bed. As if she needed one, she had found another father. Her wounds turned out to be superficial cuts, so she told the medical orderlies to leave her alone and see to the needier cases.

Three days later, and things had not changed. She sat at her desk, and plumbed the emptiness inside herself. She felt the need to visit Mother Kazuko, and not only to give her teacher whatever comfort she could during her recuperation. Mother Gadzooks O'Hara had been her confessor before she was her martial arts master.

It was like this every time. She reached the accomplishment of her purpose, and found too many important questions still unanswered. It had been a grueling assignment, and she felt she had much to confess. She knew the demon's attempts to assail her faith, in God and in herself, had been base stratagems, but she needed to talk through the feelings that had been stirred. She could never be thoroughly rid of the pictures the fiend had planted in her mind, but Mother Kazuko would help her deal with them, would help her cleanse herself. Perhaps there would be time to stay at the retreat, to pursue her theoretical work. She could do with some cloistered tranquility and contemplation.

Recently, her missions had been getting closer together.

Someone knocked at her door.

"Come in."

It was Nathan Stack. She looked up from her breviary – she hadn't been focusing on the words for over a quarter of an hour – and smiled at him.

Stack was recovering well. He was strong. He would survive. Many hadn't. The US Cavalry had airlifted the mentally and physically wounded out to a facility within the Phoenix PZ, and buried the dead within sight of Fort Apache. There had been enough to fill a new graveyard. They hadn't had individual funerals, just a mass ceremony conducted by the regimental chaplain. Chantal hadn't felt able to speak, but she had vowed to light a candle for Cat Finney in St Peter's. She hoped the woman had gone where the good sufis go.

"We've got Federico back. The Quince has run a systems check, and there doesn't seem to be any damage. The sergeant and your car are getting along famously."

Chantal got up, and went to the door. She accompanied Stack down to the courtyard. Newly-assigned personnel were supervising the repairs and reconstruction. Major General Hollingsworth Calder, the new commandant, had promised General Ernest Haycox, the overall c-in-c of the Cav, that the fort would be back on line within the week. Haycox himself had flown in from Fort Comanche to take a look at the site of the disaster. There were rumours of resurgent Maniak chapters out in the desert. And the corps were complaining about the the roads left unpatrolled.

You could tell from their faces which of the troopers had been just shipped in and which had lived through the demon download. It was in their eyes.

Quincannon saw her, and saluted.

An ops captain walked over. She was new, and didn't look anything like Finney.

"Sister," she said. "We've had a communication from Rome for you."

The woman handed over a sealed print-out, and left.

Chantal broke the papal seal, and read her orders. They were countersigned by Cardinal DeAngelis, and didn't tell her more than the basics.

"I've been recalled," she told Stack.

"I thought you wanted to go to California?"

She sighed. "I do, but it will have to wait. It's marked urgent. I have a mission. Somewhere in Europe."

Stack didn't look happy about it. Quietly, he had come to rely on her. There was something he hadn't told her about, but which he wanted to. Something he found difficult to get straight in his own mind. She could tell. She had found she could catch his moods.

"I have to go," she said.

"I know."

"And you never told me how you escaped from Lauderdale's androids."

He hesitated, "I know. It's kind of complicated."

"Save it for when I come by again."

"Sister…"

"Yes?"

"Never mind." He kissed her on the cheek, like a brother. She tried not to be disappointed. "Goodbye, Chantal."

"Goodbye, Nathan."

He walked away, and vanished into the shadows under the eaves of the fort. She turned to Federico, and keyed in her door-open code.

"Good morning, sister," it said.

She felt comfortable with Federico's leather seat under her, and experienced that slipping-into-a-warm-bath thrill she always had when she was in the car. Federico played Ivana Sukayov's "Do Svidaniya," but she didn't want to hear that. She selected Joy Division's "60 Miles an Hour."

The main gates of Fort Apache slid open, and she drove over London Bridge. Ahead of her was the Big Empty, the desert heart of America.

"Ciao," she said, mainly to herself.

ABOUT THE AUTHOR

Besides his contributions to BL Publishing's Warhammer and Dark Future series, the seldom-seen Jack Yeovil is the author of a single novel, *Orgy of the Blood Parasites*, and used to fill in occasionally as a film reviewer for *Empire* and the *NME*. Kim Newman seems to have Jack under control at the moment, but the stubborn beast flesh occasionally comes creeping back.

More Dark Future mayhem from Black Flame

GOLGOTHA RUN

by Dave Stone

UP ON THE mesa, *out past the burning remains of Las Vitas, a pollutant-mutated scorpion was in the process of laying its eggs in the still barely-living flesh of a hairless dog.*

There was no one to see this, and therefore no one to remark on how the air around scorpion and dog now shimmered, how a sickly light hazed from their forms.

Instantly, as though some switch of unlife had been thrown, both arachnid and canine flesh crumbled into their component molecular parts, leaving nothing but skeletal remains and a perfectly intact chitionous husk.

"WE GOT TROUBLES," Eddie said, slamming back into the van. "Looks like soldiers."

"TWO MINUTES TO SURRENDER," the bullhorn-voice boomed cheerfully, "THEN WE GET LETHAL. IT'S LIKE TOTALLY YOUR DECISION, GUY."

"Mercenaries," Trix Desoto said. "Delta-trained. NeoGen runs a cadre of them for hunting parties."

Eddie strained his eyes on the dead black shadows outside, imagining the stealthy figures as they silently and invisibly took up position. He didn't actually hear and see anything, of course, on account of the meaning of the words "silent" and "invisible".

He wouldn't hear or see a thing, he realised with a cold sick certainty, until they dropped the hammer.

"MINUTE AND A HALF…" the bullhorn boomed. "SAY, YOU A SPIC, BOY? YOU A CATHERLICK? TIME FOR A COUPLE OF HAIL MARYS IF YOU *REALLY* FEEL THE NEED FOR A QUICK RATTLE ON THE ROSARIES!"

"Where the fuck did *that* come from?" Eddie muttered to himself. There might or might not have been some Hispanic in his parentage – it was about as likely as anything else – but he couldn't see what that had to do with anything.

"Destabilisation tactics," Trix Desoto said. "Like the disco. Keeping us off-balance for when they come in to take the package."

"Package?" Eddie said.

Trix Desoto indicated the supine form of the unconscious man.

"THAT'S THE BUNNY!" came the bullhorn. "NICE OF YOU TO GIVE US A GOOD LOOK AT THE MERCHANDISE!"

For a second, Eddie was unaware of what the bullhorn guy had meant. He sat there in a cold sweat, looking at the van's interior light, trying to work it out.

Then he lurched towards it with a curse and shut the light off.

"CLEVER GUY!" came the bullhorn. "WE GOT NIGHT SIGHTS AND THERMAL-IMAGING SYSTEMS OUT THE ASS, MAN! YOU JUST LEFT YOURSELF BLIND AND IN THE DARK. THIRTY SECONDS!"

If there was one thing, absolutely one thing, that Eddie Kalish was not going to do it was turn the light back on again.

Besides, what with the spill-in from the big Kliegs outside, it didn't make any real difference. The guy was just trying to find another way to rattle him and keep him from doing something all resourceful and heroic.

Not that *that* made any difference, either. If the resourceful hero in Eddie Kalish was waiting to make itself known, it was taking its own sweet time about it.

"That's it, then," Eddie said. The choices had come down to sitting here and dying, or even pretending to believe in this "surrender" crap and dying in the open. "There's nothing we can do."

"Oh there's something we can do," said Trix Desoto. "There's something I can do."

Looking at her in the in the glare of the Kliegs, it finally percolated through Eddie what had been odd about her since he had made it back to the van. Gone was the delirious swinging between lucidity and alien-sounding gibberish.

Now she seemed entirely and unnaturally sanguine – and not in any sense relating to the catastrophic blood-loss from the wound in her gut.

In fact, she was looking pale but strangely healthy. The body in the comedy-nurse uniform seemed somehow bulkier and stronger.

It might have simply been the light, but Eddie thought he could see weird muscle-masses moving under the skin. Half-thoughts of vampires, of zombies, flashed through Eddie's mind. Walking corpses, monstrous after death.

"There's something I can do," Trix Desoto repeated, eyes a kind of burning black behind the slatted zebra-striping of light and shadow from the Kliegs. "And I'm going to do it now."

IN THE BURNING *ruins of Las Vitas, the flesh of any number of scavenging animals hazed instantly into molecular dust – along with the remaining flesh of that on which they were feeding.*

Is was not as if something were sucking some actual life-force, if that word can be made to mean anything in the first place. It was more as if something were feeding on some product of life-coherence...

COMMANDER THOMAS MARLON Drexler, heading up the wet-squad out of NeoGen, was suffering from a small gap in basic expectations.

The fact was that, over the years, military-grade command technology had evolved to the point where with a single and suitably controlled squad of operatives one could subvert the infrastructure and take command of an entire city or country.

Schematic analysis of anything from the power and informational grids to the plumbing, plus detailed psychologistical profiling of the principle characters amongst the enemy, ensured that force could be applied to critical targets with a zero-tolerance of error: the equivalent of assassinating Franz Ferdinand because you *really* hate a bunch of limpid individuals banging on about the corner of some forgotten field, and want to see the lot of them end up dead.

Such seriously shit-hot Control and Command equipment didn't come cheap, of course, but NeoGen supplied its Retrieval people with the best – especially if said people were going up against such an equally-matched rival as GenTech.

Such tactical control-processes had worked perfectly in the matter of setting some local jackgang on a GenTech road-train, manipulating the various factors in such a matter that the forces neutralized each other. Then Drexler and his squad had moved in to pick up the pieces... and hit that gap in expectations.

There was another factor on the board. And that factor, simply, was just some guy that nobody gave a flying fuck about.

There was not a single person who particularly knew or cared if he lived and died – and that was the problem right there. It was like some idiotic squit of a kid going up against a Grand Master in chess; the kid does things so flatly idiotic that it leaves the Grand Master momentarily flummoxed.

The kid and the package, together with the package's medical support, had fled the site of the road-train ambush just before Drexler and his NeoGen forces had arrived. Tracksat systems had pinpointed the little RV almost instantly, but the forces on the ground found themselves with a problem. NeoGen had come armed and ready to deal with GenTech or jackganger survivors; they were perfectly capable of leaving some escaping piece-of-crap van a smoking hole in the road that not even micro-engineered algaeic heal-sealant would be able to fill.

What they did not have, however, was the capacity to intercept and stop it without damaging the package irreparably.

Tracksat extrapolation had showed that the van was heading for Las Vitas, and military-spec four-wheel drive had made it in half the time, even over rough terrain. Drexler had looked around the shithole and not reckoned much to it. Too many holes and corners. Street-fighting could get messy.

So Drexler and his boys had broken out their heavy-duty armament and removed the town from the equation.

He didn't feel particularly good about that, but then again he didn't feel bad either. It was just what you had to do, sometimes.

The only other place, within practical distance and with communications, had been the junker's yard here. Strategic modelling of all available factors placed the probability of containing the target here in the upper ninetieth percentile.

That, at least, was what MIRA had assured Commander Drexler. Drexler, on the other hand, was rapidly coming to the conclusion that MIRA was at this point just making it up off the top of her cybernetic head and winging it.

"What was that shit about calling the guy a spic?" he asked MIRA. "Plus all that, you know, religious stuff?"

Ordinarily, the Mobile Intrusion and Recon Application was capable of pumping all kinds of psychological disruption to a target: insults based on their specific gangcult, dark intimations of what the subject really felt about some family member and the so forth. This had just seemed unnecessarily basic and crude.

"Yeah, well, I just don't have the hard info," MIRA said cheerfully. For all that the voice issuing from the exterior bullhorn-attachment had been deepened, roughened and masculinized, MIRA "herself" tended to adopt a female persona. That is, a lighter, higher and feminine voice, while still in some subliminal way failing to be human in any way whatsoever.

"Filesearch on the girl throws up nothing, just like all these total blanks, yeah?" MIRA said. "Like someone went through the files and wiped her footprints out. And the guy never left no footprints in the first place – he's just some kid, you know? I'm just playing the law of averages and throwing out some generic insults. I'm having to improvise."

Drexler ran his glance across the display-monitors bolted to the dash of the NeoGen-modified Humvee – or HumGee – parked under mimetic camouflage-netting outside the junker's yard and which was serving as a scratch C&C for the guys inside.

Wireframe topographics of the yard itself, thermograph readouts of the targets in the van overlaid with extrapolated bio-data. Outputs from the microcams of the three wet-operatives inside.

"Don't try to improvise when you don't have the data," he told MIRA. "It just sounds wrong. It doesn't sound like anything a real human would say."

MIRA gave what sounded like a contemptuous little snort – possibly a sound-sample designed to convey that precise effect.

"I'm a sentient-grade AI, chum, even if I occupy the lower end of the scale. You just follow the orders and do the job and come it like a frigging robot. I sound more human and alive than you do, most of the time."

"That's my prerogative, MIRA. You don't have the option."

"Yeah, whatever you say, *boss*," MIRA said with marked cybernetic sarcasm. "And speaking of time, boss, we're well over that deadline I gave the targets. You wanna give the go-word to take 'em out?"

"Do it," Drexler said. "Remember that the package is our top priority. They can do what they like, but only after the package is secure."

"Yeah, yeah, we all know that," said MIRA. "I'm relaying the order to… hang on. Something's up…

"Check the bio-readouts on the girl. Something freaky's going on with the girl and it's – oh my God…"

There was a blinding flash from outside, washing out the Klieg-illumination in the intensity of its glare, and human-sounding or not, that was the last thing MIRA ever said.

SHAFTS OF MAGNESIUM light blasted from the windows and roof-ports of the van, from the rust holes eaten in its sides. Tendrils of electrical discharge arced to the junkyard-compound's generator unit, travelling the leads to which it had been hooked to NeoGen's Kliegs and exploding them in a shower of sparks.

Vestigial petrochems left in tanks out in the junk piles spontaneously ignited; the tanks detonated. The junk began to burn. The van itself exploded – torn apart by forces within it that were not entirely physical.

And something dark burst from it. Something dark in a wholly different sense than a mere absence of cast light.

Something big. Something shrieking. Something coming now.

IN A PLACE *that has no name, a place indefinable in spatial or temporal terms – or for that matter, any terms that might apply to organic matter, let alone life – something vast and inimical and unknowable stirred.*

Something was calling to it. Something had made a small fracture in the world. A tiny imperfection, to be sure, but one that could be worked upon. Something that could be forced further apart, with time. If time had any meaning, of course, for this vast and inimical and unknowable thing, which it didn't. It had an eternity in which to operate, after all.

It would be a mistake to believe that the subsumation and destruction of all we know would be anything more than a light snack to this vast and inimical and unknowable thing. The equivalent of a quick pack of potato chips between real meals.

Then again, potato chips come in a variety of interesting flavours, and a pack of them is just the thing to hit the spot. When you're feeling peckish — as the vast and inimical and unknowable thing decidedly was.

For the moment, though, it was in the position of having worked the pack open just enough to insert a finger. Just enough, if it inserted the smallest extremity of itself into the world of men, for a small taste. And this it had proceeded to do…

HALF-BLINDED AND gibbering with terror, Eddie Kalish scrambled through the junk piles, trying to catch his bearings. Things had shifted around, of course, during the time he had spent away, but Little Deke's had never been what you might call a roaring concern. Things, for the most part, had tended to stay where they were put; Eddie still had some idea of the layout. That was an advantage.

That was, in fact, the only advantage he might have over the people out here in the dark. People and, of course, the… *thing* out here in the dark.

"OH YES, THERE'S something I can do," Trix Desoto had said, eyes a kind of burning black behind the slatted light, "and I'm going to do it now."

She had ripped her hands from the hole in her stomach, trailing strings of some viscous substance that hadn't quite seemed even organic, let alone something that a human body could produce. A mass of this stuff seemed to have clotted in her wound, tendrils of it forming and intertwining and pulsing of its own accord.

The hands had seemed bigger – impossibly bigger, like those anatomical models where the limbs and extremities are distorted to a size comparable to the area of the brain controlling them. The nails had elongated to the point of talons.

Trix Desoto had run one of these claws down her face – for an instant Eddie had thought that she was trying to claw her own eyes out in agony, but instead the tip of a talon had run gently down the side of her face, cutting a slit from the inside of which something glowed like embers in some long-banked fire.

"Run," she had told him, face deadly serious and positively demonic in the light from the slit she had made. A talon had jabbed in the direction of the pale form of the comatose old guy. "Take him and *run*."

All reasonable thoughts about armed NeoGen troops waiting out there in the junk years had vanished – indeed, it was as if all reasonable thought had shut down. The monster snarls and you just run for the tree line or the cave. He had leapt from the van without question and headed for the junk piles.

It was only after the explosion had washed over him, miraculously failing to spear him with flying debris, that he realised that he had unthinkingly followed Trix Desoto's order and taken the body of the old guy with him. It must have been her tone of voice.

Now, EDDIE KALISH decided, the old guy was just dead weight. He left the inert form sprawled by a pile of rotting tyres, gently seeping from the punctures left from being unceremoniously hauled from the med-units.

Off to one side, through the junk, there was a single muzzle-flash and the complete lack of sound from an expertly silenced gun – though any sound of gunfire would have probably been drowned out, in any case, by the high-pitched scream and the sounds of tearing flesh. Whatever it was that Trix Desoto had turned into, it was having a ball.

Or possibly two, Eddie thought, and then really wished that he hadn't.

Eddie moved on, crept around a vaguely familiar heap of panel-sections – and ran straight into one of the surviving NeoGen troops.

Eddie Kalish would never know how lucky he was, in that instant – luck that had been brought about by the confluence of three main factors. The first being that the trooper was currently packing hi-explosive shells into his big MultiFunction Gun.

This would have been singularly *unlucky*, of course, had not one Commander Thomas Marlon Drexler ordered that minimum necessary force be used until the object of their operation be secure. A single hi-ex round fired into the van would have exploded it in much the way that it just had, so the MFG was currently slung over the trooper's shoulder and out of instant reach.

The second factor was that, unlike that produced by conventional explosives, the detonation of the van had released a variety of localized electromagnetic pulse that had knocked out the trooper's infrared night-sight. He was in the midst of tearing it angrily from his face and blinking his eyes to acclimatise to the sudden darkness when he caught the moving silhouette of Eddie.

This lag in reaction-time gave Eddie Kalish the bare second he needed to let out a yip of fear and lurch back – and this was when the third factor came into play, in the form of the heap of panel-sections that Eddie himself had somewhat inexpertly stacked some years before.

These had come, predominantly, from the hulking shells remaining from automobiles of the 1950s and 60s – from before oil embargos and the like had made sheer weight an issue. They were good, solid steel plate as opposed to membrane-thin aluminium that turned to lacework at the first breath of an oxyacetylene torch.

They were an incompetently stacked accident waiting to happen, basically – and now they came crashing down on the trooper.

The screams before, and as, they hit sounded a little odd to Eddie and it was a moment before he worked out why. For some reason, Eddie realised, he'd had trouble imagining a quasi-military stealth-killer as a girl, for all that there was no reason in the world why not.

From the image that terror had etched onto his eyes, though, he now recalled that the shape under the combat-fatigues had been undoubtedly female, and damn well-built at that.

Of course, any shape she might be in now would be decid-edly unattractive and quite beside the point. This was the first person Eddie had actually killed in his life, whether by acci-dent or design. He really didn't know how he felt about that.

There was another explosion of sound and light. It seemed that it was coming from beyond the compound wire, and that was just like as to fine with Eddie Kalish. Too much had happened. His reflexes were shot.

All he wanted to do at this point was crawl away some-where and hide and let the world go to Hell in any way that it liked.

THOMAS MARLON DREXLER slapped at the inert monitors bolted onto the dash and said: "Fuck you you piece of shit!"

This was, in actual fact, the longest single string of exple-tives he had ever used. He had simply, somehow, never seen the point or felt the need, even in the heat of combat. He was a little surprised that he even had it in him.

The EMP from the explosion within the targets' RV had knocked out the HumGee's electrical systems. MIRA "her-self" was probably still alive − or, at least, sentient-grade self-aware − since her housing was rated as shielded for any-thing up to a pony-bomb nuclear blast.

The secondary systems that would make her being alive and aware of any actual use, however, were blown.

These included the door mechanisms. Drexler had remained here, trapped, while things had exploded outside. He had attempted to work out what was happening in the junkyard compound beyond the wire, but the loss of Klieg-illumination had left him with nothing useful to see.

It was the sense of disassociation from the world that was the worst thing, he vaguely realised. MIRA might have snidely called him a robot, but the fact was that a large pro-portion of Thomas Marlon Drexler's self-image resided in the fact that he considered himself, basically, a tool.

He was a part of something larger and more important than himself. He was the strong right hand – no, rather the hammer in that strong right hand – when his NeoGen mas-ters required the application of direct force.

This was his function, and he performed it without ego or self-congratulation, without compunction or remorse. Tak-ing out the ringleaders of a labour-dispute, removing some intracorporate rival together with his wife and kids, it made no odds. It was his function. This was the core of his being and his life.

Now he was stuck here, sealed off from the world and unable to affect it in any way. He was about as much use as a spare dick – and the sensation was maddening.

This was not, quite simply, what the world was and how it worked. It was almost enough to make him take the ten-gauge from where it was stowed under the dash and use it to just switch the world off.

Something big and heavy thumped into the HumGee out-side, rocking it on its suspension and flinging Drexler forward to smack his head against the padded crash-cage which – had the electrics been working – would have ordi-narily racked itself down on servos to cushion the impact.

This direct evidence of a world outside galvanised Drexler and his basic impulses took over. Now he grabbed the ten-gauge, pulling it free from its snaplocks with no thought in his head save to aim it at the HumGee's windshield and blast his way out.

The fact that the shot would have almost certainly rebounded from the impact-tempered glass and shredded him where he sat was beside the point – the mindless need to simply *act*, overwhelming as it was, had burned away any last vestige of rational thought.

Thus it was that when the entire top of the HumGee split open under a claw and inhuman strength, Drexler was already in the process of bringing up the gun and unloading both barrels.

The shot tore into the thing beyond, opening up a hole within which internal organs gave off their own pale glow.

In this light – or for that matter any other – these organs looked like the insides of nothing on or of this Earth.

For a moment, the creature recoiled, eyes rolling down to regard the wound and jaw yawning open in a moment of imbecilic, even comical, puzzlement.

"Got you, motherfucker," Drexler snarled, thereby increasing, again, the number of times he had sworn in his life by an actually measurable percentage. "Fuckin' *hurt* your ass!"

The moment of incongruous puzzlement passed. The skin of the creature liquefied and flowed over the hole and knitted. The creature brushed at itself momentarily, and somewhat fussily, with a claw.

Then it reached in, clamped its talons around Drexler's head and hauled him out of the HumGee, snapping his neck in the process.

This was probably more fortunate than otherwise for Thomas Marlon Drexler, since it meant that he could not feel what the creature did next.

From his immobilised point of view, past the foreground spray of various fluids as the creature went to work with a vengeance, Drexler could see the night sky. The stars burned brightly, in a wide range of colours due to suspended atmospheric pollutants.

The last thing Drexler saw was one of the stars visibly move and expand. Something coming.

Big light coming down.

"OH SHIT," EDDIE muttered, increasing the number of times he had sworn in his life by no particular increment at all. "Here comes the backup."

Hunched up in the lee of a caterpillar-treaded hoist, which he had operated years before under the instruction of Little Deke, life had become quite simple, containing a grand total of two possibilities. Either the thing that had once been Trix Desoto would tire of amusing itself with the NeoGen troops and come sniffing after him, or NeoGen reinforcements would arrive to shoot him in the head.

The latter, it seemed, would be the case.

The big VTOL carrier hung in the air stitching fire into the junkyard. Eddie had scrambled for cover before realising that the VTOL was merely firing tracer-flares to provide snapshot-illumination, maybe for some variety of photosensor-system. This inference gave him no impetus to come *out* from cover, though, on account of (a) a direct hit from a tracer-flare wouldn't do him much good, and (b) the little fact that if NeoGen saw him they were gonna shoot him in the head.

As the carrier banked and descended, however, Eddie caught sight of the illuminated logo on its side:

gentech

This wasn't reinforcement for the bad guys, Eddie Kalish realised belatedly. This was the cavalry.

A drop-hatch opened and a score of impact-armoured troopers hit the dirt. Each of them toted a big MFG, and it would have been more to Eddie's taste if they hadn't looked more or less identical to the NeoGen operatives he had seen, but then you can't have everything.

One of them, presumably the squad-leader, carried a small flatscreen readout, which he was busily consulting.

"*Primary target is forty metres south-southeast,*" he ordered through a miniature amplifier. "*Carter and Trant, secure the package.*"

A pair of troopers peeled off and headed in the direction that Eddie vaguely remembered leaving the comatose old guy.

"Track-and-tranque detail, see if you can't find the silly bitch. Try to take her alive. Try and shock her into latency. The rest of you clean up the area. Standard track and pop…"

Eddie decided that, on the whole, it would probably be better if he made his presence known rather than wait for the troops to come across him. Moving slow and trying to make himself look as unimpressive and unthreatening as possible, which wasn't hard, he walked from the cover of the hoist and gave the troops a small wave. "Hey, guys ..?"

Those of the squad who remained here, maybe ten in all, swung their MFGs toward him instantly.

"You!" the squad-leader bellowed. *"Give me your clearance!"*

"What?" said Eddie.

"Security key-code clearance! Now!"

"What the fuck?" said Eddie.

Automatic fire from maybe three sources stitched into him, and that was the last thing Eddie Kalish remembered.

The conspiracy deepens in

GOLGOTHA RUN

By Dave Stone

**Available now from www.blackflame.com
and all good bookstores**

NIKOLAI DANTE

The Strangelove Gambit
1-84416-139-0
£5.99 • $6.99

DURHAM RED

The Unquiet Grave
1-84416-159-5
£5.99 • $6.99

The Omega Solution
1-84416-175-7
£5.99 • $6.99

NEW LINE CINEMA

Blade: Trinity
1-84416-106-4
£6.99 • $7.99

The Butterfly Effect
1-84416-081-5
£6.99 • $7.99

Cellular
1-84416-104-8
£6.99 • $7.99

Freddy vs Jason
1-84416-059-9
£5.99 • $6.99

The Texas Chainsaw Massacre
1-84416-060-2
£6.99 • $7.99

FINAL DESTINATION

Dead Reckoning
1-84416-170-6
£6.99 • $7.99

Destination Zero
1-84416-171-4
£6.99 • $7.99

End of the Line
1-84416-176-5
£6.99 • $7.99

JASON X

Jason X
1-84416-168-4
£6.99 • $7.99

The Experiment
1-84416-169-2
£6.99 • $7.99

Planet of the Beast
1-84416-183-8
£6.99 • $7.99

FRIDAY THE 13TH

Hell Lake
1-84416-182-X
£6.99 • $7.99

Church of the Divine Psychopath
1-84416-181-1
£6.99 • $7.99

THE TWILIGHT ZONE

Memphis/The Pool Guy
1-84416-130-7
£6.99 • $7.99

Upgrade/Sensuous Cindy
1-84416-131-5
£6.99 • $7.99

Sunrise/Into the Light
1-84416-151-X
£6.99 • $7.99

Chosen/The Placebo Effect
1-84416-150-1
£6.99 • $7.99

Burned/One Night at Mercy
1-84416-179-X
£6.99 • $7.99